Cast of Characters

Michael Evans. An English master at Sudeley Hall, a trifle on the cynical side but good with the boys, and besotted of the headmaster's wife.

The Rev. Percival Vale. The headmaster, fifty years of age and a strict disciplinarian, to whom Sudeley Hall means everything.

Hero Vale. His lovely, vibrant young wife, who's as madly in love with Michael as he is with her.

Edward Griffin. The good-natured gamesmaster, Michael's best friend.

Gadsby. Another master, a battered Adonis, boring and given to drink.

Cyril Wrench. One of the younger masters, an egotist but a gifted teacher.

Sims. The French master, a human mouse with a colorless personality.

Tiverton. The senior assistant master and a born cricketer.

Algernon Wyvern-Wemyss. The headmaster's obnoxious nephew.

Stevens II. A prefect and leader of The Black Spot, a secret society.

Ponsonby. Another student, Stevens' loyal lieutenant.

Mr. Urquhart. A solicitor with a secret.

Rosa. A rather brazenly seductive maid.

Mould. The groundsman.

Superintendent Armstrong. A mountain of a man, unimaginative but exceedingly thorough.

Sergeant George Pearson. His assistant, a picture of blue-eyed innocence.

Nigel Strangeways. A tall, lanky, well-connected, Oxford-educated private inquiry agent who happens to be a friend of Michael's.

Plus assorted students, villagers, laborers, parents, and staff.

Mystery Novels by
Nicholas Bake

A Question of Proof (1935)
Thou Shell of Death (1936)
There's Trouble Brewing (1937)
The Beast Must Die (1938)
The Smiler with the Knife (1939)
Malice in Wonderland (1940)
The Case of the Abominable Snowman
APA: The Corpse in the Snowman (1941)
Minute for Murder (1947)
Head of a Traveller (1949)
The Dreadful Hollow (1953)
The Whisper in the Gloom (1954)
End of Chapter (1957)
The Widow's Cruise (1959)
The Worm of Death (1961)
The Sad Variety (1964)
The Morning After Death (1966)

Nonseries:

A Tangled Web (1956)
A Penknife in My Heart (1958)
The Deadly Joker (1963)
The Private Wound (1968)

A Question of Proof

A Nigel Strangeways mystery by
Nicholas Blake

Introduction by Tom & Enid Schantz

Rue Morgue Press
Boulder / Lyons

For

Margaret

C. Day-Lewis and Nicholas Blake

When Daniel Day-Lewis accepted the best actor Oscar in the spring of 2008 one of the people he acknowledged was his father, the late Cecil Day-Lewis. A few people in the audience perhaps recognized his father as the former English Poet Laureate. Fewer still realized that Cecil Day-Lewis was better known, especially in the United States, by his pseudonym, Nicholas Blake, under which he wrote twenty detective novels, sixteen of which featured Nigel Strangeways, a lanky, well-connected, Oxford-educated private inquiry agent.

Cecil Day-Lewis was already an established poet but forced to make ends meet by working as a schoolmaster when he published his first detective novel, *A Question of Proof,* in 1935, reportedly to pay for mending a leaky roof. While his publishers suggested the use of the pseudonym in order to keep his two literary careers separate, no real attempt was ever made to conceal his true identity. This was, after all, the height of the Golden Age of detective fiction and the form was a not-so-guilty pleasure embraced by numerous academics. A critic for London *Times* greeted his maiden effort: "A very competent and readable first essay on what may be called 'highbrow' detective fiction. The dialogue is sprinkled, as one would expect, with a number of literary quotations, but apart from this—for the style is perfectly simple and straightforward—there is nothing to show that the book is the work of a modern poet, although there is a certain significance in the fact that the plot is laid in a preparatory school."

That leaky roof turned out to be a lucky disaster. *A Question of Proof* sold well and Day-Lewis was encouraged to continue Strangeways' adventures. Mysteries paid better than poetry and after eight years of toiling as a teacher, he was finally able to support his family by his writing alone.

There is no evidence that Day-Lewis ever thought of himself as slumming when he turned to crime fiction. While he was often linked with some of the more "literary" mystery writers, for example Dorothy L. Sayers and Margery Allingham, he himself was a major fan of Agatha Christie. His second novel, the superb *Thou Shell of Death* (1936), may have been based on Cyril Tourneur's 1607 play, *The Revenger's Tragedy*, but in most respects this tale set at a snowbound country house at Christmas time is pure Christie. Indeed, his earliest mysteries were all perfect examples of the Golden Age puzzler, complete with a somewhat larger than life sleuth modeled after his poetical mentor, W.H. Auden.

Unlike Christie, however, Blake's mysteries evolved as he moved into the 1940s, 1950s and 1960s. While most Golden Age sleuths seemed immune to the ravages of time—Poirot, after all, was already retired when he first appeared in 1920 and was still going strong in the mid-1970s when he would have been well over 100—Strangeways not only aged but altered and changed his own world view. He shed some of the more extravagant attributes borrowed from Auden at about the same time that Day-Lewis moved out from under Auden's poetical shadow with his breakout book of poetry, *Word Over All*, in 1943.

Strangeways' politics also undergo a metamorphosis as the years pass that match that of his creator, who was growing uncomfortable with his own status as one of the more privileged members of society. This may explain why one of his first acts of rebellion was to very briefly drop the hyphen from his surname. A longtime committed leftist, Day-Lewis joined the communist party in 1935. His poetry during this period focused on social themes with a strong touch of political didacticism. Aspects of this social consciousness also crept into his crime fiction, where he tended to portray virtually any member of the working class as an honest, admirable convention-defying sort, especially when viewed next to a member of the upper class. He openly decried the evils of big business and championed socialism in his 1937 Strangeways' novel, *There's Trouble Brewing*. However, in his later books, he allowed that the working class was just as susceptible to the occasional transgression as any pampered Tory.

Day-Lewis' flirtation with active communism was relatively short-lived. Within three years he became disillusioned with its more doctrinaire aspects and left the party in 1938, a decision that was reaffirmed much later when the Soviet tanks rolled in Budapest in 1956 to quell the uprising. But even though he was no longer a card-carrying communist, Day-Lewis was still railing against right-wing politics in 1939's *The Smiler with the Knife* when, with an eye toward Hitler's Germany, he argued that a strongman can turn even a freedom-loving country like Britain into a dictatorship by subverting the very patriotism of its citizenry.

Other, more subtle changes also slipped into his work as the years passed. The later books showed a much greater sense of realism and relied less on the tried-and-true—and often comically absurd—hallmarks of the Golden Age novel. No longer would the murderer, the jig definitely up, be pointed to a room where a waiting revolver sits on the table and be told to do the right thing. And while literary references continued to pepper his books, he began more and more to use aspects of his own life in his fiction. An actual incident from his own experience—a near fatal hit-and-run accident involving one of his sons—was the inspiration for an early novel, 1938's *The Beast Must Die*, picked by H.R.F. Keating as one of 100 best detective novels of all time, though most other critics, ourselves included, favor other Blake titles, including two that drew upon Day-Lewis' work experiences. *Minute for Murder* (1947) is set at the Ministry of Morale, an institution similar to the Ministry of Information where Day-Lewis worked as an editor during World War II. It's a brilliant character study where the victim is poisoned in full view of a half-dozens suspects. Nearly as good is *End of Chapter* (1957) in which Strangeways investigates a murder in a publishing house that bears a remarkable resemblance to Chatto and Windus, the firm where Day-Lewis was hired as a director in 1954. Critic Nicholas Fuller opts for 1949's *The Head of Traveller* as his masterpiece, calling it a "character-driven tragedy" and offering up a personal and detailed exploration of the poetic process

By this point, the years had begun to take their toll on Strangeways. By allowing his detective to age and suffer the calamities of time, Day-Lewis was able to add a depth to his books that was lacking in the works of many of his contemporaries. The loss of Strangeways' wife in the Blitz, the explorer Georgia Cavendish whom he met in *Thou Shell of Death*, deeply affects him but is somewhat abated when he meets and beds Clare Massinger, who becomes his mistress. We learn a great deal about his personal life, but what we never really find out is how Strangeways manages to put food on the table and a roof over his head. He is described as a private inquiry agent, but money never seems to change hands. Why this amateur sleuth should enjoy the confidence of his usual ally, Superintendent Blount of the Yard, is a question that would no doubt perplex most real coppers, although any true mystery fan knows that these are topics best left alone.

The creator of Nigel Strangeways was born in April 27, 1904, in Ballintubbert, Laois, Ireland, the son of a minister who moved his infant son to London following his wife's death in 1906. While Day-Lewis continued to refer to himself as Anglo-Irish for the rest of his life, he threw his lot in with Britain after the creation of the Irish Republic and was greatly troubled by Ireland's neutrality—and unofficial support for Germany—during World War II. He was educated at Sherborne School and at Wadham College, Oxford, from which he was graduated in 1927. In 1928, he married Mary King, the daughter of a teacher at Sherborne, and began an eight-year teaching career. With Mary he had two sons, one of whom, Sean, wrote a biography of his father: *C. Day-Lewis: An English Literary Life* (1980). He also had another son (some authorities say two) by a Dorset farmer's wife in the early 1940s. Day-Lewis also had a very public and tumultuous affair with the novelist Rosamund Lehmann during the 1940s. In 1951, he and Mary were divorced and he married the actress Jill Balcon with whom he had a son (Daniel) and a daughter, Tamasin Day-Lewis, a journalist specializing in writing about food.

From the 1950s on Day-Lewis taught poetry at a number of universities, including Oxford and Harvard. In 1968, 45 years after his first volume of verse, *Beechen Vigil and Other Poems*, was published, he was appointed Poet Laureate of England, succeeding John Masefield, who had held the post for 37 years. Sadly, Day-Lewis' reign was to be a short one. He died of pancreatic cancer on May 22, 1972, at the age of 68 at the home of Kingsley Amis, where he and his wife were staying. A great admirer of Thomas Hardy, he asked to be buried near his grave.

So, was Cecil Day-Lewis a poet first and mystery writer second? Does it make any difference? There is no question that he took both fields very seriously and did his best to produce quality work no matter what hat he wore. And when it came to mystery fiction, he understood better than most that one of the most important of the literary skills is the power to entertain.

Tom & Enid Schantz
Lyons, Colorado
June 2008

Note: The editors wish to acknowledge the work of Nicholas Fuller ("The Poet's Way of Detection") and James Gindin ("Nicholas Blake"), an entry in *The St. James Guide to Crime and Mystery Writers*.

Chapter I

Enter Severally

The scene is a bedroom in Sudeley Hall preparatory school: not one of the airy, green-washed, ostentatiously hygienic dormitories so reassuring to the science-ridden mind of modern parenthood; but one of those bedrooms, resembling in its extreme narrowness and draftiness nothing so much as a section of corridor in an express train, which tradition assigns to dons, schoolmasters and the lower ranks of domestic servant. The time is seven forty-five on the twentieth of June, 193–. There is a confused noise without, the pandemonium of eighty boys shaking off dull sloth and preparing to run their daily stage of duty, punctuated by occasional explosions from the master on duty. The incidental music is provided by a chorus of blackbird, thrush and sparrow, by the motor lawn mower giving a final trim to Big Field in view of today's festivities, and by the first of our dramatis personae, Michael Evans, who is singing snatches of the "Lament for Patrick Sarsfield" to his reflection in the mirror. The lower part of his face, a not too prominent chin and an amiable mouth, are concealed by lather; but he is noting with his usual faintly surprised approval the rather haughty set of nostril and brow, the curious dark blue of his eyes, and the black hair, disordered but not, he considered, uninteresting in its general effect. "Really, you might have done a good deal worse," he apostrophized the man in the looking glass. "You are no Ramon Navarro, it is true. But on the other hand, you are not a human mouse like poor Sims or a battered Adonis like Gadsby. In good taste without being gaudy. A Beta Plus face, on the whole…. 'But far from your country you lie cold and low …' Damn this blade! … 'Ah, why, Patrick Sarsfield, ah why did you go?' "He wiped off the remains of lather and resumed his soliloquy, "Today being Sports Day we will drape ourselves in an old boys' tie. One can never be too careful about impressing the parents with one's essential old boyhood and alma maternity. Faugh, what a riot of color! What maniac could ever have conceived this blend of magenta, green and orange? Thank God it's faded, anyway. And this unseemly length of silk is a passport to respectability, and open sesame to the great heart of the British middle-classes.... Why is it that the boys are all so nice, cheerful, unaffected, honest even and intelligent; and the parents–Lord save us–nasty, dull, brutish and short, or however it goes. That, I suppose, is the baneful influence of us schoolmasters.... Beta, perhaps, rather than Beta Plus. 'No, I am not Prince Hamlet nor was meant to be.' That reminds me–must borrow a pair of property swords for that duel scene with the Fifth.... Still, Hero seems to like it all right. How lovely and sweet she is ... 'with beauty like a tightened bow' ... and what on earth is going to come of all this? And tomorrow she is going away and I shan't see her till next term. Three months, three Godforsaken months."

From which soliloquy the observant reader will deduce that Michael Evans is sensitive to color, and something of a Bolshie, as they say; that he had the schoolmaster's conventional disrespect for parents en masse; that he is a good schoolmaster; that he has a sufficiency of that double-edged quality known as a sense of humor; that he is an English master, and really quite up to date; and that he is in love. Unfortunately for Michael, who liked facts to be decorous almost as much as he liked ideas to be dynamite-ish, he was in love with the headmaster's wife. And though she returned his love with all the gaiety and abandon of her happy nature, he could not help feeling a certain distaste at being protagonist in a situation so hackneyed by the contemporary novel and drama. Moreover, they had been lovers now for nearly two months, ever since that memorable and breathless moment when they had found themselves alone and then suddenly in each other's arms in–of all places–an empty classroom: and the situation was becoming increasingly irksome for both of them. Hero was being fretted by the inevitable intimacy with her husband, whom she must have married–she said to herself–in one of her periodic fits of absent-mindedness. Michael, surprised at first to feel none of the traditional "guilt" but only a perfect naturalness in the exploits of their love, was beginning more and more to dislike the stratagems necessary for its free play. He was alarmed, too, even while he admired it, by the recklessness of Hero; she seemed utterly oblivious to the possibility of their being caught out and its inevitable consequences. Those consequences would certainly be fatal to Michael. He would never get another job and he had no private means. And even if Percival Vale consented to a divorce, which he suspected was unlikely, Michael would be no better off. For parents, however well acquainted with the divorce courts they might be themselves, had a fixed antipathy to handing over their children to be educated by corespondents.

We shall meet Michael and Hero again this afternoon, in circumstances which turned out to be compromising in more ways than they could possibly suspect, so we may leave him for the moment to run our eye over some other principals in the cast, lingering only to remark that Michael's glass did not crack, that his bust of Dante did not sweat blood, that no hailstones fell out of the flawless sky–in fact, that none of the classical portents showed to warn him of the disastrous events soon to pile themselves upon his head.

Sweeny, the factotum, a querulous and disappointed man, is ringing the ponderous bell for breakfast, unconscious of the circumstances under which he will be ringing the same bell tomorrow. Upstairs the din is cut short. A few stragglers are hurling themselves in grim silence into their outer garments while the rest marshal themselves for the procession downstairs, for the Rev. Percival Vale is a great stickler for the more flashy manifestations of discipline. A long stride resounds over the uncarpeted floors and a voice adjures some sluggard to "brace up, for goodness' sake, Smithers! I want my breakfast." It is the gamesmaster, Edward Griffin. And as he is, like most gamesmasters, a very nice man indeed, we may go up and be introduced. He is tall and bulky, thirty years of age, with a rolling walk and the genial efficient air of an explorer, an old Oxford rugger blue, his never too equable temper rendered permanently explosive by the devices of the front-row forwards of certain Welsh clubs encountered in his youth. His other accomplishments include a talent for the piccolo and a positive genius for extempore charades. He has also been infected by Michael, his best friend, with a relish for morbid psychology, exercised frequently upon those of his colleagues who meet least with his approval.

Leaving the rank and file to enjoy their breakfast for a little, we now penetrate into the private side where the Rev. Percival Vale is sitting down to his, unattended by his wife, who has pleaded the necessity for a long lie in view of the afternoon incursion of parents. He is fifty years of age, with thin lips, a rosy-apple face, a precise delivery, a keen appreciation of his position as the fixed center of a stable little universe and an outspoken contempt for all failures within it. The boys, out of hearing, call him "Pedantic Percy": within his hearing they are apt to call him "Percy," for they have realized that he is not above a little mild flattery and gets quite a kick out of the more respectful form of his nickname. He is an excellent classical scholar, a capable headmaster on strictly conventional lines, and–on the same lines–a decent enough, though unsympathetic, person. It is, in fact, rather a pity that such unpleasant things are to happen to him and his microcosm. No shadow of coming events, however, falls upon his smooth brow and uplifted egg-spoon. He is wondering which of the parents he can touch for a subscription towards the new fives-court, whether Anstruther has a chance for Winchester, and how he shall word his rebuke to Sims for the indiscipline of his French classes.

Let us return, then, to the hall and listen in to one or two conversations which may or may not have a bearing on events to follow. At the head of the high table sits Tiverton, the senior assistant master; he has a sour mouth, but friendly, sensitive eyes; he has somehow or other fallen into the position of common-room cynic–probably owing to his boyish love of a phrase, for he is really an enthusiast. On his left and right sit Gadsby and Sims, who have already figured in Michael's soliloquy. Sims is one of those nondescript persons who gravitate into education as mud sinks to the bottom of a river, but are a good deal more difficult to stir up. He has a weedy mustache and protruding teeth, and spends his summer holidays on the Continent, ostensibly to rub up his languages, but according to Griffin for more dubious reasons. Gadsby, the local bore, must once have been handsome, but now, partly from drink and partly from mental inertia, is rapidly becoming a ruin. He had been an infantry officer in France, and was not averse to fighting his battles over again: as Tiverton put it–"he has done the state some service and he'll damn well see that they know it." Beyond these two sit Evans and Griffin, and at the other end of the table Cyril Wrench is reading the *Daily Herald* with an air of defiance. He has lately come down from one of the minor Oxford colleges, an esthete by choice but an incurable petty bourgeois by nature.

"Terrible affair, this Staveley murder," exclaimed Gadsby, rustling his *Daily Express* in a marked manner. "I see they've nearly finished the fullah's trial. I always say"–Michael trod heavily upon Griffin's toe under the table–"I always say, Tiverton, that you never know what a fullah's capable of when there's a woman in the case."

Griffin and Evans sighed rapturously at this new specimen for their collection–they were confirmed platitude-hunters–while Gadsby proceeded on his remorseless way:

"Here's this chap Jones, a bank-clerk, married man, exemplary life; suddenly falls for a barmaid; trots round the corner for a packet of arsenic; does his wife in. What amazes me, Griffin, is the nerve some of these quiet little chaps have. I remember in my platoon——"

Griffin interrupted hastily to dam the torrent: "Yes, when we find you lying in a pool of gore, we'll search Sims first for the blunt instrument. He's a nasty look in his eye, has our Mr. Sims."

Gadsby gave vent to a bellow of laughter, which occasioned an acid comment from the prefects' table–"Old Gaddie's giving tongue again." Sims sniggered feebly, rather pleased by the suggestion:

"Oh, come, Griffin, I mean to say–What am I to murder Gadsby for?

After all, he hasn't got a wife."

"Don't be too sure of that," put in Tiverton, and winced at the still louder peals of laughter elicited from Gadsby by his remark.

"No cherchez la femme for me," said Evans. "If I was looking for a murderer I should look for an egotist. Wrench is my man."

The prospective culprit shot a venomous glance at him over the top of his paper. Evans turned to Tiverton, "Though I can't see any of us qualifying as a victim. It's only in school stories that the staff are always assaulting each other with umbrellas and living in a perpetual welter of bad blood."

"Quite right, Evans," said Gadsby, "all morbid nonsense. We're all matey enough here, old man, aren't we?"

"One big, happy family, as Percy puts it," remarked Tiverton distastefully.

"Well, chaps," Griffin exclaimed, "if murder's done here, it will be committed by me upon the person of that human wart, young Wemyss. Just because he's Percy's nephew he thinks he can boss the whole bloody place. Of all the slimy, overfed specimens–and he's just enough low cunning to keep out of serious trouble himself. But whenever there's a row on he's at the back of it—"

"Like one of Buchan's Napoleons of international crime," put in Evans.

"Napoleons of international—" retorted Griffin obscenely. "I'll wring his neck for him one of these days. Do you know what he did—"

We may safely leave Griffin to his cataloguing of the crimes of the boy Wemyss and tune in to another station, the prefects' table.

"What's the first race this afternoon?"

"The 440, you boob. It's all up on the notice board. Oh, I forgot, you can't read."

"Funny boy! I say, Stevens, I heard the Griffin say you might bust the record."

"Oh, rot! I haven't an earthly; anyway, old Simmie will probably muck up the stopwatch like he did last year."

"Talking of Simmie, have you heard what Wemyss did in his French class yesterday?"

"Stale! Tell us something new!"

"But seriously, it's about time that squit Wemyss was suppressed. Pedantic Percy's little pet is getting above himself. He tried to bribe Patterson to beat up Smithers at the hay battle last night."

"Well, are you going to report him to Percy?"

"Be your rank! A-ah, I strongly deprecate idle talebearing: I choose my prefects to govern, not to–hahum–gossip." This last in a devilishly accurate reproduction of the Rev. Vale's more didactic utterances.

The head of the school, a serious, comely child of thirteen, now delivers judgment:

"No, there's no use applying to Percy. But we might hold a court on him—"

"I'm prosecutor!"

"I'm executioner!"

"Shut up! It isn't a joke. It's a bit thick the way he carries on with old Simmie. Ever since he came—"

"Mother Stevens protecting her little Simmie!"

"Oh, fry your face! I'm sorry for Simmie. He's a born ass, but Wemyss goes a bit too far."

"I say, Stevens, what about getting your brother to set his gang on him? Wemyss is not one of the Black Spot, is he?"

"I don't think so; but they're jolly secret about their members. That's a crazy notion, though. I'll talk to my brother in recess."

"Secret society beats up headmaster's nephew."

"To hire mercenaries–I may even say thugs, is scarcely the a-ah conduct of a Sudeley Hall prefect or an English gentleman, etc., etc."

Let us turn from the deliberations of the prefects to another table. A small, puffy boy of eleven years or so, with a vicious expression and the usual hallmarks of too much pocket-money, is guzzling his porridge and tormenting his neighbor alternately. It is the abhorrent Wemyss, or more correctly the Hon. Algernon Wyvern-Wemyss. His neighbor is a fat youth, heavy and resentful of eye, incurably slow in speech and action; his parents are farmers and he is here as a sacrifice to their craving for social elevation. There are one or two of him in most schools, born to be baited: the parents of such, Michael was wont to say, should be prosecuted in the criminal court for sending them.

"Well, Smithers, how are the livestock doing?"

"Oh, funny!"

"Fatting 'em up, and killing 'em off?" This was a phrase incautiously used by Smithers in an expansive moment some terms ago, and had not ceased to be used in evidence against him.

"You're fat enough; we'd better kill you off, hadn't we?" Roars of applause.

"Funny, aren't you?"

"Does your father wear leggins?"

"You'd better shut up."

"If he looks like you, I bet the cows kick him when he tries to milk them."

The overwrought Smithers breaks out and clouts his tormentor on the head. The Hon. Wyvern-Wemyss sets up a theatrical screech. Cries of

"Fat 'em up and kill 'em off!" "Go it," "Prime Beef," etc., from all round. And Tiverton comes wearily down to put an end to this tableau of original sin.

One more conversation and our prologue will be over. Stevens minor, the dictator (title derived from Evans' modern history teaching) of the Black Spot society, leans close and whispers to his lieutenant, a cheerful, chubby infant, Ponsonby:

"This afternoon: immediately after lunch: in Mouldy's hut: private conclave: password 'Dead Man's Chest,' countersign–'Bottle of rum.' "

"But, you fool," hisses the lieutenant, "we're supposed to be in the day room then."

"We can easily oil out: there's no roll-call. It's a life or death matter."

It is a couple of hours later. Michael has a period off. He fills a pipe and walks down the long passage between classrooms that lead out to the grounds. On either side of him arise sounds of education, curiously antiphonal in effect; a strident, confident recitative from the master, alternating with a treble solo or unison passage. In Sims' room something halfway between a marathon of coloratura sopranos and a witches' sabbath seems to be taking place. Michael shrugs his shoulders and passes on. Tiverton's rather petulant tones on his left: on his right Wrench is teaching the youngest form–a fluky, spasmodic voice; but he is doing it well; he has a gift. I must be nicer to him, thinks Michael. But how nightmare-ish these disembodied voices sound. And no doubt mine sounds just as repellent; though I flatter myself that I speak to boys in my natural voice. Anyway, it can't be as bad as that hectoring drawl of Percy's. No, I don't like the man, I definitely do not like the man. What on earth did darling Hero go and marry him for?

He emerged into the airy sunlight, lit his pipe, and strolled down the asphalt path between Big Field and the Hay Field. Mould, the groundsman, was whitewashing afresh the lines of the running track. Big circular stacks of hay, hollow in the middle, reminded him of yesterday's hay battle. A good romp. Tomorrow they would be dismantled and carted. He walked to the end of the path where the grounds were bounded by a thicket, and turned back. Passing behind the school block and the back of the headmaster's house he came to the high brick wall of the private garden. At the far end of this, where a shrubbery ran close to the outer side of the wall, was Hero's pillarbox. Just like her, he thought–not for the first time–her strange mixture of madcap play and reckless loving, to have chosen this romantic line of communication. He looked round once, his heart beating quicker, annoyed by the word "furtive" entering his head, took out a loose brick, transferred a piece of paper from the cavity to his pocket, and replaced the brick. Then he walked back and sat down on a seat by the Big Field, and read her note.

> "Darling, I shall be in the Vth form haystack during lunch tomorrow. Yes, highly imprudent, isn't it? But please come. I must see you. I *must see* you. H."

He sat there, content to feel happy, till the bell rang for recess. Then he went in to the common room. Surely they must be able to read his secret on his face, see that he was walking in an air of glory? Wasn't Tiverton looking at him in a rather peculiar way? He endeavored to compose his features into a workaday expression. Unsuccessfully, it seemed.

"Have you taken to Kruschen, or what is it?" said Tiverton.

"No, I've just had an hour off."

Griffin came up to him, "Will you change the chaps after lunch? I want to have a last look round in case Mouldy has committed any gaffes. Oh, and I say, Sims wants to know if you'll take on the stopwatch this year."

"Certainly, if he really doesn't want to–are you sure, Sims?"

"Yes, I'd really rather you did. I made rather a bloomer of it last year. I mean, I get so excited that I forget to press the button."

"All right, then: but I shall probably commit some solecism myself."

"Well, for God's sake don't commit it during the 440," said Griffin, "I'm backing Stevens for a record. Will anyone offer me three to one against? None? Have you no sporting instincts? Two to one, then?"

"Done," said Wrench.

On which immoral note this chapter may very well close.

Chapter II

Lyric and Elegiac

"In the morning, in the morning,
In the happy field of hay,"

was lilting in Michael's mind as he hurried out of the buildings, having seen every one sitting down safely to lunch and made appropriate excuses for his own nonattendance. The kitchen windows did not give on to the hayfield. Of course, there might be a servant wandering about in the classrooms at the back. Well, if they see us, they see us. Let them. It's about time we had a showdown. The possibility gave Michael a warm, excited feeling inside, like brandy. He was a natural fatalist–the type of person who, rather lacking in personal initiative, welcomes the feeling of having definite action imposed upon him by circumstances. He gave one look at the blank rows of windows and stepped quickly through the gap in its walls into the haystack.

Hero was there already, in a green dress, with a packet of sandwiches at her side. She was fresh and straight as the green corn. Michael drew her down and kissed her, with the scent of hay in his nostrils. A little stream of wind flowed into their sanctuary, blowing her golden hair against his cheek.

"Darling, you *are* crazy. You'll be asking me to meet you under Percy's study table next."

"Do you mind?"

"I love you, my sweet."

"I think you'd better stop kissing me now. I want to eat my lunch. There are some sandwiches here for you, too."

"But 'I on honey dew have fed.' "

"My dear, you are lovely. No one else could carry off a remark like that."

"Leaving that aside for a moment, what explanation have you given to the authorities for this picnic?"

"I told Percy that I wanted to have my lunch out in the sun. He's used to my fantastic behavior by now."

"You know, I feel rather bad, the way we talk about him–as though he was your aunt, or a dog, or something."

"Yes, I suppose it is rather awful. Of course, I've never loved him; but since I have loved you, I do feel much more kindly to him. It sounds very wicked, somehow, but there it is."

"Just like a woman, making the best of both worlds." He spoke lightly, but was aware that some hidden motive of antagonism or jealousy had caused the words. She felt it, too.

"Darling, that was a cruel thing to say."

He took her hand, with a quick impulsive gesture.

"I know. I'm sorry, my beautiful. But why, why did you marry him?"

"Panic: sheer panic. Michael, you don't know what a craving women have at times for comfort, reassurance, the feeling of firm ground beneath one's feet."

"And now you've gone out of your depth again."

"But I feel different now. I've got you beside me, and it makes me seem buoyant and much stronger. I don't think I could be a coward again, unless you stopped loving me."

"Hero, you're much braver than I am."

"I don't know. One can't really tell till the emergency comes along, can one? I wish sometimes that some crashing big one would turn up, and cut this tangle we've got tied up in."

Michael stroked the feathery down of her arm; said tentatively: "What do you think about this divorce business? Would Percy—?"

"Dear, we've had this out before. I'm not sure, but I think it's a thing he would be hopelessly obstinate over. And anyway, I'm not going to ruin your career."

"My career!" broke in Michael bitterly: "an assistant master in a preparatory school. God help us! Don't you understand that if I was prime minister, poet laureate, admiral of the fleet, and editor of the *Times*, I'd rather have my career ruined by you than live without you. The trouble is, I've no money: none of your 'comfort and reassurance.' "

Tears started in Hero's eyes.

"Oh, my sweet, I didn't mean that. You know I didn't mean that. This business has just got me down. But, Hero, you would like us to be more than lovers, to be married, wouldn't you?"

"Yes."

"Well, then, let's tell him. Please. After all, I'm not a halfwit. I'm sure I could get some sort of a job. I might even degrade myself to writing novels."

"You sweet; let's hope it needn't be as bad as that. But be patient. I'm going away tomorrow, for two months. I've promised my mother. I'll think it out by myself then. I can't think when you're so close to me. And in August I'll write and tell—"

"Hero, I love you. I leave it all to you. Don't let's waste any more time talking. They'll be out of dinner soon."

So they turned to each other and kissed for a long time. Then Hero went in. And after a little Michael walked towards the thicket, hugging his pain and happiness to himself.

It is two-fifteen p.m. The Rev. and Mrs. Vale are standing at the far gate, welcoming the first arrivals of the parents. Michael Evans, Esq., B.A., has just supervised the boys' changing; sent this one to the matron for a clean pair of trousers, found the lost stocking of that one, adjured A. not to go out without his hat and B. not to carry that large duck's egg in his pocket. He has also answered in ringing tones and the negative no less than fourteen separate and consecutive queries "need we wear sweaters, sir?" All this has been done in the midst of a shindy like a rookery ten times amplified, for discipline is relaxed today, and the silence rules abandoned. As a matter of fact, Michael has noticed this uproar no more than a city-dweller notices the sounds of traffic. The preparatory schoolmaster soon learns the knack of retiring into a kind of soundproof shell: if he fails to learn it, he either takes to drink or goes crazy.

Neat in their clean white shorts and bright blue blazers and stockings, the boys stream out on to the field. Those who are expecting their parents move off separately and with restraint towards the far gate. As each recognizes father or mother, his pace quickens involuntarily for a step or two, then is controlled to a self-conscious sedateness. Only the very youngest ones run. Michael sees Griffin approaching him, with an exercise book and a large pistol. He is wearing a double-breasted gray flannel suit and looks murderous.

"Who were you thinking of shooting?"

"Can you believe it? That moron, Mouldy, put up one too many sets of hurdles?"

"I can well believe it. Look out, here comes Gadsby. Let's move off."

But Gadsby, borne along on a strong gale of whisky fumes, caught them up and held them in the doldrums of his conversation till they were rescued by Percy fussing up to Griffin with inquiries about the tape.

Michael moved away with alacrity to where Tiverton was standing, looking very cool and dapper.

"I see you've just escaped."

"Really that man makes me despair of my profession," exclaimed Michael.

"Preparatory schoolmasters," announced Tiverton sententiously, "fall into two categories–the Old Contemptibles and the Young Objectionables.

Gadsby and I are included in the former class, yourself and Wrench in the latter."

"This station will now close down," replied Michael rudely.

"I say," he went on, "old Simmie's had a wash and brush-up, hasn't he?" He pointed to where Sims, in a suspiciously creased brown suit of antique workmanship, was talking with a parent.

"Yes, he's brought out that suit for Sports Day every year since I can remember. His contribution to the universal gaiety."

Michael craned over the assembling heads to catch a glimpse of Hero. There she was, in a cluster of animated females and deferentially inclining males. A gust of unreasonable anger swept over Michael. He hated it, seeing her at home in a different world from his own; so withdrawn from him and lively and socially competent. His anger transferred itself to the company in general. The spectacle of all this painted, feathered, complacent, chattering flock made him feel sick inside. It was to maintain this portentous scum that millions sweated or starved beneath the surface. "The fine flower of civilization": but they hadn't even looks to justify them. The women were powdered, jerky skeletons, and the men like lost sheep.

"The British bourgeoisie is beginning to have rather a hunted look in its eye, don't you think?"

"If you're going to talk politics you'd better forgather with young Wrench," snorted Tiverton.

"Thank you, but I'd rather not. Where is he, by the way?"

"Dunno. I've not seen him for some time. I expect he's crouched over his illustrated copy of *Mademoiselle de Maupin*."

"Really, Tiverton, you have a most unhealthy imagination. Oh, Sweeny's just going to ring his bell. I must go over to the finish: got to time this race."

The 440 was run on a circular course twice round, the start and the finish being opposite to where the main body of the spectators stood. The boys began to shout for their favorites. "Go it, Stevens!" "Come on, Anstruther!" "Wilkinson! Wilkinson!" A large-eared, bespectacled boy was giving, not too *sotto voce*, a faithful rendering of a wireless commentator to an admiring group of friends. "This is the Sudeley Hall sports ground. The 440 yards race is about to commence. They are taking off their blazers. They are lining up. Where is Stevens? I can't see Stevens. Yes, there he is. He has the outside berth. The favorite has the outside berth. Mr. Griffin is officiating with the pistol—Mr. Edward Griffin, the celebrated gunman. Will you speak a few words into the microphone, Mr. Griffin? No, perhaps it's as well that he should not. Now! They are going down on their marks! In a moment you will hear the pistol. Hallo, what's happening? I can't quite see. (Get out of the light, Biles, you little tick!) Stevens is sitting down. Oh, he is doing up his shoelaces. Now they're ready again. On your marks! Get set! Hallo! Old Griff has got the pistol jammed. Now it's right. On your marks! Get set! Go!! That was the starting-pistol you heard. They are rounding the first corner. Anstruther is in the lead. Bravo, Anstruther!" Here the violently cultured voice broke off, and was replaced by the owner's natural shrill screams: "Come on Stevens! Steeevens!"

It was a great race. Michael, in the appalling days to come, was to remember it vividly and gratefully, as front line soldiers in the Great War remembered some scene, cricket on a village green, a farmhouse tea, shire horses standing up grandly against the skyline—which somehow grew to become their vital link with sanity and England. The brown-green short grass; the greyhound grace of the runners; the feel of the stopwatch hot in his hands; Anstruther's grim tenure of the lead round the last bend and Stevens, white in the face, coming up with a superlative rush of speed and passing him three yards before the tape. A set of pictures that was to recur again and again to Michael; as though to a man drowning, at the last crisis of breath.

Michael had automatically clicked the watch, smiling uncontrollably, tears pricking his eyes. He became aware of a hand squeezing his elbow. He looked down and saw Sims, trembling with excitement, his usually dull eyes sparkling behind his spectacles. He felt a ridiculous wave of affection for the little man. "By Jove," Sims was saying, "what a race! I say, has he beaten the record?" Only then did Michael remember to look at the watch's hand. Yes! He'd beaten it. By a fifth of a second. Every one crowded round. The time was chalked up on the blackboard, "a school record" underneath it. Yells and clapping from the whole ground. The hero was practically winded again by dozens of hands clouting him on the back.

The sports ran their course. Parents began to get bored and move about in gossiping groups. The distinguished local resident stood up uneasily behind an array of silver cups, and drew shaky parallels between running and citizenship, patriotism, Christianity and other abstract themes. More cheers and backslapping. At four-thirty it was all over. The parents had retired, some to tea with the headmaster, others to stuff their children in the neighboring village. The remnant of the boys and the staff went in to their more frugal meal, unconscious of the fact that one of their number had been lying dead for some time, his face hideously black and his tongue clenched between grinning teeth, not a hundred yards away.

Tea is over. Sims, Evans, Gadsby and Wrench are sitting about in the common room, in various attitudes of exhaustion. Griffin has gone out to supervise the clearing away of the sports apparatus.

"Well," said Gadsby expansively, "that's over. It's extraordinary how good a cup of tea tastes after a hot afternoon in the sun. Jove, we'll not see a race like that 440 for a good few days to come–eh, Evans?"

"No; it was certainly a race and all."

Wrench lit a cigarette, "The way Stevens caught him up on the last bend! A jolly good effort."

"Why, old man, he caught him in the straight, surely," protested Gadsby.

"Yes, I know. But he was coming up on the bend fast, wasn't he? Or wasn't he?" Wrench was grievously addicted to obsolete society slang.

"Didn't see you at the beginning of the race, Wrench?" said Sims. "Where were you standing?"

Wrench leaned over to flick his ash into the grate, "Oh, I was gadding around. Acquiring merit with parents and all that."

Tiverton came in. He had been doing the rounds. As he opened the door a piercing shriek was raised in the passage: "Wemyss! Wemyss!" Then a snatch of conversation. "Where is that squit, Wemyss. I want to borrow some cash off him. He's always rolling." "I expect—" The door closed. Tiverton came in and sat down, saying:

"Roll-call's at seven, isn't it?"

"You on duty, Tiverton? Don't envy you the job. Half these little devils who've been out with their parents will be sick as cats," said Gadsby.

"And Tiverton can follow them about with a spade and bucket," added Wrench coarsely.

"Ah, tchah."

But at seven o'clock it appeared that the excitement of the day was by no means over. To Tiverton, calling the roll in the day room, one name failed to respond.

"Walters?" "Sir!"

"Ward?" "Sir!"

"Wyvern-Wemyss?"

"WYVERN-WEMYSS!"

"Does any one know anything about Wemyss?"

Several *sotto voce* suggestions were put forward: "Yes, he's a worm." "He's probably throwing up into Percy's wastepaper basket." "Or boozing at the Cock and Feathers." Nothing more constructive or audible being advanced, Tiverton asked: "Did he go out with relations?"

Silence.

"Come along," said Tiverton irritably. "He must have told someone whether he was going out or not."

A small boy at the back stood up and every head turned round towards him, as though he had them on strings.

"Please, sir, he t-told me he thought he w-would not be going out."

"When did he tell you this?"

"Yesterday, sir."

A babel of voices arose.

"Sir, do you think he's run away?"

"Good riddance."

"Please, sir, perhaps he's been kidnapped, sir."

"STOP TALKING! Sit quietly at your desks. Prefects, see that there's no ragging about."

Tiverton went through to the private side and found the headmaster in his study.

"Wemyss is absent from roll-call."

The Rev. Vale turned round sharply from his desk.

"Absent? My nephew? But that's impossible."

Tiverton enlarged wearily.

"He failed to answer his name. None of the boys seem to know anything about it. Had he leave out?"

"Leave out? No, I don't remember–I'll just make sure."

He opened a drawer and referred to a printed list.

"No. No one was taking him out. This is most extraordinary. Unless Urquhart drove over–but he would have let me know. Have you ascertained whether he is anywhere on the premises?" Vale was quite flustered.

"No. I thought it best to inform you before any sort of search was instituted," replied Tiverton in his most official tones.

"Er, yes. Quite right. What do you, er, suggest?"

"Perhaps we should ask Matron first. He may have felt ill and gone to the sickroom."

The matron was sent for, a large, imperturbable woman.

"Master Wyvern-Wemyss? No, he has not come to me."

The headmaster, who had by now regained some of his composure, directed Tiverton to keep the boys in the day room and the matron to organize the servants for a thorough search of the buildings. He himself hurried along to the common room, where the masters were at supper.

"My nephew, Wyvern-Wemyss, is not to be found. Can anyone throw any light—?"

No one could.

"The matron is supervising a search over the house. Perhaps it would be well to look over the grounds too, in case he has met with some accident. Could you arrange, Gadsby—?"

"Certainly. I suppose you will be ringing up the police?" added Gadsby tactlessly.

"The police?" Vale raised his eyebrows.

"Well, I mean to say, he might have run away."

"And for what reason, pray, should he take such an extraordinary course? Are you suggesting that he had grounds for—? Really, Mr. Gadsby."

Gadsby abased himself, and the search began. Gadsby himself went over the Big Field; Sims into the far field: Evans was allotted the garden, Griffin and Wrench the thicket. Haymakers had just come to work late on the hayfield, so it was not considered necessary for the staff to search there, or advisable to broadcast a possible scandal amongst the laborers.

Michael wandered about disconsolately for ten minutes or so, thinking of Hero, cursing the search for a farce and peering perfunctorily into bushes. When they assembled again, it was without tidings of the missing Wemyss. Matron and her forces had been equally unsuccessful; and the headmaster, deciding that Gadsby's tactless hypothesis must now be entertained, rang up the village constable. A description of the lad was given, and the constable promised to make inquiries in the village and to communicate with the superintendent at Staverton, so that a watch might be set on all adjacent stations and bus-routes. Further questioning by Tiverton in the day room had elicited the fact that no one seemed to have set eyes on Wemyss in the course of the afternoon, so it appeared that he might really have taken the incomprehensible liberty of removing himself from the Rev. Vale's tutelage.

But the masters had scarcely settled down again in the common room when there was heard a clatter of boots outside, and a figure passed the window at a shambling run going towards the headmaster's private door. A few minutes after this, a message came requesting Tiverton's presence in the study. And almost before Gadsby had time to fire off a salvo of rhetorical questions, Tiverton returned, dazed and white in the face.

"Percy wants you all in his study. They've found Wemyss in the hayfield. He's been strangled. They found him when they were dismantling the haystacks. In one of the haystacks."

Chapter III

Enter a Posse

Michael's first sensation was one he had several times experienced in his boyhood, when at chapel a notice was given out that "the whole school will assemble immediately after service" and one knew that a really serious row was on and said to oneself "Thank God, it's not me." Now, as then, he felt as though his heart had dropped into his stomach and was fluttering there uneasily. He became aware, even, of feeling a curious surprise that he had nothing to do with that luckless body in the hayfield, a relief that it was not he who had committed the crime–as though the point had been undecided till now. Then his mind started working furiously and irrationally, like an engine accelerated with the clutch in. Well, at any rate this will prevent Hero going away. It's an ill wind. But why should anyone? And who? WHO? The hayfield. Why the hayfield? Why not? In the morning, in the morning, in the happy field of hay. Only it's the evening. Tiverton looked bad. Mouth twitching, like a baby going to cry. I wonder whereabouts in the hayfield. Nuisance; police about, I suppose; will mess up the work. Oh, of course, he said in one of the haystacks. How lovely Hero looked. Her body is the sunlight of my flesh. That's blank verse. Not a very good line either. One of the haystacks. Which one? Come on, say it out. Not the Fifth form stack, I hope. I hope not. Why, what on earth does it matter to you which? Five haystacks. Odds are four to one against. Please don't let it be there. Not where Hero and I were. Oh, dry up. Pull yourself together. The happy field of—

He found himself in the study. The headmaster was there, a queer bluish tinge overlaying his ruddy cheeks, spasmodically putting on and taking off his pince-nez. He glanced round at his colleagues. They were restlessly silent, like people seeing off a train. Tiverton was not there. Michael mumbled some condolements to Vale, who replied: "Thank you, Evans, thank you. I–this shocking disclosure has quite unmanned me. Such a thing has never occurred in my school before." Griffin was not sufficiently overawed by the occasion to refrain from an outrageous wink at Michael. Vale went on, his habitual pedantry of phrase contrasting oddly with his broken, almost appealing tones. "The poor, unfortunate boy! It passes my comprehension why anyone should want to–to, er, make away with him! The scandal! The publicity! I have asked Tiverton to make it known among the boys that my nephew has met with an accident, a fatal accident. It may yet be possible to prevent the–a–ah–facts from reaching the parents. I have rung up Dr. Maddox: he will be here shortly: and the police, of course. I should be obliged, Griffin, if you would meet the doctor when he comes and take him to–I do not feel capable myself. If you have any suggestions, any of you, as to other immediate steps that might be taken—?"

Michael realized that Vale was asking to be relieved of his responsibilities, and said: "Perhaps it would be advisable for me–for Sims and myself to go out and see that the men do not interfere with the–the scene of the crime. I believe that the police would wish things to remain as far as possible as they were found."

"Certainly, Evans, certainly. An excellent suggestion."

"Excuse me, headmaster, but should we not–er–get in touch with the unfortunate boy's relatives?"

Vale, relieved of the necessity for action, was in a mood to resent any further encroachment upon his authority.

"My dear Sims, it should be unnecessary for me to have to assure you that any such very obvious steps would have been taken by me, if the situation had called for them. As it happens, I am the boy's nearest living relative myself. If you have no more constructive proposals to make, perhaps you will accompany Evans and give him what assistance you can."

Sims blushed and Michael felt awkward. Vale, feeling better for his act of devastation, indicated that the audience was over, and Sims and Evans went out of doors. Michael, fearing the worst, forced himself to look towards the hayfield. A group of men with pitchforks was gathered round one of the haystacks. Yes, the Fifth form one. It would be. Half of the structure had been demolished and the last sunlight shone sadly on the red and yellow of the new wagon beside it. The laborers stepped back a pace as Evans and Sims approached. Where part of the wall had been lifted, untidily crumpled, with pieces of straw still clinging to its clothing, lay the body of Algernon Wyvern-Wemyss. He was not a pretty sight. The manner of his death had robbed him of that last consolation. Michael turned away, feeling sick. Sims was staring fascinated at the body. The foreman of the laborers walked heavily up to Michael, touching his hat:

"Tur'ble business, this, sur. Looks like he been murdered. Bill, here, he lifts up stook on fork. 'Gor,' he says, 'one of they boys has left his coat underneath here.' We lifts two more stooks, and there he was, sur. 'Gor,' says Bill, 'it's a carpse.' Gave us a fair turn, I can tell 'ee, sur; ar, that it did."

"Yes, it must have done," said Michael inadequately. "By the way, did you move it at all?"

"No, sur. Bill, he says, 'Us had better shift the poor young gentleman and make him more comfortable like.' 'Bill,' I says, 'thou'rt a bloody chump. Leave un alone. Police woa'nt have 'ee meddlin' with murdered carpses.' So I sent him in to tell Reverend Vale as how one of his boys was in hayfield. Ar, that was the size o' the matter."

"Quite right. I should think it would probably be best if you sent your men back to the village. They can do no good for the present, and the police will want to search the field as it is. If you and–er–Bill could wait till they come—?"

The foreman gave the necessary directions and his small party broke up. Wrench came half running out of the school. Michael surprised a curious look on his face as he approached. Ruminating on it later, the best analysis he could come to was that it presented a kind of alternation of relief and fear. He had no time for analysis at the moment, as Wrench, after one brief glance at the contents of the stack, retired a few paces and began to retch. He felt himself being drawn aside by Sims.

"I say, Evans, do you know anything about this sort of thing? I mean, he looks as if he'd been dead–for quite a long time, somehow."

Michael had got the same impression, though he could not say why. Wemyss did look so very dead. Sims' remark must have reached Wrench's ear, for the latter turned and said in a high tense voice:

"Well? What of it? What are you getting at?"

"Well, you see, I've just remembered that Griffin was out in the field over there this evening till we began the search, and he would have seen if–if it had happened then. And before that was the sports. So the only time left is between lunch and two-thirty–that is, if he *was* at lunch." Sims concluded his involved argument with a mildly triumphant look.

"Well?" snapped Wrench.

"What I'm getting at is that I suppose we'll all be asked where we were then. Alibis, you know," he added brightly.

The other two were silent for rather a long time, each thinking his own thoughts. Then Wrench spoke in a vicious tone.

"Are you one of the secret police, or what? All this panic about alibis just because you have had a verbal inspiration, I suppose it must be, that he has been dead a long time. No doubt you've a perfect alibi yourself?"

"As a matter of fact, now I come to think of it, I don't think I have got a very good one," Sims replied more slowly.

"Ah, well, cheer up," said Michael with forced heartiness, "the real murderer always has a perfect alibi. It's us innocent ones who are never able to cook one up."

All the same, he thought to himself, it would not be funny at all if Sims is right. He saw his objection to the body being found on his and Hero's rendezvous, which had before been merely esthetic, assuming a very different significance. Uneasy speculation was interrupted by the arrival of Griffin with Dr. Maddox. The school doctor was a round, bouncing little man, exuding urbanity and antisepsis. Michael might have been amused at another time by the delicate way his patent-leather-shod feet pranced through the dewy stubble.

"Good-evening, gentlemen," the doctor said, restraining himself with difficulty–the fancy occurred to Michael–from pirouetting up to the corpse on his shining toes. "Very sad. Poor young laddie. Well, well!" He knelt down beside the body, putting his black bag in front of him, and got to work. The others looked away. A feeble and grotesque pun, turning on the word "examinations," arose unbidden in Michael's mind. Griffin was screwing his heel round in the earth, rather in the manner of one preparing for a place-kick. Wrench threw one or two hasty glances over his shoulder, and turned back with a visible shudder. "O, they looked at one another. And they looked away," Michael found himself muttering.

"What's that?" said Wrench.

"Nothing."

Dr. Maddox straightened himself up, with a rueful glance at his soaking knees.

"Dear me, dear me!" he exclaimed. "Most extraordinary–and, er, tragic. No question about it, I'm afraid. Murder or manslaughter. He seems to have been throttled first by his assailant's hands. These bruises, you see. Then a thin cord tied round his neck. You will observe the red line: it has sunk in rather deeply."

No one cared to verify the statement. Michael wondered how long he would be able to refrain from asking the question that was on the tip of at least three tongues. After an awkward silence, it was finally Sims who took the plunge.

"How long would you say he had been dead, doctor?"

They were kept on tenterhooks for half a minute, while the doctor disported himself in a stream of technicalities.

"To put it more simply," he concluded, "rigor mortis is fully established. That means he has been dead for more than four hours; probably for six. Of course, if the body has been lying under hay all the time, that would tend to defer the process and thus extend the period. You understand we can only fix the time very roughly: I should put it between four and seven hours ago as the outside limits."

Wrench moved his right hand abruptly towards his left wrist, paused in the act, then thought better of it and uncovered the face of his wrist watch.

"Five to eight."

At least three heads did lightning calculations, but before the results could be compared, a murmur of talk was heard and a procession appeared out of the side door, led by the headmaster and a gigantic pale-faced man, the superintendent from Staverton. Behind these two straggled a sergeant, the Sudeley constable, and two other men, one bearing a camera.

"This is Superintendent Armstrong," announced the headmaster. "Superintendent, I dare say you know Dr. Maddox. These gentlemen are members of my staff–Mr. Sims, Mr. Evans, Mr. Griffin, Mr. Wrench."

"Pleased to meet you," the officer nodded perfunctorily. Polite murmurs from the members of the Rev. Vale's staff.

The headmaster continued: "Should you wish for any assistance I am sure these gentlemen—"

"Thank you, sir," interrupted Armstrong, with an indecent disregard for the rules of academic conversation, "I will certainly ask for what assistance I may need. If you gentlemen will all go indoors for the present. I shall ask for statements from you in the course of the evening. Who was it who found the body?"

The foreman stepped forward.

"You can wait. And I should like a word with you now, Dr. Maddox. Good evening, gentlemen."

At this pointed dismissal, the gentlemen trailed back into the school; Griffin and Evans were several paces behind the rest. Griffin whispered:

"Percy will get an apoplexy if he has much more of this rough stuff applied to him. What do you think of our Mr. Armstrong?"

"I do *not* like him."

"Personally, I think he's a—"

"You may well be right."

Supper was a silent affair. The boys were subdued and had their ears open for any crumbs of information that might fall down from the high table. But none did, for the masters had instructions to keep the real facts to themselves for the present–not that there was much chance of concealing them, as Griffin remarked, with a posse of police tramping about outside the back windows. Michael was glad of the absence of the usual chatter, for he was concentrating all his powers on a difficult decision. As soon as supper was over he went through to the private side in search of Hero. Luckily he found her alone, sitting rather forlornly over an uneaten meal. She looked up at him with a twist at the corner of her mouth, half provocative, half pathetic.

"Isn't this very imprudent, dear Michael?"

"Hero, listen. I was not with you at lunch today. You were alone in the haystack."

"What on earth—?"

"Don't you see, darling, they're bound to ask us all where we were; and Maddox says the murder was probably done between one and four."

"But we can give each other alibis."

"Yes, and blow the lid off everything."

Hero's smile sweetened her mocking words:

"Oh, I see, Michael being chivalrous."

They heard footsteps coming along the passage. Michael spoke urgently. "Promise."

"Very well," she whispered, adding certain reservations in her own mind. "I'll look out something for you," she said, as the door opened and her husband came in. He surveyed them with a strained and faraway look in his eyes.

"Oh, Evans; the superintendent is going to interview the staff individually after the boys go to bed. Will you hold yourself in readiness?"

Michael mumbled something and went out. He felt vaguely irritated. Hero's little deceptions were still apt to fret him.

"What did Evans want?" Vale was saying.

"One or two properties for the play he's doing with his form."

"Mm. I don't know that I approve of all this dressing-up in school. And this is a most unsuitable time to be thinking of play-acting. Hero, it is terrible. I have given my whole life to the school. Fifteen years: and now this happens. A boy to whom I stood more especially *in loco parentis*."

"Why, nobody could say it was your fault."

"Of course not," he replied irritably, "that's not the point at all. But you know perfectly well that any suspicion of scandal is enough to ruin a place like this. And where shall we be then?"

"Well, I suppose we shan't starve. We come in for some money now, I take it." Hero was exasperated into a callousness of phrase that quite startled her.

"My dear, that was a most brutal and uncalled-for remark. As though I— really, Hero, you can scarcely be yourself tonight. I should have expected a little more sympathy from my wife on such an occasion as this."

Hero sighed wearily. The old appeal for pity. And the trouble was that it always worked, operating on the part of a woman's nature that was beyond her control. No, she said firmly to herself, I love Michael. I'm not going to be emotionally bullied into doling it out to anyone else. Love is not indiscriminate charity. She looked more dispassionately at her husband. He was quite white, and breathing heavily. She said:

"I'm sorry. I expect I'm a bit overwrought myself."

"Yes, yes, it is a difficult time for us all."

She tried to laugh him out of his concern, saying lightly:

"Especially for us who are under suspicion."

"Under suspicion? Are you mad, Hero. Good heavens, you mean the money. Why, you don't really suppose—?"

"Well, the police will presumably look for a motive."

Hero still was speaking in jest; but, looking up, she was dismayed to see her husband's face taut with fear God, she thought, he's going to break down in a minute. One might have supposed he really had done it himself.

Two small and highly malleable noses are pressed against the window of the Third form classroom, which gives on to the hayfield. Their owners– the intrepid leaders of the Black Spot–with their usual flair for smelling out or getting into trouble, have detected the presence of the detectors and have cut evening prayers in order to keep an eye on their activities. They are busy getting what the papers call an "exclusive story."

"Look, Stevens, that must be the head policeman–that one in the flat cap."

" 'Inspector,' you ass, not 'head policeman,' " observed the dictator crushingly.

"Isn't he a whopper? He's fatter than the Griffin."

"I bet he's not so strong, though. Do you remember Griff holding me and Pongo above his head–one in each hand?"

"Jolly hard cheese on Wemyss; though he was a bit of a worm. I wonder what the accident was."

"Accident? You poor simp, you don't really think it was an accident, do you? They wouldn't have a crowd of bobbies all over the place if it was an accident."

"Crumbs! Do you mean—?"

"Murder. Mm. Bumped off. That's what I mean. And what's more," added the dictator darkly, "I've got an idea who—"

"Oh, whoopee! Tell me! Are we going to track him down? Who is it?"

"Don't breathe all over the glass, you boob, I can't see." Ponsonby rubbed the moisture away with his sleeve. "I shan't tell you yet," Stevens proceeded, "you'd only go yapping it all round the school."

"Oh, Stevens, I wouldn't really–I say, what's that bloke with the camera doing?"

"Photographing the remains. We always do it in murder cases. Gosh, don't you see, that proves it's murder."

Ponsonby goggled in admiration of his leader's flight of logic; then doubled his nose up against the pane.

"Look, they're lifting him up. They're going to put him in the hay cart. I can't see any blood, can you? Doesn't he look horrid? I think I'm going away."

The dictator was made of sterner stuff. "You go away if you like. I'm going to see this through. Quick! Come back! They're turning the hay over: looking for clues, I expect." Ponsonby returned to the window. "Now they're driving the cart away. Wonder where they're taking him. Cemetery, I suppose."

"Do you think we'll get a half-holiday for the funeral?"

"Might. Gosh, look, the inspector's found something. He's taking it up in his handkerchief. Fingerprints, you know."

"Oh, flip! Will he take ours?"

"Shut up! I can't see—it's getting so dark. It's a bullet, perhaps."

"No, it's a pencil—a silver pencil."

Chapter IV

Viva Voce

The sun has finally abdicated his noonday eminence, unperturbed by dark deeds, fear or passion. He looks in at the dusty common room, where masters are chatting spasmodically, trying without much success to cover up with commonplace this sudden chasm in their lives. The police have quartered the hayfield now and found whatever was to be found, and the hay cart is carrying its normal load. A line of lapwings flies along the far edge of the playing field, their black and white showing alternately like ripples of light or waves on a moonlit lake. Tiverton, watching them out of the day room window, toys with a mental image of death and life, crime and innocence, black and white. Every one in the school, for that matter, except a few very young boys who are so small that the whole affair passes over their heads, finds his eyes drawn magnetically to the windows and what lies beyond them.

Soon the superintendent comes in to the day room. The boys eye him in that deceptively polite, appraising silence with which boys in the mass are wont to receive a stranger. Armstrong looks almost fidgety, if such a human Everest could be said to fidget. But, encouraged by the receptive looks of his audience, he passes his forefinger once round the inside of his collar, assumes his most avuncular expression, and plunges in:

"You have all heard that an unfortunate accident has occurred. I have been sent to inquire into it, and I hope that if any of you young gentlemen can give me assistance, you will do so." He has begun well. The most captious juvenile critic can find nothing to lay hold of here; and the idea of assisting the police has gone down splendidly. The superintendent feels that he is passing this test with honors, and resumes more expansively: "Now all I want to know at present is, did any of you notice whether your playmate was at lunch, or see anything of him afterwards?" An invisible shudder passes over the assembly, starting from the veteran critics of the Fifth form at the back, and communicating itself like a groundswell to the small boys at the superintendent's feet. Yes, he has put his foot in it all right. One word has changed him from a potential hero to a figure of fun.

33

For some weeks now the word "playmate" is to be a stock joke and a great weapon of offense, and it would take him many more weeks to live down the effect of it. He realizes that he has "lost his audience," and ceasing to attempt any further imitation of Agag repeats his questions in a harsh, official tone. Wyvern-Wemyss had not appeared at lunch; several boys had had leave out to lunch with parents, and those who ordinarily sat next to Wemyss assumed that he had leave out too. No, no one had set eyes upon him afterwards, or knew where he had gone. Nor had anyone been outside the buildings till just before the sports began. Armstrong may have a kestrel's eye, but he cannot be expected to pick out, amongst eighty boys, a small hand slightly lifted and as quickly lowered at his second question, or two small pairs of features becoming tense and obstinate at his third. He strides down the room and out of the door, rather hurriedly for him–but not so quickly that he escapes the beginning of a short variety turn by a youth with outstanding spectacles and ears, in which the unfortunate word figures as the *pièce de résistance.*

The superintendent is closeted with a headmaster distinctly conscious of the fact that he is being interviewed in his own study, and feeling, no doubt, something like Kronos when Zeus turned up out of the blue and started to put him through his paces.

"Now, sir," the superintendent was saying, "let me see if I've got the facts right so far. The boy was last seen, as far as we know, during the last period of lessons today. His absence was not noticed till seven p.m. when a search was instituted. From the evidence of Morley, the foreman of the laborers, it is clear that the body was well concealed."

"It might have been placed there in the course of the evening, any time after the murder," the headmaster added.

"Why, of course, sir; that had not occurred to me," said the superintendent mendaciously, adding in a heavily humorous tone that caused the Rev. Vale to wriggle slightly in his chair, "we shall be having you in the force before long, sir." He went on: "All your staff been with you for some time, sir?"

"Yes, except for Mr. Wrench; he came last term."

"What sort of a man is this Mr. Wrench?"

"Well–er–I've always found him satisfactory in his teaching capacity. Not a scholar, of course, not a scholar; but conscientious, and a very fair disciplinarian."

"I was not referring to his teaching capacity so much as to his general character." It was curious the way no one seemed to be able to converse with Percival Vale without being infected with his measured mode of speech.

"Oh, his general character? His college gave him a very fair testimonial. I can't say I've come into contact with him a great deal outside our scholastic duties. He strikes me as reserved; and he has a rather regrettable leaning towards estheticism. I doubt if his politics are altogether sound. But, of course, he is not quite a–not quite, a-ah–that is—" The headmaster broke off, looking a trifle confused.

"Not quite a gentleman?" Armstrong suggested. "Well, that may be said of quite a number of us. However, to resume. The search proved unsuccessful, and you got in touch with us. May I ask, sir, by the way, why you did not ring up the police as soon as the boy was found to be missing? We had no word from you till seven-thirty."

"I was unaware at the time that my nephew was murdered," replied the headmaster acidly. It was the superintendent's turn to wriggle slightly in his chair.

"You imagined that he had just run away, or something, I take it," he counterattacked.

"Your second hypothesis is more correct than your first," returned Mr. Vale. "I supposed that he had met with some accident. My boys are not in the habit of–a-ah–running away."

"No, quite so. And you were first informed of the tragedy at seven twenty-five by Morley, who told you of his discovery?"

"Yes."

"You then sent for Mr. Tiverton and told him to inform the rest of your staff; and you telephoned to Dr. Maddox and the police?"

"That is so."

The telephone rang in the lobby outside. The headmaster began to rise from his chair, but Armstrong lifted a large hand and said:

"Don't trouble yourself, sir. Sergeant Pearson will take the message." The headmaster relapsed into his seat, saying with a rather sickly smile:

"You seem to have garrisoned the place already."

The sergeant entered and told his superior that Dr. Maddox was on the phone. After a short conversation Armstrong returned.

"Now, sir," he continued briskly, "may I ask you few more questions; just a matter of formality?"

"Certainly."

"If you will give me an account of your own movements between one and four."

"Oh, well, let me see. I was in school till quarter to one. Then I signed leave outs till lunch time. In hall till one-thirty."

"All your staff at lunch, sir?"

"Yes. No, I'd forgotten. Evans asked to be excused attendance." Armstrong made some cryptic hieroglyphics in his notebook.

"Give any reason?"

"No, I do not consider it necessary for my staff to—"

"Exactly, sir, and then?"

"I was talking in here with my wife for about a quarter of an hour. After that I went up to my dressing room and changed. By then it was time to go and meet the parents. Today was our Sports Day, you see."

"And when did they begin to arrive?"

"Why, about two-fifteen, I suppose. I really don't see what—"

"You were in your dressing room from one-forty-five to two-fifteen– changing?"

"Well, I dare say I lay down and rested for a part of the time. You cannot expect me to remember every trivial action."

"You will excuse me asking, sir, but have you anyone who can confirm this? Servants coming in? Your wife?"

The headmaster bent upon him that look which had quelled many an unruly parent and could reduce small boys to a state of total aphasia. It bent and broke upon the superintendent's adamantine front.

"This is outrageous! I did *not* commit this murder and I *was* in my room from one-forty-five to two-fifteen. If you do not take my word for the one, you are not likely to take it for the other."

"No, sir. We can't afford to take people's words in murder cases. I have my duty to do. If I can't get information from one person, I must try to get it from another." There was an inflexible ring in the superintendent's voice, and Percival Vale recognized it. He said, abruptly, and rather sulkily:

"My wife was in her bedroom for part of the period. It adjoins my dressing room. We spoke a few words to each other through the door. That's all the proof I can give you."

"About what time would that be?"

"Mrs. Vale came up shortly after two. We went downstairs together."

Armstrong relaxed his moral pressure at this point, and drew the remaining facts from the headmaster comparatively painlessly. These were: that the boy's parents were dead and he was the nearest living relative; that he shared the duties of guardianship with James Urquhart, Esq., solicitor, of Staverton; that no one had asked to take the boy out for the afternoon; and that he was unaware of anyone who could possibly want to make away with his nephew. The superintendent also listened graciously to a theory that some tramp must have killed the lad–he was accustomed to have a considerable amount of money, for a boy, in his pockets; and declared that this no doubt was what had happened. It was only after the superintendent had gone out to "have a few words with Mrs. Vale," that the headmaster began to realize, with a nicely balanced blend of indignation and apprehension, that his inquisitor had had him in the

hollow of his hand, as Gulliver held the King of Lilliput, and that there
had been a sinister absence of inquiry about the extent to which "his
nearest living relative" would benefit by the Hon. Algernon Wyvern-
Wemyss' death.

The Superintendent Armstrong who interviewed Hero Vale was a very
different man from the official inquisitor of Percival Vale. His eyes ex-
pressed a polite admiration of her beauty and his voice a polite recogni-
tion of the unpleasant circumstances in which she was involved.

"This must have been a severe shock for you, madam. But if you could
just answer one or two questions; a matter of routine?"

"Why, of course."

"After lunch–you didn't happen to notice if your nephew was at lunch,
did you?"

"No. I couldn't. I wasn't there myself."

The superintendent gently uncrossed his legs, and said in his mildest
voice:

"Oh, I hadn't realized that. To be sure. You were lunching out? With
friends?"

"No, by myself. I took some sandwiches out–into the hayfield. My
husband will tell you I often behave in an eccentric way."

"Quite natural, I'm sure: I mean, to prefer one's meals out of doors on
a fine sunny day. I take it you didn't see anything of your nephew–or
anyone else, while you were in the field?"

"No, I couldn't very well. You see, I was in one of the haystacks–the–
I'm afraid it was the one where they found him."

"You don't say. This must make it still more distressing for you. But,
really, it's very lucky for us."

"For you?"

"Why, yes. Don't you see, it narrows down the time during which the
murder could have been committed. Unless, of course, the body was placed
there later."

The superintendent's eyes were twinkling enthusiastically at her, like a
benevolent uncle's exhibiting a new toy to his nephew. Hero realized that
he was making great efforts to put her at her ease–"did that mean off her
guard," she thought–and that he knew she realized it. He continued a
trifle brusquely:

"And after that?"

"I went in, just before the end of the boys' lunch. I was with my husband for a bit. Then I was superintending the catering and chairs and
things for the sports, till I went up to dress."

"Which would be about—?"

"I went up just after the hall clock struck two."

"Did Mr. Vale go up with you?"

"Oh, no. He was in his dressing room when I went into my bedroom."

"I see. Thank you very much, Mrs. Vale. I hope I shall not have to trouble you again."

The superintendent was feeling slightly ruffled when he sat down in the morning-room and prepared to interview the staff. He was fortified, however, by the presence of Sergeant Pearson with a large notebook in the background, and a certain solid piece of metal in his own pocket. Tiverton was the victim. He had been in the common room the whole time between lunch and two-thirty, except for occasional visits to the day room, to see that the boys, who were sitting there till they should be told to change, were doing nothing outrageous.

"Which of the staff were with you?"

"Let me see. Mr. Sims was there most of the time. He went out, at about two o'clock—to change, I think: I didn't notice him after that till just before the first race began."

"You did not go up to change, yourself, sir?"

"No, I had put on my festive garments before lunch."

"What about the other masters?"

"Well, really, I'm not my brother's keeper, you know. They were in and out, most of them. Gadsby, I believe, went in to the village shortly after lunch. Wrench turned up soon after two o'clock and went out again. Evans came in to change the boys: that must have been just before two-fifteen. Who else is there? Oh, yes: Griffin had a cigarette here before he went out to look over the arrangements for the sports. I cannot answer for the headmaster," he added mischievously.

"Did all the masters attend the sports, Mr. Tiverton?"

"Yes, they were all there. I didn't see Wrench till the end of the first race. Talking to parents or something, I believe."

"And you have no suggestions, sir, as to the perpetrator of the crime?"

"No. No—except that I can't conceive what motive any of us could have that makes you inquire so searchingly into our whereabouts."

"A matter of form. Thank you, sir; that will be all for the present," said the superintendent indifferently. "Could you ask Mr. Gadsby to step this way?"

Gadsby came in and embarrassed the superintendent by a hearty hand-shake. "Well, putting me on the mat, eh? Fire away then."

"If you could just tell me where you were between lunch and the sports, Mr. Gadsby. We have to inquire into these things."

"That's all right, old man. Fullah's got to do his duty. 'S'matter of fact, I popped into the village for a quick one. Have to get primed for these social riots, y'know. Not a society man."

"Quite so, sir. And how quick was the one?"

Gadsby went into a paroxysm of laughter. "Ha! ha! ha! That's a good one. Damned smart. Must tell it to the chaps. Ha! ha! 'How quick was the one?' Well, to tell you the truth, it was quick all right, but more than one. Two or three. Good beer at the Cock and Feathers, and I settled it down with a couple of whiskies. Old Tompkins, keeps the pub, y'know, super-intendent; he'll go into the witness box for me."

"I'm sure that won't be necessary, sir," replied the superintendent play-fully, a remark which also went down very well with the hilarious Gadsby. "You were there, how long, sir?" he prompted.

"Left about two-fifteen. No distance in a car."

"Oh, I see, you were in a car. I see. Then there is only one further question. Can you think of any reason for this boy's being done to death? Ever heard anyone threaten to–it might have started as a practical joke on the part of some boys, for instance."

Gadsby leaned forward with what Tiverton called "his schoolgirl's con-fidence" expression. "I don't mind telling you–though it seems a bit hard on the poor little fellow, talking like this just now–most of the school hated him like poison. I wouldn't put it past a good many of them to screw his neck a touch too violently. Funny thing, that: only at breakfast today—" he broke off suddenly.

"At breakfast, sir, you were saying?" the superintendent prompted.

"Oh, we happened to be talking about murders, that's all," Gadsby re-plied lamely. Then, as though feeling that something more was expected of him, "Curious what coincidences you run across every now and then, isn't it, superintendent? I remember in '17—"

But Armstrong was in no mood for reminiscences of that sort. He inter-cepted the garrulous Gadsby before he could get into his stride, and skil-fully elicited from him the substance of that breakfast conversation which had already been recorded. The sergeant scribbled furiously.

It was Sims' turn next. He came hesitatingly into the room, an uncer-tain smile looking coyly out through his reedy mustache.

"Good evening. Er–I believe you wished to see me."

"That's right, sir. I have to ask you a few questions. Will you just tell me your movements after lunch today?"

"Oh, dear, I'm afraid I've a hopeless memory for that sort of thing. Now, what *did* I do? I went into the common room for a bit. Tiverton was there, I remember. Then I changed; upstairs. Then I came down again. I'm afraid this is all rather inadequate."

"Have you any idea what time you came down, sir?"

"Well, it struck two as I was going up the stairs. And one takes about a quarter of an hour to change. So I suppose—"

"I see. You came down about quarter past two. Then you went into the common room, didn't you?"

"Yes." Sims shot a quick glance at the superintendent. "No, I'm wrong. Whoever told you? I went outside and had a cigarette."

"Whereabouts did you go?"

"Oh, out at the back. Along by the hayfield, you know. I walked up and down the path. Griffin must have seen me, you know. He was out on Big Field."

Armstrong did not fail to note an apprehensive timbre in the tone of Sims' last statements, but he gave no sign of it.

"Quite. And I take it you saw nothing out of the way?"

"No, of course not. I should have told you. There was no one out on that side of the house but Griffin. Evans came in just as I was at the door."

"Thank you, sir. Then, if you have no suggestions to make, will you be so good as to send along Mr. Evans?"

Unless he is lying—no, unless he and Mr. Griffin are in collaboration, and if Mrs. Vale's evidence is correct, that would seem to fix the murder between one-thirty and two-fifteen, unless, of course, it was committed somewhere else. Far too many "ifs" and "unlesses," thought Superintendent Armstrong, fingering a certain envelope in his pocket.

"Ah, good evening; Mr. Evans, isn't it? Have you any theories about this crime?"

Michael was conscious of antagonism; a very faintly contemptuous accent on the word "you" (had some one else been bothering the superintendent with theories?), and a general air of dangerous quiescence in the superintendent's big body slumped back heavily in his chair.

"Me? Oh, Lord, no."

"You have never heard anyone threatening to murder this boy?"

"Of course not. Do murderers commonly proclaim their intentions in public?"

The superintendent's brow contracted. He said, "You do not recall a conversation at breakfast today?"

"What on earth? Surely you are not suspecting Griffin? It's too ludicrous. Why, anyone might talk about screwing a boy's neck. I do myself about twice a week."

"Very well, sir, we'll pass that over." Michael had an uneasy feeling that Armstrong was by no means passing it over. Was he just an ordinary police numskull? No, there was a formidable intelligence in those small eyes. Then why go off on this ridiculous tack about Griffin? Perhaps he is trying to put me off my guard. Be careful.

"Now, just a few formal questions, sir. I am told you were not in school for lunch."

"No, I went out–into the wood beyond the playing fields."

"Did you see Mrs. Vale?"

O God, now it's begun. What has she told him? Chance it.

"No."

"Oh, I thought you might have. She was having lunch in the hayfield."

Thank God. It seems all right so far.

"Did you have anything to eat, sir?"

"Yes, I took some sandwiches with me." That should be safe enough.

"I see.... I expect they were busy in the kitchen today." The superintendent's voice was just a shade too offhand. Michael sensed the trap.

"I keep a loaf and butter in my room." Well, so I do. Damn and blast! I should never have said that. I should have waited till he asked. Out of one trap into another.... Armstrong, however, made no comment.

"I take it you saw no one in the wood, or on the hayfield?"

"No. Griffin came out not long after the bell rang. He and Mould, the groundsman, were in Big Field all the time, I think, after that."

This was going fine. Nothing to be afraid of in this fat official in blue. Just my guilty conscience.

"I understand, then, that you didn't go into the hayfield at all, sir? You were in the wood from one-thirty to about two-fifteen?"

"Yes."

The superintendent creaked forward in his chair, rummaging in a pocket, and pulled forth an envelope; allowed something to roll out of it on to the table in front of him.

"And how do you account for this pencil of yours being found in the haystack where the body was? These are your initials, aren't they?"

Hell and damnation! That's torn it. Must have dropped out when I was kissing Hero. Didn't miss it this afternoon. He tried to assume a look of injured innocence.

"Well, I really don't know. Unless it dropped out during the hay battle yesterday. I was ragging about with the boys a good deal."

"Oh, you missed it yesterday, did you?"

Michael became vaguely aware of another pitfall. Always keep as near the truth as possible when you're lying–he seemed to remember as a convincing maxim.

"No. I'd no idea I'd lost it till you turned it up in that rather melodramatic way." Michael was amazed to feel a wave of apparently genuine righteous indignation surging up in him. He added, with some heat, "And I may say, if these are your usual methods of interrogation, I don't wonder the papers make a fuss about the third degree."

"Perhaps we are both being a little melodramatic, sir," said the superintendent, retreating in as good order as possible from his false position. To tell the truth, he felt considerably nonplussed, as Michael might have noticed if he had not been too occupied wondering whether the superintendent could have failed to observe the gaping and guilty chasm between his first question about the pencil and its answer. However, Armstrong began to show signs of apology rather than suspicion. Michael found himself giving a lively account of the hay battle, and in the end left the presence with a feeling of doubt as to whether its Machiavellian maneuvers had not been a product of his own guilty imagination.

To him succeeded Griffin, evidently prepared to lose his temper on the least provocation. This was duly given to him by the superintendent's question about his unwary breakfast table remark.

"Oh, my holy heavens! If that's what you're getting at, you'd better arrest every schoolmaster in England on suspicion of murder."

The superintendent handled this highly combustible article with great delicacy. "Come, sir," he said, "you must realize that we policemen have to go into every detail, however trivial it may seem. You remember the case of Jones-Evans?"

"Jones-Evans? The Llanttyprid forward? Do I not. I always said that fellow would come to no good. Bit my— ear once in the scrum. Yes, I see what you mean."

"I take it, then, that your remarks were not meant in earnest?"

"Oh, I don't know about that. I might well have screwed the poor little blighter's neck for him. But, as it happens, I didn't, if that's what you want to know."

"Exactly. You were out in the field, weren't you, after lunch? See anything peculiar?"

"No, except Mouldy–he's the groundsman; descended from a long line of village idiots, I think. Found he'd put out one too many sets of hurdles this time."

"What did you do about it, sir?"

"Oh, I spoke a few words to him on the subject. Then we put them back in his shed again."

"About what time was that?"

"Ten or fifteen minutes before the sports began, I should say. Why?"

"Well, sir, it is possible that the body was not placed in the haystack till some time after the murder. I am naturally wondering where it might have been hidden in the interval, if this theory should be correct."

"No, there were no bodies lying about in the shed when we went in. Couldn't have been hidden, either, because Mouldy yammered something about his sacks having been moved, and shifted them all back; so we should have seen if there'd been anything behind them."

Armstrong creaked slightly in his chair. "Well, that is about all then, sir. You didn't happen to see Mrs. Vale after lunch, did you?"

"I think she came out by the garden gate once or twice, to see about the seating accommodation."

"Anyone else about?"

"No, I don't think so. Oh, yes, Sims walked up and down the path for a bit. Came out as we were bringing hurdles in. And, I was forgetting. Just before that Evans walked along, from the direction of the wood. That's all."

"Then I won't trouble you any further. Can you send me Mr. Wrench?"

Armstrong beamed upon Wrench as he sat down. If he noticed the nervous tic in the master's left eyelid, and the way his hands gripped the arms of his chair, he certainly did not betray the fact.

"Now, sir, I expect you younger gentlemen know some things about the boys that the older ones don't. Perhaps you may be able to give me some suggestion as to why anyone should want to kill this lad?"

"Oh, really, I've no idea. Of course he wasn't popular with the boys, though some of them played up to him because of his money; or with the staff, either, for that matter."

"How do you mean?"

"Well, he ragged anyone if he thought he could get away with it; in a nasty, malicious way, too."

"I see. Though I don't imagine, from what I've seen of your colleagues, that he would get much rope from any of them."

"Good Lord, he twisted Gadsby round his finger, and as for Sims—" Wrench broke off in some confusion.

"I quite understand your hesitation, sir. Very natural under the circumstances. But, of course, even we policemen are not so stupid as to suppose that anyone would commit murder from such a motive. All I'm trying to do is to get an idea of the psychology of the victim. It often gives one a line on the murderer, you know."

"Oh, well, if that's all," said Wrench, still rather uneasily, "I suppose there's no harm in telling you that Wemyss did his best to make Sims' life a hell for him."

Armstrong elicited some circumstantial evidence for this; then, feeling Wrench to be "ripe," as he put it, moved to the attack.

"All I want now, sir, is an account of your own movements between lunch and two-thirty."

Wrench visibly braced himself in his chair, and began to finger his pink tie. Armstrong noticed a slight coarsening in his accent as he began to speak.

"Aow. I was in the school—mucking about, you know."

"You must try to be more explicit, sir."

"Well, after lunch I went up to my bedroom, and lay down for a bit; feeling rather seedy. Then I felt better and thought I'd read. I remembered I'd left my book in the common room and went down to fetch it. Tiverton was there, and—"

"May I ask what was the book, sir?"

Wrench looked up quickly, blushing. "I really don't see what–it was a French book, if you want to know, *Mademoiselle de Maupin*," he spoke defiantly.

"I see. A school textbook. They didn't teach us French when I was at school. And then?"

"Then I read for a bit, and changed, and came down."

"You were late for the first race, weren't you, sir?"

"Late? No. Who put that in your head?"

"Oh, I'm sorry, sir. Some mistake. I understood that you were not with the other masters at the beginning of the sports."

"No more I was. I was talking with a parent."

"Who was that, sir?"

"Funny thing, I don't know," said Wrench slowly. "Tall, blue-eyed chap, in a brown suit. He came up and asked me how 'Tom' was getting on. Hadn't an earthly who he was, but I told him 'Tom' was doing all right. That often happens at these beanos. Parents come up to you and expect you to know who they are and all about their boys."

"Very difficult it must be, sir. Well, that is all I need ask you. Thank you. Good evening, sir."

Chapter V

Obverse and Reverse

Evening of the next day. They have cleared supper away in the common room. Tiverton, Evans and Griffin have congregated in the former's sitting-room; Wrench is on duty; Gadsby and Sims are in the village, and expected back presently. The superintendent, who has been poking and pottering about all day, is finally gone, and with his going the oppression in the air seems to have lifted a little. Other persons, too, have come and gone, leaving the atmosphere still acrid and poisonous, as though after a gas attack; reporters from local and London newspapers, smelling out scandal for their titled proprietors like jackals scenting down a corpse for rather seedy lions. Reporters with notebooks; reporters with telegraph forms; reporters with cameras, rather baffled to find no "sorrowing relatives" whose contorted features they may serve up next morning as a breakfast relish for their great public; reporters courteous, insinuating, truculent, well-meaning, ignoble, acute or obtuse the whole swarm has swept down and swept away. The night air seems to sigh with relief, and even the murder-stained hayfield may be feeling cleaner for the departure of the carrion birds who hovered over it. Millions of eyes have fastened avidly upon the news which, in its local evening paper variety, Tiverton is now declaiming to Evans and Griffin.

SHOCKING FATALITY AT PRIVATE SCHOOL TITLED VICTIM

HAYMAKERS' SENSATIONAL 7:15 P.M. DISCOVERY

CORD ROUND SCHOOLBOY'S NECK

"Haymakers working in a field adjoining Sudeley Hall Preparatory School late yesterday evening were horrified to find the body of a boy underneath one of the stacks. The fatal discovery was immediately communicated to the headmaster, the Rev. P.R. Vale, M.A., who identified the body as that of his nephew, the Hon. Algernon Wyvern-Wemyss, a pupil at the school. The deceased, it transpires, had been brutally strangled, a

45

thin cord tied round the neck being the cause of death. Superintendent Armstrong and Sergeant Pearson, of the Staverton force, were quickly on the scene and our correspondent learns that they have discovered clues which should lead to a speedy arrest. The headmaster, who is also president of the Staverton and District Archaeological Society, in an interview stated that he suspected the crime to be the work of some vagrant and attributed the wave of violence which has lately been sweeping the country to the disastrous policy of the late Labour government. In reply to a question, the Rev. Vale strongly deprecated the suggestion that a practical joke might have been at the back of this shocking fatality. The deceased, who was universally popular with his schoolmates, was the son of—"

"Blah! Blah! Blah!" interrupted Griffin rudely, "give it a rest."

"Oh, here's something more to your taste," went on Tiverton. "Mr. Edward Griffin, the old Oxford rugby blue, who is on the staff of Sudeley Hall, on being asked for his theory about the crime, intimated that he had nothing to say."

"I intimated that that reporter would get shot out on his face if he didn't clear off pretty quick."

"Which was impolitic of you, Edward," said Evans. "He'll have it in for you now. Don't you see, he's already contrived to make you look slightly suspect."

Griffin snatched the paper and read through the whole column. "Good Lord, I believe you're right. What with him and the bobbies, I shall be getting a hunted feeling before long."

"The superintendent got after you, did he?" Tiverton asked.

"Did he not? A nasty, suspicious blighter. Some fool must have told him what I said at breakfast in the morning."

"Not guilty," said Tiverton.

"Nor me," said Evans. "As a matter of fact, I think I'm the chief suspect at the moment. The 'clues which should lead to a speedy arrest' were my silver pencil. He found it in the haystack."

Griffin looked concerned. "I say, that's bad. I take it you are not the perpetrator of the outrage; or if you want any lying done, just tell me." He spoke lightly, but Michael became aware of a faint undercurrent of anxiety in his voice.

"That's very nice of you, Edward, but I hope it won't be necessary. Curiously enough, I am not the murderer."

"That pencil's a bit awkward, though," said Tiverton. "How did you explain it?"

"Well, I told him it must have dropped out when I was ragging about during the hay battle."

Tiverton looked as if he was about to ask another question, but refrained, saying instead, "In detective stories it would have been planted there by the criminal to throw suspicion on you."

"Perhaps it was," laughed Griffin, "as the most unpopular master at St. Botolph's, you must have plenty of enemies."

Michael reached forward to the table, took up a pile of books, and sprayed them with great deliberation over Griffin's head.

"*My* books, thank you," Tiverton said. "But look here, seriously, are you sure you lost your pencil at the hay battle? I thought I saw you using it yesterday morning. I mean, if you *did* have it yesterday, or some one found it after the hay battle and didn't give it back—well, you see, it follows that it must have been planted there, *and by some one in this place.*"

The tone of the assembly suddenly grew rather grave. Michael was feeling ashamed to be deceiving men he was fond of. But was he deceiving them? He couldn't for the life of him remember when he *had* used the pencil last. After all, it mightn't have dropped out when he was with Hero at all. But who on earth could want to—?

"I see what you mean," he said slowly. "Yes. It's an unpleasant thought, isn't it? If this person dislikes me sufficiently to want me hanged, he is presumably willing enough to bump me off himself if the law fails to come up to scratch."

Tiverton, who had been manipulating a coffee machine in a rather spinsterish way, poured out three cups.

"I'm inclined to think, though," he said, "that you may get a reprieve. Has it struck you two what is the oddest thing about this business?"

"No."

"Proceed, Holmes, I am all attention."

"Well, where did Wemyss go after school yesterday? As far as we know he seems to have vanished off the face of the earth. And secondly, who or what could have induced him to go off in that curious manner, apparently without letting anyone know or leaving any trace behind him? I believe, if we could answer the second question, the mystery would be solved."

How right Tiverton was in this conjecture they were not to realize for some time.

"You amaze me, Holmes," said Griffin, "but I must confess that I still don't see where Evans' reprieve comes in."

"Unless he was running away or playing truant—and I don't think that very likely, apart from the fact that as far as we know no one saw him in the village or on the roads—some outside agency must have induced him to leave the premises."

"A fine period," commented Griffin with admiration.

"I suggest it must have been a note of some sort from some one he knew, or he wouldn't have gone; but not from anyone on the staff here, for masters do not make written assignations with boys. Wemyss would have felt there was something fishy about that."

"I sincerely trust they do not," said Griffin primly. He turned to Evans. "By Jove, Michael, he's right, isn't he?" Griffin had the faculty of spontaneous enthusiasm, and Tiverton's face reflected the warmth of his approval.

Evans said, "So we look for some one outside the school who knew him?"

"Or a boy in the school. Don't forget that possibility," said Tiverton. Further exploration of the subject was interrupted by the arrival of Gadsby and Sims. Gadsby was unusually Cock and Featherish, and even Sims appeared, for him, quite on top of the world. Gadsby sat down and helped himself, unasked, to coffee and a cigarette. Then he delivered an ominous gargling noise and got under way.

"Just been taking old Simmie along for a quick one. He seemed a bit down in the mouth–police been chivvying him or something–so I prescribed a dose of mother's special, didn't I, Simmie?"

"That's right."

"Thought we should never get there, though. Sims saw a yellow-bottomed gorse-tit or something in the hedge, so we had to stop while he stalked it. Can't think what you see in these Godforsaken birds, Sims. Oh, and talking of birds, where's Wrench? Stalking the fair Rosa, I suppose."

"What on earth are you talking about, Gadsby?" said Tiverton, with a voice like a cold douche. Gadsby was too well lit up to be extinguished by this. He continued:

"Meantessay you haven't noticed her making eyes at meals? Dirty work at the crossroads, you mark my words. It's a case."

Griffin and Evans shuddered ostentatiously. Sims drew himself upright in his chair; he was pink and trembling. He stuttered, "R-really, Gadsby, that's a most unneces-nerecess, er, uncalled-for remark. That sort of thing's d-disgusting–t-talking about 'bub-bub-birds'; j-just because some people– these s-stuck-up s-society people–choose to bub-behave like amilals, ani-mals–I don't think it's f-funny at all," he concluded, in dignified confusion. Every one was rather embarrassed, except Gadsby, who opened his eyes in an exaggerated fashion and said:

"Good Lord, who'd have thought it? Sims turning pious. I say, Simmie, how many did you have when my back was turned?"

The following silence was so acute that it penetrated even Gadsby's hide, and he remarked, a bit huffily, that he supposed the subject had better be changed. This he proceeded to do, crashing his gears merci-lessly.

"Well, as we seem to be in the drawing room, I'll tell you a nice, clean joke. Oh, I say, that reminds me of a thing the superintendent said to me last evening–damn smart, I call it. Decent fullah, that."

The company was duly regaled with the superintendent's witticism, and the talk drifted in his direction. Tiverton doubted the ability of his mind, Griffin the legitimacy of his birth. Gadsby thought he was a clever fullah and a sportsman. Sims remarked with some truculence that he was not going to be bullied by any great hulking lout in a blue uniform. Michael, appealed to as the thumbnail character-sketcher of the party, admitted that he'd been too frightened by the superintendent to get more than a blurred impression of him, but felt that his cleverness or stupidity, which- ever it was, was on the grand scale, and that either would therefore be equally dangerous.

At this point the alleged philanderer, Wrench, came in. A certain awk- wardness made itself felt in the atmosphere, a general looking sideways and fiddling with teaspoons and relighting of pipes.

"Have some coffee, Wrench?" said Tiverton. "Been putting the boys to bed?"

"Thanks. Yes, they're a bit worked up tonight."

Sims blurted out, "There you are, Gadsby," and grinned apologetically as four pairs of eyes shot meaning glances at him. Wrench looked about him in a puzzled way. "What *are* you talking about? Is this a bet?" The silence grew even more sultry. Tiverton broke it, like a thunderclap, "Gadsby apparently thought you were putting Rosa to bed."

"Here, I say, hang it, old man," stuttered Gadsby.

Wrench went very white. His eyes narrowed and his nostrils distended: all humanity seemed to have left his face. He rose to his feet, still holding the coffee cup, glaring at Gadsby:

"You dirty rotter!" he said, in a taut, brittle kind of voice. "You poor, brainless sot! Get to hell out of this!" His voice rose to a shout and cracked. He threw the coffee cup full in Gadsby's face.

Gadsby staggered and blinked. Blood and coffee were running down his cheek. He growled in his throat, then lurched towards Wrench and knocked him several feet into a corner, where he lay with a heap of Tiverton's golf-clubs tumbled over him, whimpering. Evans was on his feet, feeling full of blind, undirected rage. Tiverton had a queer, puzzled look on his face. Only Griffin seemed to be himself. He stood up like a cliff in front of Gadsby, took him by the shoulders, twirled him round and put him into the passage, saying quietly: "You seem to have done enough mischief for tonight; your presence will not be required any more." Then he turned round and got the sobered Sims to help him bring Wrench up to his bedroom. Tiverton and Evans were left alone in the devastated room.

Tiverton still had that strange, faraway expression, as though he were trying to think out the answer to a conundrum.

"Now what on earth," he said slowly, "what on earth made me say that?"

"We all seem to be a bit bedlamite this evening," answered Michael lamely. "Well, I think I'll go along. Good-night."

And he went to bed, where he lay awake for hours, coming to realize how the dirty work of murder was only beginning when the victim was dead: going over details of the past day, and as it were piecing together thus the new, changed relationship amongst his colleagues. For there was a change: a kind of reservation beneath the surface. It came upon him with a sickening impact that he and they felt that the murderer was one of their number, and that the events of the evening had been a violent revolt of masked suspicions. He was very glad indeed that Nigel Strangeways was coming.

While the Sudeley Hall staff were showing these premonitory signs of a collapse of morale, Superintendent Armstrong and Sergeant Pearson were holding an informal council of war over whiskies and sodas in the former's house. Sergeant Pearson made his report first. He was a young, keen, open-faced officer. His curly flaxen hair and general air of blue-eyed innocence made him a favorite, especially with middle-aged women, and a success as an interviewer. His face so accurately mirrored his mind, which was entirely straightforward in its workings, that criminals were apt to open their hearts to him as to a brother, or else–hopelessly rattled by his extreme ingenuousness–suspect that it concealed a diabolic cunning and tie themselves up accordingly in knots of duplicity.

His report was long but apparently barren. He and the Sudeley constable had first verified Gadsby's alibi at the Cock and Feathers. He had arrived and left at the hours stated. He had been alone in the private room for five or six minutes after his arrival, but had then sought the more congenial atmosphere of the public bar. Pearson had then gone the rounds of all the parents living in the vicinity who had attended the sports. None of them had seen the unfortunate Wemyss. Only one recollected talking to Mr. Wrench at the sports, and that was after the 440 yards race; neither had he blue eyes nor a son called "Tom." None of them had noticed Mr. Wrench talking to a blue-eyed man in a brown suit at any time before or during the sports; though several fathers had had the requisite color of eyes and clothing.

Meanwhile some of the sergeant's men had been combing the neighborhood; but, if the boy had left the school grounds at all, he apparently had done it in a cap of invisibility. An extensive inquiry had also been set on foot into the whereabouts of that class described as "having no fixed abode"; the results of this were still coming in, and no support for the headmaster's theory had as yet been found. The laborers who had found the body had been put through a searching examination, the result of which was nil.

All these facts Pearson retailed in a regulation voice, sitting bolt upright and gazing dreamily at a picture of some anatomically deformed angels above the superintendent's head. He now relaxed, transferred his attention from angels to whisky, and waited for Armstrong to speak.

"Well, George," the superintendent said, "you've done a good day's work. I didn't really expect those lines to lead anywhere, but it narrows down the field to be shut of them."

He then proceeded to outline his own activities. He had first examined the rumble and front seats of Gadsby's car; there had been no sign of either having recently been occupied by a body, though that by no means eliminated Gadsby as a possible murderer. He had next interviewed the whole staff of servants at Sudeley Hall. They were now practically exempt from suspicion, having been underneath each other's noses–if not actually tumbling over each other–either in the kitchen or the garden, during the hectic period between lunch and the sports. At this point Armstrong made a pregnant pause. Knowing his superior's weakness for a dramatic effect, Pearson said, " 'Practically' you were saying, sir?"

"Yes. I stumbled over two curious pieces of evidence. The groundsman, Mould–he's a bit lacking in the upper story–but he was quite certain that a number of his sacks, full ones, had been moved since he went into his shed that morning. When he and Mr. Griffin went in, he said, he found them in a sort of lean-to position against the far wall. They were placed in such a way as to make a possible hiding-place–I got him to put them back for me as he remembered finding them after lunch."

Sergeant Pearson whistled in a way cunningly calculated to express both astonishment and admiration. The superintendent continued:

"My other exhibit is Rosa. She is one of the maids. She was in the kitchen, helping to wash up, till just before two. Then she said she felt unwell and went up to her bedroom to lie down. We have no corroboration of her movements from then till she joined some of the other servants at a dormitory window watching the sports–soon after two-thirty. Miss Rosa is a pretty hot piece of goods, I can tell you, and what's more, she's frightened. I didn't press her at all. I'm just leaving her to simmer for a bit."

Armstrong leaned back, took a good swig at his glass, breathed stertorously, and beamed upon the sergeant.

"I got some interesting sidelights from the servants, too. Mr. Evans, it seems, is quite the gentleman but a bit standoffish. Mr. Wrench is the reverse, in both particulars. Mr. Sims gives no trouble; Mr. Tiverton a good deal–'fussy old geezer,' were the words, I think. Mr. Griffin and Mr. Gadsby are 'jolly, pleasant-spoken gentlemen,' though the latter does keep whisky bottles under the bed. The Rev. Mr. Vale seems to be a holy terror, with a tongue 'like I never did'; in fact, no one would stay on for a minute if it wasn't for Mrs. Vale, who is 'a real lady and ever so nice,' though 'some do say as how she's a bit flighty and who wouldn't be with an old devil like that for a husband.' "

The superintendent filled up his glass and the sergeant's before proceeding to relate the rest of his activities. After his interview with the domestic staff he had made a thorough search of the wood; result–nil. Had tested all suitable surfaces in Mould's shed for fingerprints; result–hopeless. Had verified from several boys that Tiverton had been in and out of the day room after lunch. Had found a copy of *Mademoiselle de Maupin* in Wrench's room, the illustrations of which caused him to amend his views about school textbooks. Had finally left the school and paid a visit to Mr. Urquhart in Staverton.

"He told me, after the usual lawyer's demurring, that Mr. Vale, as the deceased's next-of-kin, stood to come in for a considerable sum of money; he would not like to stipulate the exact amount, etc., etc. He himself had managed the boy's financial affairs since the parents' death, Mr. Vale seeing to the educational side. Mr. Urquhart is the sole executor of the will, and only comes in for a small legacy himself, so he tells me."

Armstrong hovered again, as it were in midflight, and the sergeant gave the requisite cue.

"You are not satisfied with his story, sir?"

"Mark my words, young man, that fellow's frightened of something. Half the people in this case are, as far as I can make out. But I'm coming to the funny part of it. I asked him for his movements on Wednesday. He blustered a bit–all these lawyers do–then he told me a very curious story. Says he got a typewritten anonymous note by the morning post, with a Sudeley postmark, asking him to be in Edgworth Wood, that's less than a mile from Sudeley Hall, you know, at one-forty-five, when the sender would tell him something to his advantage. 'Absolute secrecy,' 'burn this note'; all the usual stuff."

"And did he?"

"Did he what? Oh, yes, he burnt it, so he says."

"I meant–did he go, sir?"

"Aha, George, you're coming on. You're wondering why a respectable solicitor should take any notice of a shady communication like that."

Pearson hadn't thought of this at all, but he nodded his head portentously. "And I suppose nobody turned up," he said.

"You suppose right, my boy, if Urquhart is to be believed. Now if the thing was a genuine hoax he would probably not have destroyed the note. On the other hand, if he really did meet someone, he would be eager to produce that someone to prove an alibi. Anyway, I've left him to simmer, too. We're going to see him again tomorrow, though he doesn't know it. I've put a tag on him, of course, and I've sent Wills and Johnson to inquire whether anyone saw him or his car anywhere about Edgworth. It's a deserted sort of place, though."

"You mean, you think it's possible that he—?"

"He might have done it; yes. But I doubt it. He doesn't stand to gain much by the boy's death. No, I've other ideas about Mr. Urquhart. Lives very well for a solicitor, don't he?" the superintendent added irrelevantly. "Big car, posh house and all. Well, well, we shall see. Now, George, what is your theory about this crime?"

This was another favorite gambit of the superintendent's, and Pearson made the conventional movement in reply. He scratched his head, stared dismally into his whisky and soda, and mumbled something about not seeing the wood for the trees yet. Armstrong took so deep a breath that his buttons threatened to fly off and expelled it to the visible perturbation of his mustache; his decks thus cleared for action.

"All right, then," he said, "let's take a look at the trees. Assuming for the present that Wemyss was murdered where the body was found, some time between one and four p.m. Can we narrow the time down?"

"Well, sir, no one but a loony would have killed him during the sports. Hayfield's in full view of most of the sports ground and that particular haystack is only about thirty yards from where some of the spectators were standing."

"Twenty-six and a half, actually," said Armstrong with elaborate negligence. "Yes, you're right there. We can take two-thirty as one limit. Probably two-twenty; because people were coming out on to the field by then. Now, Mrs. Vale says she was in that haystack till about one-twenty-five, and she wouldn't be likely to admit it if it wasn't true. What do you think of her, George?"

George grinned sheepishly. "She's a bit of all right, she is."

"Aha! Fallen for a skirt again. You'll never make a detective, young man," rallied the superintendent ponderously. "Now, if you ask me, I'd say she was a deep one. Got nerve, too. Wonder if she's got enough nerve to take her lunch beside a corpse."

"Good Lord, sir, you can't mean that?" The sergeant was genuinely shocked.

"I should say she'd strength enough to strangle a young whippersnapper like that. And there's the money, don't forget that."

"Well, if you're thinking of that motive, what about old Brimstone?" said Pearson disrespectfully.

"Mm. Took half an hour to change, he says. Had plenty of time to slip down before his wife came up. Mr. Urquhart told me the school was prosperous, though, and I can't see Brimstone taking a risk like that unless he was on his beam-ends–if then."

"Surely that applies equally to Mrs. Brim–Vale, doesn't it?" said the chivalrous Pearson.

"From that point of view, perhaps, though we don't know that she may have run into debt privately. Dresses pretty expensively. But you're forgetting what the servants said."

The sergeant stared uncomprehendingly.

" 'Flighty' was the word. I couldn't get 'em to say any more. But that's another possible motive. Supposing she'd been carrying on with someone, and Wemyss caught 'em at it, she and someone would want to stop his tongue for him, I fancy."

"B-but, she's a lady, sir," was all the sergeant could find to say.

Armstrong smiled good-humoredly. "And ladies never do anything worse than leave their cars unattended outside shops. Well, let's get on to the other trees. Take opportunity only. Tiverton? Out of the question. Gadsby? Might have croaked the lad before, after or between drinks and hid the body in the rumble seat. But when did he plant it in the hayfield? Must have been after the sports. I'll have to find out where they all were between four-thirty and seven; should have done it before. Then there's Sims; out in the field after two-fifteen; but Griffin and Mould were outside too–far too dangerous. Griffin? Mould is *his* alibi and a pretty strong one. Evans? In the wood all the time, he says, till two-fifteen. A nice, quiet place for a bit of strangling, though I didn't find any marks of a struggle. But when could he plant the body?"

"Mr. Griffin smoked a cigarette after lunch, so no one would be outside till about one-forty," suggested Pearson.

"Good for you, me lad, I'd forgotten that. Though it'd be a pretty risky business carrying a body from the wood to the hayfield. There aren't many windows looking that way, but he couldn't be certain no one would come out. Still, there's that pencil…. You know, it'd have been much easier if he'd been in the haystack with Mrs. Vale."

The sergeant looked pained again. Armstrong grinned at him. "Well, if you won't have that, what about Wrench? Another of the frightened brigade. Poor alibi. Says he was in his bedroom most of the time. Seemed a bit disconcerted when I asked him what book he'd been reading. Could have done it between lunch and one-forty, when Griffin went out–though

there again, he couldn't be sure no one wouldn't come out. Then there's
Mould. He's a bit simple–that type's often homicidal–and the sort of person Wemyss might have ragged the head off, but he was having lunch in
the kitchen till he went out to meet Griffin. Last of all, Rosa. Poor alibi
from two to two-thirty, but the same objection to her as to Sims. There
remains the mysterious individual with blue eyes and a brown suit. Nobody saw him till the opening of the sports–and I doubt if anyone saw
him then."

"You mean, Wrench is making it up?"

"I'm sure he is, and I should very much like to know why. It's about the
feeblest effort at a faked alibi I've ever heard. Well now. In point of opportunity, Mrs. Vale or Evans–or both of them together–win in a canter.
Don't look at me in that nasty way, young feller, you've got to keep your
susceptibilities out of this. Next come Mr. Vale, Gadsby and Wrench in a
bunch, and Wrench is the dark horse of that lot. Tiverton, Griffin, Sims,
Mould and Rosa are left at the start."

"And for motive, sir?" There was a mixture of respect and apprehension in the sergeant's voice.

"Three possibilities so far. Money, revenge, and silence. Vale or Mrs.
Vale might have been actuated by the first; Sims or Mould by the second;
Mrs. Vale and the unknown someone by the third," said the superinten-
dent succinctly.

Pearson shifted uneasily, "It certainly don't look too good for Mrs.
Vale."

"Revenge seems to me least likely. Grown men don't kill boys just
because they've had their tails twisted by them. Money? Well, as I say,
the Rev. Vale seems to have enough of it; his wife is more open to suspicion on that count. But I put my money on the third. If the boy knew of
some intrigue going on, he was just the sort who'd be likely to blab about
it. Mrs. Vale is one obvious party, though I'm not forgetting Rosa. As for
the other party, the someone—" Armstrong paused significantly.

"Evans?"

"You've said it. Young, good-looking; just the opposite of that old fos-
sil of a headmaster. *And* his pencil was in the haystack. *And* he and Mrs.
Vale both took their lunch out; curious coincidence, that. I'm going to
keep a pretty sharp eye on those two birds."

The sergeant emptied his glass and stared at the bottom of it, presumably for inspiration. Finally he said, "I don't quite understand, sir, why
you haven't considered the possibility of it having been done by one of
the boys."

"Don't you worry about that. I'm not forgetting the possibility. Of course,
if it had been, it could only have been a rag that went too far. Boys don't

murder each other—besides, I forgot to tell you. I had a little chat with several of the head boys; prefects, they call them. Anyone leaving the room had to ask their permission. No one did. But even supposing someone had got out unnoticed. Supposing they had set on this young Wemyss. They might have pretended to throttle him, *or* to garrotte him with the cord, but the medical evidence suggests that he was first strangled with hands and then the cord tied round to make certain. Nobody would do that as a joke. It's deliberate murder. And I don't believe any boy could make those bruises, either."

The sergeant felt that this reasoning, though specious, had been rather flimsily constructed by Armstrong as a defense against a possibility which he had not explored with his usual thoroughness. Pearson loyally repressed an inclination to wonder whether his superior was not marshalling the facts to fit his own theory, though indeed the case against Mrs. Vale and perhaps Evans did look far stronger than any other. After rather a long silence he said tactfully:

"Well, sir, I presume the chief constable is not going to call in the Yard at present. After your work in the Crawleigh murder last year, I don't suppose he thinks we shall need their help."

"No, he is leaving it to me for the present," replied the superintendent, not without gratification, "but a fellow called Strangeways is coming down; he's a nephew of the Assistant Commissioner. Private inquiry agent he calls himself, an amateur, but he's done several pretty enough pieces of work. Evans wired for him this morning. He's a friend of his, apparently, so I suppose he'll be doing his best to put a spoke in our wheel. Still, he'll be living in the school and he may be able to find out what I want to know more than anything else."

"And what's that, sir?"

"How the murderer got Wemyss into position for the murder."

Chapter VI

Two Balloons Go Up

Once again Sweeny, the factotum, is ringing his bell. He mutters to himself the while, but whatever he may be saying is drowned by the harsh peremptory tongue which tells the school that another day has begun. The shadow of death still lies upon the school, but it is checkered now, a kind of half-mourning, here lying heavy as original darkness, here shot through by the returning rays of a normal sun. In the dormitories, where boys are scurrying to and fro, thinking of a lesson unprepared, a cricket match, holidays to come, the shadow lies lightest. Here the elastic mind of youth has thrown off whatever weight tragedy may have laid upon it and bounds forward irrepressibly on its natural course, though even here there may remain one or two dark patches not yet dissipated by the sun. In their cramped, monastic bedrooms the masters are dressing. Though morning smiles happily outside their windows, night still holds the upper hand within. Is it from one of these rooms that blackness emanates to infect all the rest? Is it here–the core and center of evil–hidden away from sight like an ancestral monster? And is that monster dormant again now, satisfied with one disaster, relapsed again into a period of sleep? Or is it waiting, the Adversary, ambushed behind a smile, an old acquaintance, an ordinary face?

Thus pondered Michael, deliberately trying to multiply his apprehensions to their highest power, skating fancy figures over the thin ice which he already could hear cracking beneath his feet. That pencil. How much did the superintendent really know? Was it possible that no one had seen Hero and himself in the haystack? How innocent and safe it had all seemed then. There had only been two people in their world, but now the world was closing in on them, as on growing children, and the end of innocence in sight. "The wages of sin is death"–the final, remorseless phrase marched into his mind. He shook his head impatiently. Surely one had got rid of that outdated superstition. But no, it seemed to have taken on a new lease of life. He remembered the half-laughing words Nigel had once spoken, "We're not meant to be happy. You may think you've got away with it at

last, but that's just when They come back at you." Well, at least he'd keep
Hero out of this. The fact of their love remained, and if some sacrifice
must be offered in return for it, to appease the jealous gods, let them take
him. Let them take him and break his neck on the end of a string. God, he
thought, I'm talking as if I had done it myself; talking melodrama like
any wretched egoist of a murderer writing his last confessions. I'm not
guilty. They don't hang innocent people. Oh, don't they just? Anyway,
Nigel will find out the truth....

The Rev. and Mrs. Vale are having breakfast. Well, I asked for it, Hero
is thinking; I asked for a crashing great emergency to turn up and cut the
tangle, and it has. At least, it's turned up, but it only seems to have made
the tangle worse so far. I can't leave Percy now, just when he feels everything is breaking up for him. It's not honor and dutifulness. One can fight
pompous abstracts, but not this imperative woman deep inside oneself.
Oh, Michael, your hands, your exquisite touch. I wonder what Michael
did say to that policeman. "Yes, Percy, Mr. Strangeways?" she said: she
had the successful wife's faculty of keeping her ears for her husband and
her thoughts to herself.

"This Mr. Strangeways is, I understand, able and well-connected. Evans
suggested that he should wire for him, as you know, in order that we
might have someone to—a-ah—watch the case in the interests of the school.
I have just heard that he will be arriving at Staverton by the twelve-forty.
Evans has the last period off and intended to meet his friend at the station. Perhaps you might care to go in with him and drive Mr. Strangeways
back."

"That's a good idea. We might all have lunch there. I've some shop-
ping to do." Even Percival Vale might, at any other time, have noticed the
over-studied negligence in her voice. But he had other things to think of.

"I am not at all sorry he is coming, my dear," he confided, "I am by no
means happy at the course the investigation is taking."

"Why, Percy? Has the superintendent been bothering you about the
will?"

"No. He has not, in fact, touched upon it at all. I really can't understand
it. But I strongly resent members of my staff being held in suspicion."

Hero's hands suddenly clasped themselves tight under the table. She
spoke sharply, "Whatever do you mean?"

"Perfectly ridiculous on the part of the superintendent. He found Mr.
Evans' pencil in the haystack where poor Algernon was murdered. He'd
dropped it there, of course, during the hay fight. But Tiverton has told
me, in confidence, that the police seem to be attaching importance to it.
Quite erroneously, of course. A member of my staff connected with an
occurrence like this! Fantastic."

The headmaster was quite heated at the idea. But his wife's heart dropped below zero. God, it's come. What fools we were, tempting providence like that. One can't tell how brave one is till the emergency comes, I said. Well, here it is. Go on, be brave! Think hard! What are you going to do now? Thank heavens I shall be able to talk with Michael before that foul policeman turns up again. Michael will know what to do. That's it. Put it all on to him! Get into a panic again like a blasted schoolgirl!

But it was not given to Hero to discuss the new development with Michael until discussion had become useless. At ten o'clock Armstrong arrived at the school and asked for a few words with Mr. Evans. Michael went into the morning room. The superintendent received him amiably enough, but he was not an unknown quantity now; Michael felt the force of authority behind him and a certain indefinable menace. Armstrong began seriously:

"Now, Mr. Evans, I have come to ask you one or two questions which I am afraid may be distasteful to you. But I am sure you realize that in a case of this grave nature the interests of justice must overweigh all private considerations."

Michael relaxed slightly. This didn't sound like an address to a suspected murderer.

"Certainly," he said.

"When you were in the wood, Mr. Evans, you said you were looking out in the direction of the hayfield some of the time?"

"Yes—I think I did—once or twice."

"Did you happen to notice Mrs. Vale there?"

This is getting difficult. Tell the truth when in doubt. "No—she was in the haystack, wasn't she. One can't see over the top from the wood."

"I see. And you would be prepared to state on oath that to your knowledge no one else came out on to the hayfield while you were in the wood?"

"Yes, but it doesn't seem to help much. As I say, I hadn't the field under view for more than a few minutes altogether."

Armstrong rubbed his chin and his brow contracted. He said, with apparent hesitation, "It's a pity. If only you'd been looking in that direction most of the time—well, as it is, it only helps to strengthen a theory which I was most reluctant to form." He paused in an indecisive way.

"What on earth are you getting at?" said Michael, a premonition of what was to come sharpening his voice.

"Look here, sir. I have come to a tentative conclusion, and I'm going to take the risk of telling you what's in my mind; I shouldn't be sorry, as I say, if somebody could prove it wrong. Even we policemen don't much fancy accusing a—you realize, sir, that everything I am going to say is in strict confidence?"

"Yes. Go on."

"Well, then, the most tenable explanation of the crime so far is that it was committed during lunch by Mrs. Vale, with or without the connivance of her husband." The superintendent blurted out this last speech, as though trying to conquer his own doubts as to its truth. His eyes looked at Michael with a rather apologetic expression, but they looked at him very hard. Michael sprang to his feet in a swirl of emotions–shock, indignation, fear and a certain utterly base relief.

"Stop! You must be mad," he was almost shouting. "I won't listen to this! It's absolutely wicked. It's sheer lunacy to imagine that—" Armstrong gestured with his hands and interrupted.

"Please sit down, sir, and hear me out. I'm afraid I put it too abruptly. It is only fair that you should know the facts that have compelled me to take up this position."

He mentioned the will in the Vales' favor and asserted that he could find no other possible motive for the crime. He suggested that it would be far easier for the headmaster or his wife than for anyone else to ask the boy to come to the haystack, or wherever he was murdered, without arousing his curiosity. A picnic might have been proposed, for instance, immediately after school. "What's more," he added, "the movements of every one else about the school are accounted for satisfactorily with the exception–to be frank–of your own. And in your own case there is obviously no motive; to mention only one difficulty."

Had Michael's brain been capable of its usual activity, he could not have failed to see the gaping holes in Armstrong's jerry-built case. But the unexpected grouping of events into such a different and staggering pattern had taken his wits away, and he could only think what his own attitude should be to the new situation. Armstrong was relying on this, and without giving Michael time to dispose his forces, went on, looking keenly at him the while:

"I am not, of course, asserting that this theory is correct; but it is the only one which fits the facts at present in our possession. The difficulty from your point of view–believing quite naturally that Mrs. Vale is innocent–is that she was alone in the hayfield during a part of the critical period. That's why I asked you if you'd seen anyone else there. Any evidence that tended to prove that Wemyss was not in the haystack with Mrs. Vale would naturally decrease the suspicion against her, or remove it altogether. As it is—"

The superintendent shrugged his shoulders with an admirable simulation of regret and seemed about to end the interview. Michael's brain was running round in demented circles. Should he confess to the murder? Or was that unnecessarily quixotic? No, he'd never be able to make the details fit the facts convincingly at such short notice. If he said he'd been with Hero, that would almost certainly mean exposure and disgrace for both of them, but at least it would clear her of the more terrible suspicion. Yes, he must take the risk. The superintendent's hand was already on the door handle; his broad back prevented Michael from seeing that the knuckles were white and tense.

"Just a moment, superintendent."

Armstrong turned slowly, a faintly surprised expression on his face. One could not possibly have guessed that he was seeing a weak card bluff the trick.

"Sir?"

Michael was trembling uncontrollably. Even his voice seemed out of control. "You have told me something in confidence, and I'm going to make the same request of you. If what I am going to say turns out to have no bearing on the case, will you promise to keep it to yourself?"

"Well, sir, that's rather a difficult thing to promise. But I can assure you that if we solve this problem, we shall not bring forward any evidence without it is necessary to incriminate the murderer."

"Very well. I was with Mrs. Vale in the haystack from one to one-twenty-five." The words tumbled out, as though eager to rescue Hero. The superintendent gaped for a moment, then pulled himself together and said:

"You realize this is a very serious business, sir? You have been obstructing the police in the course of their duty—you and Mrs. Vale—by the false statements you originally made."

"Yes, I know, I know. But you must see that we couldn't let it become known. The scandal—"

The superintendent shaded his face with his hand, "I see, sir: that certainly seems to let Mrs. Vale out, though it is not too easy to credit your second story when your first is admittedly a tissue of lies." He paused.

"You must believe me," said Michael frantically. "You said that if anyone had been with Mrs. Vale it would remove the suspicion against her." He commanded his voice and spoke soberly, "I swear to you that Mrs. Vale and I were together and that we saw nothing of her nephew."

Yes, you were together all right, thought Armstrong, but I think you saw more of her nephew than was good for him.

"And, if you need any further explanation," continued Michael, "we were there because we love each other."

"So I gathered," said Armstrong dryly. Then he smiled in a more friendly way, and added, "Well, sir, you've led us a pretty dance, but I'm inclined to believe that you're telling the truth now. I shall not let this go further unless it becomes absolutely necessary. And I'm asking you to keep our conversation–all of it–entirely to yourself; that is, with the exception of Mrs. Vale."

"But–Strangeways—"

"Oh, yes, I was forgetting him. Yes," the superintendent seemed oddly disconcerted, "I think you'd better let me tell him as much as I think necessary first. Then you can, if you wish, communicate to him more fully the position between yourself and Mrs. Vale. Now there are just two more questions. What did you do when you left Mrs. Vale?"

"I went into the wood, and stayed there, as I told you, till two-fifteen."

"And secondly, what were your movements between the end of the sports and the roll-call?"

"I was in the common room. We were all there for tea, as a matter of fact."

"And then?"

"Well, I stayed there reading till seven o'clock. Tiverton was on duty, so he was in and out all the time. And Griffin went out after tea to see if Mould tidied up the ground properly. The rest of us remained in the common room."

"Till seven? You're sure of that?"

"Absolutely."

Armstrong declared himself satisfied and rose. Michael went back to his classroom feeling a vast relief. The balloon had gone up certainly, but that was almost bound to happen. It might be kept dark for a bit even now, and Hero was safe; that was all that really mattered. That superintendent was not such a bad stick at all. Michael would have had cause to reverse his opinion if he could have heard what Armstrong was saying to himself, as he went to have his few words with Hero. "The motive! And out of his own mouth!" he exulted, clenching his right fist hard in his pocket. That the superintendent was a brilliant, if unscrupulous, tactician, is sufficiently obvious by now. But he lacked the comprehensive view of the strategist, or he might have asked himself why a man who had committed murder to keep the secret of his guilty love should so easily be induced to betray his motive.

Oblivious of the suspicions they were leaving behind them, Michael and Hero drove towards Staverton. It was the first occasion they had been alone together for any time since their mad half-hour in the haystack. Michael's hand was on her knee. They felt much older since then; happy, but exhausted, as though the shore lights were in sight after a stormy passage. Hero's driving was an index of her character; cool and efficient up to a point, but she was apt to grow impatient with the process, and then it became a headlong one. In an emergency she sometimes lost her head for a fraction of a second. The luck of the careless carried her through this blind moment, and after it she got her grip again very quickly and was cool and efficient till the next one. She turned the car up a lane out of the main road and drove bumping through a gate. Here, where they were hidden by the hedge, she took Michael's hand and leaned back on his shoulder.

"Darling, I'm glad it's all out. I am, really. But what made you change your plan and tell the superintendent?"

"My hand was forced. You see, he thought–" even now Michael could scarcely get the words out–"he thought you might have done it yourself."

"Me? Are you sure? Why, I was told that it was you he suspected. My dear, it was terrible. Percy said this morning that they had found your pencil in the haystack, and I thought of them putting you in prison and tying a rope round your neck." Hero's body shook and she began to cry.

"Hero, my beautiful, please don't cry. I shall start in a minute. It makes me feel as if my inside had all collapsed."

She laughed tremulously and wiped her eyes on his sleeve, "You know, I'm much softer than I thought I was." Then she told him what the superintendent had said to her: Mr. Evans had altered his evidence and would she corroborate his new story. "So of course I did. Michael, it's a shaming thing to have to tell you, but I must. I thought at first you'd done it because you'd lost your nerve. Please forgive me."

Michael forgave her with many kisses, "Well, I suppose I did," he said, "it broke me up altogether when he said that he believed you'd done the deed. I could have killed him."

"I wish you would, Michael. I don't like him at all; his horrid pig's eyes and his smarmy manners. I believe he's capable of anything–he's probably ordering ropes for both of us now," she added, laughing.

"Oh, I don't think he's as bad as all that. After all, he might have made a nasty fuss about the lies we told him. And he did give me every chance to prove his theory wrong."

"Well, I wouldn't trust him an inch. You know, Michael," she went on irrelevantly, "I feel as if I'd just been reprieved and let out of prison. The grass is extra green and the sky extra blue and the birds singing specially for us. I feel good. I think we ought to be good. I think we ought to tell Percy."

"Get in our word before it all comes out in the general washing of dirty linen. Your psychological motives are highly questionable."

Hero flushed and stiffened a little. "You have rather a mean mind sometimes. I hate this talk about psychological motives. What's the point in rooting out all the bad reasons that one does a good thing for?"

"I didn't say 'bad reasons.' "

"Oh, don't be silly. You know that whenever you say 'psychological motives' you mean to imply the worst. Presumably there are psychological motives behind our loving each other, but you don't talk about them. No doubt you'll start to when you get tired of it."

"Hero, don't turn away from me like that. We mustn't start quarreling now. It's this damned murder business which is upsetting me. You can't imagine what it's like in the common room. Every one seems on the point of flying at every one else's throat. Gadsby and Wrench have had a dust-up already, and Tiverton simply snaps every one's head off. Griffin seems the only one of us left who is not qualifying for the loony-bin. But I think you're right. We ought to tell Percy."

"I'm so glad. My sweet, you know I didn't mean it–about your having a mean mind. Let's wait a few days, though, till he's got over this shock."

"Is he taking it badly?"

"Oh, just what you'd expect. The school will be ruined, and so on. He's forgotten all about Algernon, I think. But one oughtn't to talk about him like that. Poor dear, the school is the only thing he can see."

"*L'école, c'est moi*. Well, let's hope that Nigel finds the murderer outside it."

"Tell me about Nigel. We'd better start off again. You can tell me on the way."

"Nigel? Oh, he's a very good stick indeed. Up at Oxford with me–for goodness' sake keep your eye on the road and not me; you nearly ditched us then—"

"You look so nice, I can't take my eyes off you."

"Up at Oxford with me, I repeat. Could not stick two years of the place, the spectacle of so many quite decent youths being got at and ruined for life was too much for him. Heard that at Cambridge the hearties were still heartier and the intelligentsia even less intelligent, so decided to dispense with any further education. So he answered all his examinations in limericks–very good answers, I believe–he's a first-rate brain, but it alienated the dons, they have no taste for modern poetry, and he got sent down. Traveled about for a bit, learning languages. Then settled down to investigate crime; said it was the only career left which offered scope to good manners and scientific curiosity. He's been very successful; made pots of money. He did all the stuff in the Duchess of Esk's diamonds affair and several high-hat blackmail cases which have figured less prominently in the press."

"But what's he like?"

"Like? Oh, like one of the less successful busts of T.E. Shaw. A Nordic type. He's rather faddy, by the way; his protective mechanism developed them, I daresay. But you must have water perpetually on the boil; he drinks tea at all hours of the day. And he can't sleep unless he has an enormous weight on his bed. If you don't give him enough blankets for three, you'll find that he has torn the carpets up or the curtains down."

"Sounds crazy to me."

"Oh, you'll like him all right. He's a simple soul, really...."

The figure that emerged from a first-class carriage and advanced towards them with rather ostrich-like strides did not, Hero thought, live up to Michael's lurid description. Nigel Strangeways blinked at her short-sightedly and bowed over her hand with a courtliness a little spoilt by the angularity of his movement. He made one or two flat remarks, which his loud and exuberant voice somehow redeemed from banality, then they moved down the platform and got into the car. Hero hoped to improve the acquaintance over lunch, but, as it happened, lunch had to be postponed. Her husband had given her a note to take to James Urquhart. She stopped behind the solicitor's Daimler, which was standing outside his house. But as she was on the point of ringing, the door opened suddenly and a small, pouchy-faced man emerged, carrying a suitcase. "Why, James—" said Hero, but the man leapt down the steps, collided with a nondescript-looking individual who suddenly rose up in his path, sent him staggering away into the road, and flung himself and his suitcase into the front of the Daimler. Heavy footsteps could be heard thundering down the stairs, but by the time the superintendent and the sergeant were out of the house, Urquhart had started his car, thrust off the nondescript man who had picked himself up and was trying to get his hands on the steering wheel, and was twenty yards down the street. Armstrong glanced at Hero and Michael, hesitated a second, then rapped out a few orders to his sergeant and jumped into Hero's car. Michael had moved into the driving seat, anticipating action.

"Follow that car," shouted the superintendent, "he can't get away for long, but the sooner we catch him, the better."

Hero bundled into the back seat, where Strangeways took her arm in the most friendly and reassuring way, remarking, "I seem to have plunged *in medias res*, as you might say." Michael jumped the car forward in second, skidded neatly between a bus and a sandwich man at the corner, and hurled them in a series of swoops and jerks through the traffic of the High Street. "O death," sang Strangeways, in a raucous baritone, "how bitter art thou to him that liveth in peace, to him that hath joy in his possessions and liveth free from trouble." The broad back of the Daimler slipped coyly round a corner, fifty yards ahead, its red rear lamp winking an offensive challenge. Michael changed down at forty, the car swayed and seemed to hang like a lift at the bottom of its descent, then he accelerated into the side street and was confronted by a level crossing, with the gates just beginning to close. Michael in control of a fast car was a person in whom one would scarcely recognize the decorous, slightly neurotic schoolmaster of Sudeley Hall. He put his car at the gates like a seasoned huntsman. Nigel murmured to Hero:

"Does your vehicle jump?" Then gently closed his eyes as they rocked over the metals with the gates scraping and jarring at their rear wings. The superintendent shot an apprehensive glance at Michael, but he was staring ahead, smiling serenely, apparently not contemplating further addition to his tale of victims.

They were out in the country now, drumming in third up a long incline. Trees pounced at them and withdrew, hedges-moved endlessly past like conveyor belts, the tires purred on a different road surface, and the Daimler kept its distance. They bucketed over the top and a steep hill fell away at their feet. Michael went down it like an airplane diving. The speedometer needle surged up from fifty to sixty, to seventy, to seventy-five. Armstrong, putting his head outside, found his eyelids fluttered up and down by the wind's pressure. The Daimler looked bigger now, and they could see the figure inside bumping up and down hunched over the wheel. Strangeways held Hero closer, remarked that this was better than the movies and began singing an aria from "Israel in Egypt." Hero's golden hair was floating above her head as though she were sitting over an electric fan, her eyes were sparkling and her mouth curved ecstatically. Even the superintendent forgot his fright in the general excitement, and to the astonishment of the company began to deliver hunting cries in a high tenor.

A red triangle flicked past; a blind crossroads ahead. The Daimler was over them. A baby Austin nosed out from behind a barn on the right; the owner gave a startled glance at the projectile leaping at him down the hill, flurried with his hands, and stopped almost in the middle of the crossroads. Michael's left hand dropped on the brake and his right forced the wheel steadily over to the right. They swung behind the tail of the Austin, then Michael jerked the wheel to the left and braked hard. The tires screamed, a wall sprang at the right side of the car, seemed to halt in mid-spring as Michael put the wheel right over again, was snatched away. They were through.

"Michael *darling!*" said Hero.

"God's truth!" said Nigel.

"Well done, sir," said the superintendent, opening his eyes again, then pointed ahead. The Daimler was lurching from side to side of the road like a maddened bull. Urquhart must have fatally glanced back, expecting his pursuers to be smashed at the crossroads. A tire burst. The Daimler went off at a tangent into the ditch. Her huge body pirouetted on its front wheels, was tossed up into the air like a toy, twirled over the hedge, and fell devastatingly into the field beyond, jerking clear a small black figure, a suitcase and several cushions, which came to earth scattered and severally, as though vomited out of a volcano. They all listened, expecting to hear the dreadful thump of the body, though even the Daimler's crash had been scarcely audible through the roar of their own engine. When the body dropped out of sight behind the hedge, they winced and felt as if they were going to be hit hard in the wind. Michael pulled up and scrambled with the superintendent into the field. The Daimler looked like a scrap-heap. Urquhart, too, was in a sorry mess, but a bush had broken his fall and he was not dead. They got him quickly into the nearest village, where a doctor attended him till the ambulance came from Staverton.

Armstrong proposed to remain by Urquhart's bedside in the hospital till he recovered consciousness; if he ever should. But he thanked Michael, a little awkwardly, for his help and promised to come up to the school that evening if he could, and tell them all about it.

"Is he—James—the man, the one you're looking for?" said Hero, as Armstrong was preparing to depart.

"Well, no, he's not the murderer, ma'am. At least, I should be very surprised if—but if he ever gets over this, he'll see the inside of a prison all right, I can promise you that."

With this they had to rest contented for seven hours or so. After dinner that night, when the headmaster and his wife, Michael and Nigel were discussing the affair in the drawing room, the superintendent was announced. He walked gravely up to Percival Vale, "I'm afraid this will be a terrible shock to you, sir. Mr. Urquhart is dead. Before he died he made a confession. One which, I may say, confirmed my own theory about him. He had been playing fast and loose with your nephew's fortune. He had appropriated a considerable part of it from time to time for his own uses, then speculated, unsuccessfully, in an attempt to make good the estate. I think he knew that I suspected this, for when I went to interview him this morning he sent in a message that he would see me in five minutes, and he spent those five minutes in collecting whatever remained and was accessible of Master Wemyss' property. I had posted a plainclothes man at the door, but he got past him. For the rest we have to thank Mrs. Vale for her car and Mr. Evans for his fine driving."

The headmaster sank into a chair, his face was buried in his trembling hands, and Armstrong could only guess what emotions were being concealed. He went on:

"And, of course, that means that the murderer is still at large. Mr. Urquhart would be the last person to kill the boy, since his death would inevitably lead to his own immediate exposure. I take it that you had no suspicion of what was going on, Mr. Vale?"

The headmaster raised the face of one who saw the last props of a shaken world give way, "It can be scarcely necessary for me to say that I had no idea of it," he answered hopelessly.

"I have a reason for asking the question, sir," said Armstrong, and proceeded to relate the incident of the anonymous note which had brought the solicitor to Edgworth Wood. "You see," he explained, "I couldn't imagine what would induce Mr. Urquhart to keep such an unprofessional appointment, unless he himself had something on his conscience and the note referred to it. Now that we know he *had* something on his conscience, we can infer that the writer of the note must have known of it or guessed it—"

"It might have been a shot in the dark," interrupted Strangeways.

"That is barely possible, of course. Do you know of anyone who would be likely to have discovered Mr. Urquhart's frauds, sir? Anyone, that is, who also had personal connection with your nephew?"

"No."

"That is a pity, sir, because there doesn't seem much doubt that a person who fulfils those two qualifications wrote the note, and the person who wrote the note was the murderer."

Chapter VII

About it and About

The next day Strangeways spent in getting the feel of the place, as he put it. He had a great advantage over the superintendent here; not only was he understood to be "on our side," for so the common room looked upon it, but he had an uncanny knack for fitting into the different kinds of circles and societies into which his profession brought him. He did this, not as most "mixers" do, by altering himself to suit the environment, or by any apparent exercise of social tact. It was his obvious and genuine interest in the person he was talking to—a far more sincere form of flattery than imitation—that was his passport to so many differing types of individual. This interest was actually far less flattering to the individual than it seemed on the surface, for it proceeded from scientific and not sentimental curiosity, but its ultimately impersonal nature was concealed by Strangeways' personal vitality and good manners, and very few of those who were subjects of it realized that they were dealing with a kind of human microscope.

Let us follow him as he steers an erratic, seemingly aimless course through a school day. He has had breakfast with the staff. Work has begun. He moves slowly down the corridor between classrooms, as Michael did three days before. First on the left, the headmaster taking Latin. The real, genuine old pedagogue's voice, matured in the wood, snapping and buzzing away like electric sparks in a tense, strained silence. That man, thinks Nigel, has not passion enough for one kind of murder, and surely his mind is too complacent and academic for the other. The school is the symbol and vindication of his own ego. His reaction to the crime, Hero and Michael agree, is a feeling that his life work had been badly damaged; a kind of blow, not simply at his reputation, but at himself. That feeling is real, not assumed; I can see that for myself. It is unthinkable that such a man, in order to get hold of a property which he does not need, would commit a murder bound to damage the school and therefore to violate his own ego.

He moved on. Gadsby. A common enough type. Good-looking once, the life and soul of the party, a great success in a small, mentally confined circle. And then he grows older, loses his looks and youthful zest, the circle is broken up and he is left defenseless. There remains drink; "love affairs"; some kind of drug to make him forget his losses. He is almost burnt out, a bonhomous automaton. Almost burnt out, but perhaps not quite. The sort of person who might be found mixed up in one of these squalid "crimes passionnels." The sort to commit murder from fright, not for revenge. Wonder how he supports this monastic life. He doesn't talk to the boys like a homosexual, repressed or otherwise. I must have a look at the servants, that was a handsome wench waiting at breakfast.

A devilish hubbub broke into his thoughts. He moved over to the door on his right whence it proceeded, murmuring, "*Mon Dieu, quel hulerberlu! Quel*, I might even say, *tohu-bohu!*" Feet were clattering on desks, books falling, or, more likely, being thrown, hoots, groans and scuffles. A jerky, ineffectual voice said, "Stop this noise, won't you! You two, sit down at once. What's all this disturbance about?"

"Please, sir, Pompo's lizard has escaped. Wooh! Look out, sir, it's going up your trouser leg."

"Lizard? What on earth are you talking about?"

"Don't you know what a lizard is, sir? A reptilian quadruped, common in tropical regions, with a long tail, and knobs on."

"Ponsonby, none of your insolence or I'll report you to Mr. Vale. Now then, Bastin, what's all this about your filthy lizard?"

"Sir, he's not filthy, sir, his name is Gloucestershire, because he's got a long tail, you see, sir."

"Chew yourself, Pomps. We beat your moldy old Middlesex anyway."

The anguished voice of Sims blurted out again. It was just like a sheep strayed on the mountains, Nigel thought, "The next boy who talks without permission will be kept in this afternoon. Now then, what do you mean by bringing a lizard into form?" Dead silence. "Will you answer me at once."

"Please, sir, you didn't give me permission to speak."

Sims laughed, an uncertain, would-be ingratiating laugh, "The point is well taken. You may speak."

"Well, sir, he was so lonely by himself in my desk—oh corks! Look out, you chaps, he's trying to get under the door!" There was a trebly increased rumpus, several bodies crashed against the door, then an angry wail arose, "Curse you, Stevens II, you've pulled its tail off! I'll give you such a conk on the nut." "I'm frightfully sorry, Pompo. It just cime awiy in me 'and: oh, you would, would you?" Crash, bang, thump, screech. Strangeways moved off at a brisk walk, as he heard the headmaster's door opening, and stopped again at a discreeter distance. Mr. Vale entered the inferno. Medusa herself could not have had a more petrifying effect, "The whole of this form will stay in this afternoon and write out lines for me. You three, Stevens II., Bastin and Ponsonby, will also come to my study at twelve-forty-five for a thrashing. A word with you, please, Mr. Sims." Strangeways moved hurriedly into the common room while the outraged headmaster swept past, towing Sims, as pale as dead Hector, at his chariot wheels. Strangeways unashamedly put his head to the study door and heard a dressing-down which made his ears tingle. Poor little devil, he thought, no one has ever given him a chance. Just like Vale to take up this line with him. Sarcasm, biting contempt, talking to him like he talks to one of the boys. Of course, Vale is really angry, indiscipline lets down the school; ergo, is an insult to himself. My hat, though, if anyone spoke to me like that I'd break his head. But Sims is too crushed for that; the slave mentality. Chock-full of inferiority feeling no doubt. The way the boys seem to treat him would do it alone. Is there a point at which such slaves rebel? I wonder does a worm turn, in actual fact. Must find out whether Wemyss was numbered amongst his oppressors.

Sims returned, flushed and shaken, to his classroom, and Strangeways resumed his promenade. He smiled involuntarily as he stood outside Griffin's door. He was teaching history, Nigel realized at last, full of flagrant inexactitudes and gross caricatures of eminent personages. Nigel left him as Henry the Eighth, decapitating wives right and left with a ruler. There was enormous competition amongst his form for the place of honor on the block. No, if murder is there, thought Nigel, I'll eat all my hats and join the nudists. He moved farther down the passage. Tiverton's room. There was order here, but maintained at the cost of incessant nervous effort. The boys answered questions in respectful enough tones, but one felt that they would break out if the master let up his nervous pressure for a moment. There was no real sympathy between him and his pupils; they were not even united by the bond of fear, like the headmaster and his. I doubt if Tiverton is in the right job; he has enthusiasm, but no channel to communicate it here. Might have made a good scientist if he'd had more brains, or an expert connoisseur, perhaps, if he'd had the money. Murder? I doubt it. Too spinsterish and comfort-loving. I imagine he's got a soft center, too. But not absolutely off the cards.

Strangeways moved across the passage and stopped, quite startled, outside Wrench's room. Good Lord, what have we here? This man has something very near a genius for teaching, and at breakfast I thought he was just the usual scrubby prep-school nonentity. The silence in the room was one of rapt attention. Wrench's voice was confident and incisive, the faint Midland accent lending it a curious kind of distinction. Patient, illuminating, right on top of his work, Nigel said to himself. He's obviously got brains. Brains enough to plan a subtle murder, and the single-minded desire of the bright lower-middle-class lad to get somewhere. I can imagine him remorseless against anything that stood in the path of his ambition. But how could Wemyss? Supposing there was something that threatened to ruin his career; supposing Wemyss knew of it? Stop! We only want impressions so far; theories must wait for facts.

The bell rang for the end of the hour. Doors vomited forth a stream of boys. Evans came along and dragged his friend towards his own classroom. "You've got to come and take the part of Hamlet, if we succeed in doing any work at all. The boys have heard that there's a new sleuth on the premises, so you'll probably have to give a lecture on crime." A few minutes found Nigel, stripped to the shirt sleeves, a lath sword in hand, confronting the Laertes of Anstruther. Nigel was no actor; but, if he lacked dramatic talent, he was equally lacking in self-consciousness, and his boisterous abandon soon affected the other players. There was, perhaps, more sawing of the air, o'erdoing Termagant, and out-heroding Herod than the refined Prince of Denmark would have cared for; still, the Elizabethan gusto of the actors compensated for much. Laertes was truculent, Hamlet elaborately ironic. A smallish, rabbit-faced boy, representing the king in a purple tablecloth and a pie-frill crown, began to declaim:

"Set me the stoups of wine upon that table." Two advanced bearing lemonade bottles, while the court made ribald comments, not unconnected with the weakness of Mr. Gadsby.

> "If Hamlet give the first or second hit,
> Or quit in answer of the third exchange,
> Let all the battlements their ordnance fire;
> The King shall drink to Hamlet's better breath;
> And in the cup an onion shall he throw—"

The King was not allowed to proceed any further. Yelps and howls of mirth convulsed the company. Michael realized that it would take them the rest of the hour to recover from giggling fits, so he suggested that Strangeways might be willing to answer any questions they liked to ask. The form leaped at the chance and plied him for many minutes, with the thirteen-year-old's quaint blend of sophistication and naïveté. Then Anstruther asked him how he would have gone about solving the mystery of his father's death, supposing he had been Hamlet. This opened the floodgates, and Nigel talked on and on to a spellbound audience. As the hands of the clock hovered over ten-thirty, he noticed that one of his audience had conceived an idea and wished to deliver it. He broke off. "Did you want to ask something special?"

"Sir, excuse my interrupting–" it was Stevens, the head boy, speaking–
"but wouldn't it be fine if we could find out who killed Wemyss by acting
the murder over again, like Hamlet made the players do before the king."
Strangeways received the suggestion with perfect gravity. "Yes, that's a
good idea. I'll remember it. And by the way," he said, striking while the
iron is hot, "if any of you have any ideas about this business, I shall be in
Mr. Evans' room after lunch. Remember, anything you know about Wemyss, any little detail you noticed that struck you as queer, however unimportant it may seem, may help a great deal." The bell rang, and Nigel
left the room having made twelve hero-worshippers, allies, and possibly
too zealous assistants.

Michael and his friend strolled into the common room, where they were
received with friendly nods. Tiverton stretched out his cigarette case to
Strangeways, looking at him quizzically. Strangeways took one, lit it, and
said, "Anything wrong? They aren't opium, are they? Or have I a smut on
the end of my nose?" Tiverton smiled, "Another illusion shattered! I've
never read a detective story in which the great man didn't 'carefully select a cigarette from the case,' and I've always wondered how and why he
did it when the case was generally full of Players."

"Just padding," said Wrench, "they can never spin a single crime over
three hundred pages, so they either have to fill up with carefully selected
drinks and smokes or make their criminal commit a few more murders."

Sims looked over the top of his *Daily Mirror*, "Let's hope our local
criminal doesn't adopt your second alternative."

Wrench frowned and exclaimed irritably, "Oh, God, why is everybody
always bringing up this subject? Need we all become monomaniacs just
because we all suspect that one of us *is* a maniac?"

There was a painful silence. It was the first public appearance of a
truth, so to speak, and it got the welcome that truths usually get on their
first appearance. Nigel looked down his nose in a noncommittal way,
seemingly absorbed in his own thoughts–actually listening hard for the
intonations of voices. Griffin pushed back his chair and said:

"A deep wedge of depression is moving quickly down from Iceland.
There will be local soul-storms tomorrow."

"Look here, Wrench, that's a nasty thing to say," exclaimed Sims. "I
mean, do you really think the murderer's a maniac? It's not a very agree-
able thought."

"Don't you worry, Sims, nobody would hurt you," Wrench replied, the
contempt in his voice scarcely veiled. Sims ducked back behind his paper. Gadsby, who had been trying in vain to get a word in, rasped in his
throat, collected eyes like a hostess, making a marked exception of
Wrench's, and said:

"Rather a morbid subject this. Let's change it. Well, Strangeways, getting any forrarder?"

"That is not changing the subject," remarked Wrench belligerently.

Gadsby ignored the objection, and continued to stare expectantly at Nigel, with his rather grisly animation of face–the expression of a galvanized corpse.

"Early days yet, Mr. Gadsby," said Nigel. "At present I'm so interested in the workings of a preparatory school that I have almost forgotten what I came here for."

"And what is your opinion of our workings?" asked Wrench, a little on the defensive.

"I think your boys are very lucky to be at school now and not thirty years ago. Nice common room you've got here. I've a dim recollection of the one at my own private school; no windows, one dusty skylight, a foil without the button in one corner and a broken brassie in another, on the table a Latin grammar without a cover, a bottle of invalid port, and a tooth tumbler. A very good expressionist picture of early twentieth century education."

There was general laughter, to which Gadsby added a rather puzzled contribution, "There's something in what you say," he remarked. "Talking of education, that reminds me, can't find my French prose book." He got up and began looking into lockers that lined the far wall. "Suppose it can't have got among your books by mistake, Tiverton?"

Tiverton turned round abruptly in his chair, "No, it could *not*. And will you kindly keep your nose out of my locker. You know perfectly well that there's an unwritten law here against snooping into other people's belongings in the common room."

Sims looked up in a worried way and Strangeways looked down his nose again. The aggrieved Gadsby said, "Oh, very well, very well. Seem to have put my foot in it again. Got *Lady Chatterley* tucked away in there, have you?"

A further outburst from Tiverton was averted by the entrance of the headmaster, "Oh, there you are, Strangeways. Getting acquainted with the–a–ah–genius loci? Now, is there anything you want, any assistance we can give you?"

"Well, yes, I should very much like a cup of tea."

"Tea? Ah, yes, to be sure, tea. I will have a cup sent in to the morning-room for you."

Nigel, looking, for him, almost bashful, asked if it might be a pot; to which the headmaster consented, though with the defeated air of one invited to take part in a round game whose rules he does not know. Nigel had only just poured out his third cup when Armstrong was announced.

One or two preliminary remarks were passed, which made it clear to Nigel that the superintendent was sparring for a verbal opening, and he decided to get in his own word first.

"As you know," he said, "I have come down with a rather vague commission to investigate this case in the interests of the school. I should like to assure you at the outset that I shall be doing so in no spirit of antagonism to yourself. Naturally, I hope that I may be able to find a solution which will help to restore the school's reputation or, at least, damage it no further. But if I am forced to conclude that the criminal *is* connected with the school, I shall do my best to assist you in proving his guilt."

"That's fair enough, sir."

"Like a cup of tea? No? A cigarette, then. Now, as to my line of action. I know that you professionals get sick to death of amateur theorizing. I therefore suggest that we pool the facts, but each keeps his theories to himself until he has a pretty complete case."

Armstrong studied his toecaps for a moment or two. He was faintly resentful of Strangeways having taken the initiative thus, nor was he too keen on a pooling of the facts, when all the facts at present were to be contributed by himself. On the other hand, the amateur was in a far better position than himself for the making of further discoveries. So, on the whole, it seemed best to strike the bargain. He therefore proceeded to give Strangeways a detailed and lucid summary of the course of the investigation up to date, "And you can see for yourself, sir," he concluded, "though we have decided to keep our theories to ourselves, that the facts so far are all pointing in one direction."

"Mrs. Vale and Evans?"

"Yes," said Armstrong, rather surprised by the other's matter-of-fact admission, "though I shouldn't have expected you to agree so readily."

"Why not? Evans is one of my best friends, but I shan't help him by shutting my eyes to all evidence against him. If I may sum up your own position, it is this. The murder was committed either by someone outside the school or someone inside. The movements of all vagrants known to be in the district have been satisfactorily accounted for, and besides, there was no sign of the body having been robbed. This, and the entire absence of possible motives, puts the first alternative practically out of court, though one must not altogether leave out of one's reckoning the man whom Wrench said he spoke to at the beginning of the sports. Take the second alternative. The time-limit appears to be fixed as from one to two-thirty p.m. From about one-forty-five to two-thirty the hayfield was in full view of Griffin and the groundsman. From one-thirty to one-forty-five, there was no one about outside, but the murderer could not reckon on this and it would have been dangerous in the extreme for him to have murdered the boy in the haystack or carried his body to it at a time when anyone might come out of the school. There remains one to one-thirty, when every one's movements are accounted for, except those of Evans and Mrs. Vale, who admit that they were actually on the spot where the body was found."

"That's it, sir, the case against them seems the only possible one. But—"

"But you haven't got a single fact to support it except a piece of string that might come off anyone of millions of balls, and a silver pencil, which seems to be rather a broken reed itself."

"It's extraordinary, Mr. Strangeways. I've never heard of a case where there were so few material clues. I've been over that field and all the grounds till I was sick. I've badgered the servants. I've searched the masters' rooms, though you needn't tell 'em that. Not a blessed thing to be found. And yet the motive: Mr. Evans and Mrs. Vale seem to have so much the strongest one."

"By the way, superintendent, I'm surprised that you had so little difficulty in obtaining confirmation of this motive."

Armstrong looked uncomfortable, but he could not ignore the question in Strangeways' remark, and was compelled to give an account of the stratagem he had employed in his last interview with Michael. Nigel stared ruminatively down his nose during this account, then said, "Well, you certainly don't use kid gloves. Don't think I am criticizing you. You people wouldn't have much chance of catching criminals if you kept to the rules which they break. But there are two points which counsel for the defense can make—"

Armstrong, who had started very much on the defensive against the amateur, was now entirely at ease and asked him to expound.

"First, it seems unlikely that a murderer would admit from the beginning having been on the spot when the murder was committed. One would expect them either to have cooked up an alibi, or to have put the body somewhere else."

"It might be a bold kind of bluff, sir, to sidetrack suspicion by putting themselves in the most obviously suspicious position at the start."

"It might. That has been done, I know, but—well, anyway, my second point is this. Supposing the murder had been done from the motive you suggest, it's unnatural that a murderer should be so easily induced to betray his motive. One doesn't give up one's key position without making a fight for it, more of a fight than Evans seems to have made, at least."

"I see your point, sir. Yes, I admit that hadn't occurred to me. Of course, he might just have lost his nerve; though, after that little affair yesterday, my opinion of Mr. Evans' nerve has gone up considerably. Well, I must be getting along. I can see that you don't need much advice from me, but there is one line which I'd like to suggest. I can't manage to get anything out of the boys myself—"

"Damned little snobs, most of them, I bet," interrupted Nigel.

"That's just it, sir," said Armstrong gratefully, "and I believe that they are the only ones who might give us a line on—"

"On what it was that made Wemyss conceal himself so successfully till the murderer was at liberty to finish him for good?"

"Good Lord, Mr. Strangeways, either you're a thought reader, or else you ought to be running this case instead of me," said the superintendent with real admiration. And refusing another offer of tea–to Nigel's considerable relief, for there was little left, and he wanted a sixth cup–he took himself off.

Until lunch Strangeways wandered about in the school grounds. He tried, not very successfully, to visualize them as they were on the Sports Day; the running track, the flags, the crowd and the haystacks. He poked his nose into Mould's hut and pondered the question of the sacks. Someone must have moved them. The murderer? If so, why should he have transferred the body to the hayfield at all? It was hidden just as well in the hut. Why, you poor fool, because he wanted to gain time. He knew the hut would probably be visited before the sports, whereas the hayfield almost certainly would not be. He *knew*. You are already assuming that the murderer is familiar with the school arrangements. But, granted all this, the main difficulty is unresolved. *When* was all this done? You believe Michael and his young woman to be innocent; well then, that leaves from one-thirty to two-thirty. One-thirty to one-forty-five, unless the murder was committed while Griffin and Mould were on the big field. That has been assumed to be impossible. Is it? The walls of the haystack, Armstrong said, were tall enough to conceal a man stooping inside, therefore the murder might have been committed there unseen. But there still remains the fact that either the murderer, or his victim, or both, would be seen going from the school to the haystack. Of course, Griffin and Mould might have had their backs turned for a moment every now and then; but the murderer couldn't rely on this; it wasn't like dashing across a deck between waves. A murderer who has covered his traces so well is surely not the man to have trusted to luck at the most crucial point of his actions.

Try again. Is that two-thirty fixed? Medical evidence puts four p.m. as the outside limit. Was the murder done during the sports after all? But if it is not reasonable to suppose that a murderer would risk being seen by two people, surely it's far more wildly unreasonable to imagine that he would have taken the risk with two hundred or so. Supposing it was not done in the haystack at all, and the body put there later, say, when every one was at tea. That means it must have been done by someone outside

the school, for boys and masters are all accounted for from tea time on-
wards. All very fine, but why in the name of the saints should anyone take
the trouble of carting the corpse back and dumping it down in a haystack.
That's the most fantastic idea of all. The haystack. Why the haystack,
anyway? Surely the solution lies there. If one could only grasp why the
murder was done–or at any rate the body deposited–in such an eccentric
place, such a public place, such a wildly paradoxical place, one would
have the key of the riddle in one's hands.

Nigel strolled slowly back into the school, deliberately overlaying this
crucial question with other minor ones, hoping it would soon dive into
his unconscious mind and emerge in due season bearing the answer with
it. It was not long, indeed, before other matters turned up which effectu-
ally diverted his attention. He was sitting in Michael's room after lunch
when there was an impetuous knock at the door and a body entered with
that unwilling and unseemly haste which, in a prep-school, usually indi-
cates propulsion from behind by a bashful associate. The first figure shot
several feet into the room, revealing itself as Anstruther. He was followed
by Stevens, looking elaborately unconscious of his companion's uncer-
emonious entry.

"Please, sir," they both said simultaneously, and stopped with a common blush.

"You go on, Stevens," said Anstruther.

"Please, sir, may we say something to Mr. Strangeways?"

"You may," Michael smiled affectionately at the head of the school,
contrasting his unstudied diffidence with the contained and natural arro-
gance of his slight figure.

"We thought we ought to tell you, sir," the boy addressed Strangeways,
"on the morning that Wemyss was murdered, there was a conversation
about him at the prefect's table." Nigel suppressed a faint smile at the
stilted opening, and Stevens continued.

"You see, sir, he was becoming rather a menace, I mean, he was a
ghastly tick, really, and we thought it was about time he was suppressed."

Michael stirred uneasily. Heaven forefend that this should turn out to
have been a joke that went too far. And Stevens, of all people.

"Of course, we couldn't do anything ourselves. Percy–Mr. Vale–
wouldn't stand for us reporting a boy for ragging a master. So we decided
to get my brother and his gang to deal with him."

"And did you?"

"I talked to my brother in recess, and he said he'd get some of his gang
to beat up Wemyss after the sports. They call themselves 'the Black Spot';
a sort of secret society, it is, sir. Rather a childish business, but it seems to
amuse them." Stevens spoke with an indulgent, one-man-of-the-world-

to-another air, but there was an entirely boyish note of apprehension in his tones as well. It was at this point that Strangeways might very well have lost the battle. If he had taken up a stern moral attitude, or, worse still, if he had tried to laugh off the whole thing, the sensitive Stevens would have retired forever into his shell, and the train of events which finally led to the solution of the crime would never have been started. But Strangeways was neither a moralist nor a hearty blunderer.

"I see," he said, "that must have made things rather difficult for you and your brother, but I think you were quite right to tell me. And, of course, you needn't worry about it. I'm quite sure that neither of you is the murderer. But if you or he can give me any information, I'd be extraordinarily grateful, and it won't go any further than me, unless I think it absolutely necessary to tell the police about it."

Stevens gave him a smile of great sweetness, "That's jolly decent of you, sir. Of course, my brother didn't do anything. But perhaps it would be better if he told you himself. He wasn't funking it, you know, but— well—he thought at first you might be a mess, like that policeman johnny."

"I'd like to see your brother very much; how about this afternoon?"

"Well, he's been kept in then, but he could come up before tea, about half-past five, if that would do."

"Would he like to have tea here with me? Could that be arranged?"

"I'm sure he'd love to. But I don't know whether Mr. Vale would allow him," Stevens added dubiously.

"I think I can manage to get his permission," said Strangeways with unimpaired gravity. Stevens and Anstruther departed, casting glances of shy admiration at him, as unconscious as he that they were putting one end of the long and tangled clue in his hand.

Chapter VIII

Initiation of a Detective

Strangeways looked forward to his tea-party with mild curiosity. He went into the village and bought suitable cakes and a good supply of chocolate. Returning, he filled in time on the cricket field, in that pleasant mood composed of esthetic rapture and expert attention which the cricket devotee shares only with the lover of music and the fisherman. In the middle of Big Field the first eleven were bowling against a second team stiffened by the inclusion of Griffin and Tiverton. For the second time since he had entered the school, Nigel was made aware of class; Wrench's teaching, and now Tiverton's batting. The man was a born cricketer. As Nigel watched him, dealing in his offhand manner with some by no means despicable bowling, he found himself most irrationally crossing Tiverton off his list of suspects. No man who could bat like that would commit a mean and cowardly murder. Nigel seemed to have been there only a moment or two, held as he was in that timeless trance of the sky, green grass and gracious action, when he looked at his watch and found that it lacked but ten minutes till his tea-party.

He hurried indoors, boiled water, put out the food, and awaited his guest. There were two of them, as it happened. Stevens II put his head round the door, gave Strangeways a frank stare, and asked, "Can I bring someone else?" "Of course, if you like, fetch him along." "That's O.K., sir, I've got him outside here." The face disappeared. A highly audible colloquy took place beyond the door. "Come on, he says you can come." "But look here, what will Percy say?" "Bother Percy! He'll have to do what the detective jolly well tells him." "What's he like?" "Decent. Do come on! There's milk chocolate on the table." "Oh, all right. You needn't pull my ear off." Stevens II. entered the room, towing a chubby, fiery-faced child behind him, whom he introduced as follows: "This is Ponsonby. He's my lieutenant. Don't trip over the table, you silly gowk."

Ponsonby, under the influence of cakes and chocolate, quickly became his natural self. The dictator had no reserve to shed; he discussed the merits of different kinds of iced drink, told Nigel all about his fleet of model airplanes, and becoming even more convivial, related several grossly scandalous anecdotes about members of the staff. When there was not a speck of food left on any of the plates, he summed up, "A jolly good binge, sir. Better than eating train-grease on cardboard in hall."

"Train-grease on cardboard?"

"He means toast and butter, sir. That's what we have for tea on Saturdays," explained Ponsonby.

"Butter!" said Stevens darkly. "Be your rank! Any fool knows it's margarine, or worse."

Nigel cut short what threatened to be a lecture on dietetics, "Well, I suppose we'd better be getting down to business. You were going to tell me something about Wemyss."

Stevens knitted his brow. He looked very like his elder brother now, but much more the man of action, the rough diamond, the potential leader.

"It's rather difficult," he said. "You see, it's not really about Wemyss at all. And if I tell you, it's betraying a secret of the Black Spot."

"Punishment—expulsion and disgrace," added his lieutenant portentously.

"So we thought perhaps—that is, if you would become a member of the Black Spot yourself—"

Strangeways just avoided saying, "It would be a great honor," realizing that Stevens was not the person to accept grown-up politeness.

"I see what you mean."

"The trouble is that every one has to pass a test before we allow them into the society," continued Stevens doubtfully.

"A test?"

"Yes. An ordeal, sort of. To prove their courage and all that sort of thing."

"Couldn't I go through the ordeal?"

"Well, sir, we make them do rather funny things. I mean, it's all very well for boys, but I don't think it'd do for grown-up people," said the realist Stevens.

"Couldn't we make him an honorary member?" asked Ponsonby.

"Shut up, Pongo, I thought of that long ago, so snoo to you."

"I'd rather be a proper member, if you don't mind," said Strangeways; thereby, as he came to realize later, making a decision that was to lead him to the criminal.

"Oh, flip! That's fine! Are you sure you don't mind, sir? You could have the test tomorrow. We'll work it out tonight."

"You'll give me the same test as you give every one else?"

"Well, we make up a different one for each new candidate. It's more fun like that. But they're all the same sort of thing. You'll get your instructions tomorrow morning and report to me when you've finished, that is—" the boy broke off with a little confusion. There are limits to a dictator's scope of dictation.

Strangeways affected not to notice this and a time and place were arranged for the next meeting. From then till it was time to go, Stevens discarded his official dignity, he and Ponsonby finally leaving the room with repeated volleys of, "Thanks *awfully*, sir!" "Thanks *frightfully*, sir!" which made Nigel feel as if he had presented them with half the kingdoms of the world. They had scarcely gone when Stevens returned again and, putting his head in at the door, whispered, "I say, sir, you'll not tell anyone about the test, will you, sir? It's supposed to be awfully secret." Nigel reassured him, though he felt by no means reassured himself. The boy had said that what he had to tell him was not about Wemyss at all. That was bad enough, and now he had to waste some valuable time tomorrow undergoing a probably most undignified initiation. Yet an intuition, which had helped him more than once before, told him that he was beginning to grow warm.

If he went to bed that night vaguely uneasy, a paper which was put in his hand the next morning as he strolled towards the common room sent him into a real panic. This is a bit too much, he thought, rereading his instructions. I shall be landed in prison by this evening. It was a ragged piece of exercise-paper, with enough thumbmarks on it to make it a fingerprint expert's paradise. There was a round splodge of ink at the top, the Black Spot, no doubt; underneath, in laborious capitals, ran the following legend:–

"IF YOU WOULD BECOME A MEMBER OF YE ANCIENT AND HONORABLE SOCIETY OF YE BLACK SPOT, YE MUST PERFORM AND COMITT BEFORE 2 P.M. TODAY THE FOLLOWING EXPLOITS. TO WIT:–

1. Chalk a white mustashe on the nimph of ye drynking fountain in Sudeley.
2. Ask Higgins, resident in ye hamlet aforsaid, to show you his famous scales, and bring back a description thereof.
3. Remove one rabitt trap from ye phesant cover of Lord Edgworth and keep ye same till the society demands it.
N.B.–Exploits to be purpetrated in ye above order.

P.S.–If thou shirkest or failest in any you shall cease to be elligible for this society.
P.P.S.–Burn this paper. And if you divulge its contents, or any part of its contents, or anything whatsoever pertaining to ye Black

Spot, to any living soul, the Black Spot will be put upon you and
you may expect no mercy.
"R.I.P.

"(Singed) THE OFFICERS OF THE SOCIETY."

This rigmarole, attesting alike to its author's wide reading and inventiveness, caused the sweat to stand out on its recipient's forehead. It appears
to be either the jail or the nearest lunatic asylum for yours truly if he
attempts to "perform and comitt" these fantastic feats, thought Nigel. But
the adventurousness which had led him into many strange places made
up his mind for him. He put a match to the sinister document, and went in
quest of a bicycle, some information about Lord Edgworth's "phesant
cover," and a piece of chalk. He chose a bicycle–the oldest one he could
borrow–because some means of escape was clearly desirable, and a car
would be far too conspicuous. Lord Edgworth's coverts were a couple of
miles from the school, he learned, in the opposite direction from the village and separated by a fence from the wood in which Urquhart had kept
his fruitless vigil. The coverts, he was also told, were the haunt of all the
local poachers and possibly not unfrequented by some of the Rev. Vale's
young gentlemen. They were jealously patrolled by keepers. You may
well say "R.I.P." thought Nigel.

It was after ten o'clock when he started. A morning heat haze, which
was just giving way before the brassy stare of the sun, promised that his
ordeal would be a physical as well as a mental one. His bicycle, too,
creaked rheumatically, and he was conscious of a marked discrepancy
between its plebeian frame and his own well-worn but still gentlemanly
suit. As the village came in sight, Nigel found himself pedaling even
slower. Practical jokes and crazy exhibitions were all very well in the
heat of the moment, but this cold-blooded lunacy was a far different cup
of tea. Apprehension became sheer horror when he arrived on the green
in the middle of the village. The "nimph" was a substantial woman of
uncertain age, her charms partially concealed by verdigris, standing in a
eurythmic attitude in a large and unsavory-looking basin of water. Moreover, she was attended by a group of village swains, wearing their Sunday best, who sat on the parapet of the basin. Nigel's nerve all but failed
him. He was on the point of turning back, when the face of Stevens II rose
up mutely reproaching before his mind's eye; what would that intrepid
youth say if the great detective returned, a failure? He braced himself,
leaned his bicycle against a wall, and approached the group.

"Good-morning! A fine day!"

"Ar."

"Does Mr. Higgins live near here?"

"Ar. Keeps shop down street."

"I hear you've had a murder in the neighborhood. A nasty business."

"Cor, Bert, that's a good 'un, that is. Detective gennulman from Lunnon 'e says, 'I hear you've had a murder in the neighborhood.' That's a bloody good 'un, that is." Hoarse guffaws. A swain expectorated rudely at the eurythmic nymph. Nigel stuck to it. His brain was working furiously.

"I didn't know you'd heard about me."

"Found any clues like, mister?"

"One or two. We're getting along slowly."

"Detective gennulman asks we does Mr. Higgins live here. Gennulman be going to arrest Mr. Higgins, see?" remarked one logician.

"Gennulman better mind out. Mr. Higgins always drunk Saturday nights. Mr. Higgins powerful raging Sunday morning."

"No, I'm not going to arrest Mr. Higgins," Nigel assured them, to their visible disappointment. "Talking about clues, though, there's something I'm looking for. I want it badly. In fact, I'd give five shillings to anyone who found it for me." At this point he clearly began to hold his audience. "Do you fellows know of anyone who'd like to earn five shillings?" he added.

"See here, mister, what be looking for? Us might oblige 'ee."

"That would be very decent of you. I've got a theory that the young gentleman was murdered on the road between here and the school. His handkerchief is missing, and if my theory is correct, it should be somewhere in the ditches, or along the road, or perhaps it was thrown over the hedge," Nigel lied luxuriantly. "It'd take me a long time to do the whole search myself, and I don't want to ask the police, they're so busy. That handkerchief is worth five shillings to me. I'm always to be found at the school, if anyone discovers it." His last remark was made to the vacant air, for the group had melted away like dew and were already halfway out of the village.

The green now seemed uninhabited; Nigel swung his leg over the parapet and waded through scum-covered water up to the nymph. He cast a glance over his shoulder, feeling rather like one about to commit an offense in Hyde Park. Luckily, he was too short-sighted to observe the windows on the edge of the green, at each of which one or more faces peered out from behind the curtains, deeply interested to see a "detective gennulman from Lunnon" at work. Many and heated were the arguments conducted throughout the next two days on doorstep and in public bar as to the exact meaning of the gentleman's activities. One school held that he was looking for more bodies in the basin, another that the brazen nymph had yielded up some vital clue to the mystery. The thick white mustache

which, after the detective's humid departure, was found on her upper lip–
and which, Nigel thought, rather improved her appearance–was zealously
preserved and pointed out to visitors with pride as one of the local curiosities. The boys of Sudeley Hall, walking to church half an hour later,
beheld it with uncontrolled glee. And there it remained, a mystery to all
but three persons, till many days after a greater mystery was cleared up;
till rain came and shaved it slowly away and restored to the nymph her
proper femininity.

Nigel pocketed his chalk again and turned round. Twenty faces whisked
behind curtains, as he climbed out and pushed his bicycle towards the
next adventure, "Mr. Higgins, resident in ye hamlet aforsaid." He was so
relieved to have got away from the nymph unarrested, that he failed to
make the obvious connection between the nature of Mr. Higgins' resi-
dence and the object of his second quest. "Scales," he thought to himself,
"a description thereof." This is just to test the candidate's powers of observation, it'll be as easy as drinking tea. He knocked at the door. After a
long interval it was opened, disclosing a huge, bald man, with bloodshot
eyes, in a state of bad temper and deshabille.

"My shop ain't open on Sundays," this individual barked; "you 'ikers
are a disgrace to the country, profaning the Sabbath, and tearing about the
country in the nood."

"You've got me wrong, Mr. Higgins," remarked Nigel affably. "I am
not a hiker, and if you look a little more closely you will observe that I am
the reverse of noo–nude. And I'm sure no one could tear anywhere on
this ghastly bicycle they've lent me."

"Well, what the 'ell do you want, then?"

"I'm staying in these parts, and I was told that I shouldn't go before I'd
had a look at your famous scales. I'd be obliged if—"

Nigel broke off in considerable alarm. Mr. Higgins' whole head was
rapidly going through a series of color gradations, from tomato, through
beetroot, to dark plum. He wheezed apoplectically in his throat, then lunged
at Nigel, roaring out, "Corbooger, another of these blasted inspectors, are
yer? I'll inspect yer." Nigel left two buttons and some shreds of cloth in
Mr. Higgins' clutching hands, leapt on to his bicycle, and pedaled fast
back along the way he had come, vowing vengeance on Stevens for leading him up the garden to that dishonest tradesman. When he had slowed
down out of earshot, he began to realize that it was not a leg-pull on the
boy's part. The keen, but closely limited imagination of a boy of that age
had made Stevens assume that Strangeways knew all the local scandals,
and the second test called for at least as much audacity to a boy's mind as
the first.

Nigel had passed the frenzied handkerchief hunters, and was now breasting the last hill before Edgworth Woods came in sight. He wheeled his bicycle into the wood, leaned it up against the high wire fence that separated neutral ground from no-man's-land–or rather, Lord Edgworth's land, bent down to take off his trouser-clips, straightened up with one hand on the wire–and found himself face to face with a very broad man in corduroy breeches carrying a gun.

The broad man stared at him in that curiously somber and incriminating way that gamekeepers, park-keepers, and policemen have. But Nigel was not in the least intimidated. His blood was up now, he felt on top of the world. Had Stevens II witnessed his subsequent conduct, there can be little doubt that the dictator would have abdicated in his favor. Nigel put a hand through the wires and exclaimed genially:

"Lord Edgworth, I presume?"

"Naw," said the broad man, his stony stare wobbling a little.

"A gamekeeper, then, I daresay?"

"May be."

"Well, I should have thought you would know whether you're a gamekeeper or not. However, that is your affair. We will leave it aside for the moment. Do you—"

"Yurr," interrupted the broad man, pointing to a notice behind him, " 'Trespassers praasecuted,' see? So doan't you come climbing over this yurr fence."

"That's just what I was coming to talk to you about. Do you allow the Sudeley Hall boys in there? Because I've just seen two of them getting through the fence about a hundred yards down."

"Drat they boys!" exclaimed the keeper, "I'll skelp 'em." And he hurried off in the direction Nigel pointed out, leaving him to climb through into the preserve at his leisure. That was about all the leisure Nigel got for the next quarter of an hour. He had not penetrated ten yards into the wood when a pheasant rose up at his feet, honking like a flustered motorist. His heart almost leapt out of his mouth, and he could hear the keeper come pounding back at the noise. Nigel plunged into a patch of fern on his left and lay down panting under the lofty fronds.

The riot in front died down and stopped. The gamekeeper appeared, looked about him suspiciously, and approaching the patch of fern began to prod into it with the muzzle of his gun. Nigel was within a foot or two of being stunned by one of these prods, but then the danger receded, and after a few minutes he emerged from his lair and cautiously resumed the search for rabbit-traps. This time he walked very slowly. The birds had got used to him now or they were somewhere else, or something, and soon he was rewarded by the sight of a grassy, sandy bank, perforated with many rabbit holes. He approached, peered about him, ah! a wire noose on a stick. That must be a trap all right. He bent down and tugged it out of the ground. There was a rustling above him. For a second time that morning he straightened up to see the broad man staring at him.

"Caught this time, hey?" rasped the broad man, and bore down on him.

"Not quite, but here's one of the traps they set–little devils!" Nigel peered into the trees, and suddenly shouted, "By Jove, there they are! Quick! We'll get 'em this time," pocketed the trap and rushed wildly off, drawing the bemused keeper after him. He had not run long before the keeper was outdistanced, and soon he was climbing through the wire fence again. His bicycle was nowhere to be seen, but he took his bearings by the sun and began to walk along the leafy path in the direction of the road. He had not gone more than a hundred yards when he heard voices in front. Thinking that the keeper might have moved with reinforcements to intercept him, he crept slowly towards the sounds. Then he stopped dead. He had recognized one of the voices; it was Wrench; he was talking to a woman.

"I tell you there's nothing to be frightened about. You keep your mouth shut and we're safe as houses," Wrench was saying.

"I can't help it. I'm afraid of that Mr. Armstrong. I'm sure he suspects something. He looks at me fair awful. I know he'll make me tell him."

"I'll wring your pretty neck if you let out anything till I give the word. Don't you see it'll ruin me if you tell the tale? That old swine Gadsby has started dropping hints, and God knows how soon they won't come to Vale's ears as it is. You'll damn well keep quiet, my girl. Time enough to come out with the story if they begin to suspect–the other thing."

"I don't believe you care for me a bit, Cyril. I'm just a toy, that's all. All you care about is your rotten old reputation. Oh, sir, why did you ever—?"

"Shut up!" snapped Wrench, "don't talk like the films. Anyone'd think you were a poor, innocent little thing seduced by the villain, instead of—"

"Damn you, I hate you."

Nigel had been pushing cautiously forward, wishing to identify the woman; her voice seemed somehow familiar. A flaunting red dress; a servant's Sunday finery. "Curse my short sight. What the hell's the use of a short-sighted detective?" He edged nearer still. "Yes, it's that girl Rosa." His foot slipped and he lurched heavily sideways in the undergrowth. The girl screamed. Wrench sprang to his feet and ran, dragging her with him. Nigel could have kicked himself. What might he not have missed? Well, at least they hadn't seen him. He was sure of that. He allowed a decent interval to elapse, then walked on, found his bicycle, and rode slowly back to the school, deep in thought.

Michael had told him about the fracas between Wrench and Gadsby, and the superintendent had mentioned his suspicion that Rosa knew more than she would say. Wrench, a thruster, eager to get on, one of the children of this world. Rosa the flesh, and probably the devil too. Let's get it clear. She was not to tell the tale unless the police began to suspect "the other thing." If she told the tale Wrench would be ruined. What sort of thing would ruin Wrench? Obviously the discovery of his intrigue with Rosa. But under what circumstances would Wrench ever allow this intrigue to be made public? Surely only if some worse danger threatened—the "other thing," in fact. And what could that be but the suspicion of his having committed the murder. How could confession to an intrigue remove this suspicion? It would have to be in the form of an alibi. Nigel remembered the account of her movements Rosa had given the superintendent. She had felt unwell and gone up to her room about two o'clock, remaining there till a few minutes after two-thirty. The "tale" then would be that Wrench was with her during that period. But might it not be true? Wrench was given to slangy expressions. He might have meant "tell the true tale," and again, he might not. His alibi for two to two-thirty was weak enough—reading in his room. But why two to two-thirty? How could Rosa help him by saying he was in her room then, when all the evidence seemed to show that the murder must have been committed before that period? Look at it from the other side. If Wrench did the murder, he must have done it between two and two-thirty, that being the time for which he is reserving his stronger alibi. No, not two-thirty, a few minutes after. The superintendent said that no one saw Wrench during the first race. But Wrench himself trotted out a yarn about a man in a brown suit, to give the impression that he was in the field when the sports began. That is probably a part of his first and weaker alibi. He will say he made it up in order to avoid confessing that he had been with Rosa. If he committed the murder, then, it was between two and a few minutes after two-thirty. But Griffin and Mould were on the field from two to two-fifteen, and after that more and more people were swarming on to it. Nigel's head grew dizzy with these tail-chasing arguments, and he was glad to find himself back at the school, ready to hear whatever Stevens II had to say.

The two boys came up immediately after lunch. Nigel was eager to begin questioning them, for the idea conceived after his second exploit had been greatly strengthened by the third. However, he had first to undergo the ceremony of initiation into the secret society. He gave an account of his adventures and handed over the rabbit-trap. He was then blindfolded, while the dictator read a kind of confirmation service over him, in the course of which he was compelled to swear a number of very solemn and magniloquent oaths. Finally, the bandage was removed, a large black spot of ink was printed on his right wrist, and he was a full member of the society. The dictator and his lieutenant now changed into

Stevens II. and Ponsonby. The hunt was up.

"Sir, it's about the day Wemyss was murdered. At breakfast me and Ponsonby arranged to meet in Mouldy's hut to transact important private business of the society," the dictator reeled out the last phrase in character, and was immediately transfigured into Stevens II again. "We oiled out as soon as lunch was over–it's quite easy, you know, sir–and hid—"

"Behind the sacks, against the right-hand wall of the hut as you go in," interposed Nigel nonchalantly. The boys' eyes rounded. Ponsonby said, "Gosh, sir, how did you know that? You must be a jolly good detective. Are you head of Scotland Yard?"

Nigel was unaccustomed to the point-blank praise of small boys, and blushed a little, "No, far from it. But do go on, this is frightfully interesting."

"There isn't really anything more. We talked for a long time. You see, my brother had asked me about the gang's beating up Wemyss, so we had that to arrange too. Then we hurried back into school just before changing time."

"Why, Stevens wanted to tell you, sir—" broke in Ponsonby.

"Put a sock in it, Pongo! We thought we ought to tell you, sir, because the policeman asked if anyone had been outside the house after lunch and of course we couldn't tell him because it was the Black Spot and deadly secret."

"I see," said Nigel, thinking that they had been very lucky in not giving away their secret to Armstrong, for it could not have failed to put them under official suspicion. "So I take it you didn't set eyes on Wemyss while you were going in or out."

"No, sir, I'm afraid we haven't been much help," said Stevens, with pathetic eagerness.

"You've cleared up one difficulty, and I rather think that if you will answer some more questions, you will have done more than anyone else could to solve the mystery."

"Oh, whoopee! Ask me, sir!" "Ask me!"

"Well, then, first of all, I suppose Wemyss wasn't a member of the Black Spot?"

"I should think he jolly well wasn't, slimy little chizzer!" Stevens clearly did not subscribe to the de mortuis doctrine.

"Is it possible that he could have thought he had a chance of being elected?"

"Oh, I should think so; he was sidey enough, anyway."

"Now I want to get it quite clear. How do you go about the business of deciding on new members?"

"Stevens generally decides himself," put in Ponsonby, with a certain air of grievance. Nigel could well imagine it.

"Slit your gullet, Pongo! We have a general meeting of the gang, sir–
there are supposed to be six besides the dictator and the lieutenant–then,
if every one agrees on a person, we give him an ordeal, like we did you."

"Supposing the person doesn't want to be a member? I mean, how do
you find out if he wants to be? Do you sound him about it beforehand?"

"Sometimes, sir. Generally we just give him the instructions straight
away."

"But do most people in the school know about the Black Spot? What I
mean is, when you just give the instructions without talking to the person
beforehand, how does he know it's not a leg-pull? Would he have heard
about the society's method of initiation?"

"Oh, yes, I think so. At least, he'd know about the Black Spot. Of course,
it's supposed to be absolutely secret, but I expect most of the school know
about the sort of things we do." The realist spoke again.

"So if a boy got a set of instructions, and wanted to become a member
of the society, he would follow them out without telling anyone about
them?"

"Mm. Rather."

Nigel sat back and lit a cigarette. So far, everything seemed to be bearing out his bizarre theory. He went on again, approaching the crucial
question.

"You said yesterday that you made up a different test for each new
member. What sort of tests have they been?"

"Oh, all sorts of things. Playing jokes on the masters, altering the school
clocks, hiding Sweeny's bell, scouting about the country like you did, sir,
and so on."

"Stevens had a jolly nippy idea for one last term, sir," said Ponsonby,
"only it never came off. He was going to tell a chap to disappear for an
hour. He could go anywhere he liked in the school or the grounds, but no
one must see him."

Nigel's heart leapt strongly. So he had been right, after all. His fantastic theory was vindicated. He controlled his voice and said carelessly:

"That was a good one. Why didn't it come off?"

"Well, sir, you see, it was like this. We'd written out the instructions,
and folded them up and passed them along to the chap in form, but the
master saw it and confiscated it."

Glory be, thought Nigel, this is too good to be true. He went on, "But
didn't the master make a fuss about it? I should have thought that would
have been the end of the Black Spot. Or did he just tear it up without
reading it?"

"No, sir, Simmie was jolly decent about it. He's not a bad sort of beezer at all, if he wasn't such an absolute ass. I didn't see him tear it up, but he can't have reported it to Percy or we should have got tanned. Percy is frightfully down on all that sort of thing. Simmie just gave us some lines for passing notes in form and didn't say anything more about it."

Sims! Good Lord, Sims! Well, well, well. "Why does every one rag Mr. Sims, if he's a decent kind of man?"

"Oh, well, sir, he is such an ass. I dunno. You just can't help it. It's quite safe, too, he never does anything but set you some lines, and he generally forgets to collect them; at least, he used to; but now he writes them down in that black book he carries about with him. 'Doomsday book,' he calls it."

"It doesn't always seem quite safe to rag in his room," remarked Nigel meaningly. Stevens and Ponsonby shifted uncomfortably on their seats.

"That was just bad luck. We'd forgotten Percy was in school that hour. I say, my bim's jolly sore still. Isn't yours, Pongo? Old Pedantic swings a pretty hefty cane."

"Well, here's a bob to buy some medicine. Chocolate, applied internally, is quite a good remedy, I'm told."

"Thanks *awfully*, sir." "Thanks *frightfully*, sir. I say, sir, have we really been any help?"

"Don't let out a word of our conversation to anyone. You've as good as told me how the murder was committed."

"*Gosh!*"

Chapter IX

Retrospects and Prospects

As soon as the boys had left, Nigel went to look for Sims. The question was, how to bring up the subject of the paper that Sims had confiscated without arousing his suspicion. No, thought Nigel, that won't do. If he is the murderer, and worked on the lines I'm certain the murderer did work on, he is bound to be suspicious. And if he is innocent, he'll still be automatically on the defensive; he's probably got a first-class persecution mania, and that'll make him morbidly sensitive of trouble in the air, however much I try to conceal it. No use trying tact or tactics. He'll be put most at ease if I appeal to him as to an equal and put the facts straightforwardly.

Sims' room was like himself, colorless, ineffectual, rather pathetic. He had tried to liven up the regulation school environment with a few touches of his own, Nigel noticed–a second rug, a couple of reproductions of Dutch masters, a huge and elaborate desk; but somehow they made no difference; they seemed to have absorbed their owner's air of failure–they looked as out-of-place and stranded amongst the ordinary furniture of the room as did Sims himself amongst his colleagues. The books, too, Nigel observed, while Sims trotted about looking for cigarettes–what an incredibly miscellaneous collection! Novels representative of the whole possible gamut of taste, thereby betraying the complete absence of it in Sims; a whole shelf full of the Christian mystics and meaty-looking tomes of evangelical sermons; the most boring of modern poets rubbing shoulders with the most respectable of classic ones; elementary textbooks on almost every conceivable branch of human knowledge, as though Sims had hurried from subject to subject looking for his métier and always been disappointed. The bookcase was a museum of false starts and broken hopes. It filled Nigel with pity. He felt as if he was about to vivisect a lost dog.

"Is one allowed to ask how you're getting on?" said Sims.

"Oh, rather. I've found out quite a lot today, entirely by accident. I'm beginning to think I've got the explanation of the difficulty that has been holding up the case."

"Have you really? Dear me! You mean—?"

"Well, you have no doubt wondered what it was that induced Wemyss to disappear so mysteriously after school that morning."

"I–why, yes, it did seem very unaccountable, unless he was murdered almost at once. Surely he must have been. Someone would have seen him otherwise, wouldn't they?"

"That does seem probable, on the face of it. But the problem still remains, what made Wemyss go–like a lamb to the slaughter, so to speak– at all? What made him miss lunch, for instance? And, though you couldn't have guessed it, you've had the answer in your own hands."

Sims blinked and looked worried. "I? Dash it all, Strangeways, whatever do you mean?"

"Do you remember last term confiscating a note that was being passed in form? Written in capitals, with a round splodge of ink at the top, something about the Black Spot?"

"Bless my soul! However did you get to hear of that? Yes, it was some ridiculous nonsense about a secret society telling somebody he was to disappear for an hour. Disappear!" Sims' eyes blazed behind his thick spectacles, "Great Scott, Strangeways, I see what you're driving at. You mean, one of the boys sent a similar note to poor Wemyss–but that implies that this boy killed him. No, I can't believe that. They're perhaps rather too high-spirited at times; but murder–no, no, it's impossible."

"There again I'm inclined to agree with you, though I don't know how the superintendent will take it. Tell me, what did you do with the note? Is it possible that one of the servants could have got hold of it?"

"Oh no; we destroyed it. You see, I happened to make some comment or other about it in the common room, and we–er–in short, we decided to destroy it."

"We?"

Sims looked more worried than ever. He bent his head in thought. "Look here, Strangeways, is the superintendent in your confidence?"

"I haven't told him about this development yet, but of course I shall have to."

"I see. I hate the idea of getting other people into trouble, but—"

Nigel said gently, "In so far as the knowledge of this note is potentially incriminating, you are bound to be technically under suspicion yourself, I'm afraid."

"Oh dear; yes, of course. How awful! But that does seem to make it a bit better. Well, let me see: Wrench had a look at the note. Who else was there? Oh, of course, Evans. I remember that because it was he who suggested that we should let it go no further. He said something about these secret societies being a sign of vitality and inventiveness, and that it would be a pity to stamp it out. I daresay he's right. He knows a great deal about boys–but then, he is so popular with them. Somehow I never seem to have got the knack of it like he has."

"I heard two of them singing your praises just now, anyway."

"Did you really?" Sims' face quite lit up. "That's very gratifying. I'm afraid you must form a poor opinion of me, getting so much pleasure out of a little thing like that. But it's the breath of life to us schoolmasters–to find that our labors are sometimes appreciated."

Nigel managed tactfully to arrest the heart-to-heart talk which seemed imminent, and after making certain that the knowledge of the Black Spot note had been confined to Sims, Wrench and Evans, took his leave. It was now time to let Superintendent Armstrong into these discovered secrets. He had only paid one visit to the school in the last two days, though there was always a constable about the place–"just to see that none of us makes a bolt for it," as Griffin said, to the general discomfiture of the common room. Armstrong was evidently relying on Strangeways to provide an opening for his next move. Nigel asked Mrs. Vale if she would mind driving him in to Staverton before tea. Hero was quite willing. She had only seen him in company up till now, and felt a recurrent jealous impulse to measure her influence with Michael against his.

Nigel was sensible of the faint antagonism beneath her offhand manner–she resents my being able to do more for Michael than she can, he thought–and set himself to dispel it.

"How is your husband feeling about things now?" he asked.

"The condition is unchanged. The bottom of his world has been knocked out, but he'll grow a new one soon enough unless the parents start removing their boys." She spoke bitterly. Nigel winced inside himself. He disliked superficial cynicism in women, just as much as he liked their natural, deep-centered irony. There was consequently a marked evasiveness in his reply when she asked him how he was getting on with the case. Her hand tightened on the wheel and she wrenched the car petulantly round a corner.

"The flippancy of the postwar woman distresses you, I see. Don't you realize that my husband means simply nothing to me now? I love Michael and I don't care what happens as long as he is happy."

"I know that you love Michael and that no one could make him so happy as you. But I imagine your husband meaning nothing to you now is more of a wish than a fact. You can't live with a person for several years without forming some relationship, and personal relationships don't suddenly vanish into thin air. The truth is, you're angry with yourself for not being able to break the ties between yourself and your husband."

"You win, Mr. Strangeways–Nigel," she said, touching his hand. "You seem to know so much about me that I'm sure you'll forgive my exhibition of bad temper. Oh, it's terrible. It's like a nightmare. There is Michael, stretching out his hands to me, wanting me so badly, and I try to run to him and it's like running through deep sand. Tell me, they don't still suspect him, do they?"

"I'm afraid they suspect both of you. You see, the case against you is the only possible one that can be built on the facts the superintendent has got so far. However, I've something to tell him now which may change his ideas. By the way, I shall be some time. You'd better not wait for me. I'll get a bus back."

"No, I'll wait. But what makes *you* so sure we didn't do it?"

Nigel laughed. "Oh, I'm not a very good detective. If I was the proper inhuman, cold-blooded, scientific sleuth, I should probably be suspecting you hard. But I'd always believe my friends sooner than the facts."

"You *are* nice, Nigel. I shall stop being jealous of you."

They soon reached the Staverton police station, whence they were directed to Armstrong's own house. Here arranged to call back for Nigel in three-quarters of an hour and he went in to see the superintendent. Preserving a discreet reticence about the events that had led up to it, he related the conversation he had heard in Edgworth Wood, and then told Armstrong of the confiscated note, the procedure of the Black Spot and his talk with Sims. Armstrong was not slow to draw the same deductions as Nigel had.

"Well, sir, I always suspected that some of those boys must have known more than they cared to let out. But it's you who've proved it and I'm very grateful. The chief constable is getting a bit restive, though he hasn't been able to suggest any other lines that I could work on. Now I shall be able to make a move. I'll come up this evening and chivvy that Rosa first. Once we've got the real story out of her, we can deal with Wrench. It seems pretty clear that he was either with Rosa after two o'clock, or committing the murder. But the question still remains–how? We've more or less decided that it couldn't have been done after one-forty-five, when Griffin and Mould came out."

"Well, we've just got to find a loophole, that's all."

The superintendent shifted in his chair and fingered his top coat-button. "Sims and Evans knew about this note, too," he said with some hesitation. Nigel looked down his nose. "What I mean is," went on the superintendent, "I take it we are agreed that the murderer wrote a similar note to Wemyss, telling him that he was to remain hidden from twelve forty-five–for an hour, or till the Black Spot came and found him, or something like that–told him to hide in the haystack, to my way of thinking," Armstrong concluded firmly.

"He couldn't have hidden there at once. Evans and Mrs. Vale were there," replied Nigel with equal firmness. The superintendent shrugged his shoulders. "You're welcome to your own opinion, sir, but you can't expect me to alter mine. Evans knew the contents of the Black Spot instructions. What's more, it was he who originally suggested that Sims and Wrench and himself should hush it up—"

"Which proves absolutely nothing at all," interrupted Nigel sharply.

Armstrong's brow furrowed. "You don't need to tell me that, Mr. Strangeways. Nor does the fact that Mr. Evans is your friend prove that he didn't commit the murder. Anyway, it was simple enough for him to have slipped a note in Wemyss' desk, say, telling him to hide in the haystack immediately after lessons, and then to have slipped out himself at one o'clock and strangled him—"

"With Mrs. Vale applauding loudly from the front row of the stalls!"

"You will have your little joke, sir. Well, at least you must admit that she and Mr. Evans had about a hundred percent better an opportunity to pull it off than anyone else–to say nothing of motive."

"Oh, yes, I admit all that," said Nigel wearily, "but you'll not get me to believe that either of them strangled that wretched youth, unless you produce about three independent eyewitnesses. And what about that anonymous note to Urquhart? How on earth was Evans to know that he had been embezzling Wemyss' money?"

"It is possible that Mrs. Vale had found out. Or, as you said yourself, sir, it might have been a shot in the dark."

"Seems to me a mad sort of thing to have done. Unless the murderer was pretty sure that Urquhart had been up to some dirty work, he could not have relied on his burning the note."

"Well, at any rate, he did go to the wood. His servants confirm his absence, and my men report that his car was seen outside the wood at one-fifty. By the way, Tiverton, Wrench, Evans and Mr. Vale himself own typewriters."

Nigel leaned forward earnestly. "Look here, let's assume–just for argument's sake, if you like–that the murder was not committed by Evans and Mrs. Vale or till after one-thirty. What follows? First of all, that Wemyss could not have been in the haystack. That implies that he was given instructions to perform more than one exploit. Now I happen to know"– Nigel spoke rather hurriedly here–"the sort of things Stevens' gang make people do: practical jokes they are, mainly. Do we know of anything in the nature of a practical joke that took place that day?"

"No, I don't thing anything came to light–by Jove, though, how about that extra set of hurdles? Mould swore he'd put out the right number."

"Good for you, Armstrong, you've got it! A perfectly sound practical joke, and it would have come off if Griffin hadn't gone out to make sure that Mould hadn't committed one of his apparently frequent bloomers."

"Perhaps it *was* one of his apparently frequent bloomers," said the superintendent slyly.

"And perhaps not. Assume it was not. We can begin to get some idea of Wemyss' movements. He couldn't safely do his hanky-panky with the hurdles before lunch, because some of the day room windows look on to the field. For the same reason he couldn't have done it after lunch. Therefore he must have done it during lunch–the dining-hall faces the opposite direction. Well, then, on my theory he hid somewhere from twelve forty-five till one; then put out the extra hurdles; then hid again till he went into the haystack–or there might have been some other feat he had to perform before that. Or he may have been told to go into the haystack as soon as he'd done with the hurdles, but found that it was occupied and had to wait till Evans and Mrs. Vale went in. There were five other haystacks to hide in."

The superintendent was shaking his massive head slowly and ponderously. "Thin, sir; much too thin, and all resting on what was very likely an ordinary mistake of the groundsman's. Besides, sir, I just can't stomach all this coincidence: the murderer *and* your friends choosing the same haystack; the murderer and his victim conveniently waiting till your friends were gone before they did their act. Here, sir, are you feeling ill?" Nigel had gone pale and his eyes were bulging in his head. He shook himself. "No, thanks, I'm quite all right. You've just put a pretty staggering idea into my head. But I'm going to exercise our agreement to keep theories to oneself–just for a bit, at any rate. It's thin, you see–very thin."

He wagged his head with an impertinent imitation of the superintendent, which caused that worthy to chuckle fatly in his bull neck, and to opine that Mr. Strangeways was a one. He then suggested that Mrs. Vale might take him back to the school with Nigel. The three-quarters of an hour had not quite elapsed, so Armstrong shouted to his "old woman" to brew their guest a pot of tea. By the time he had drained the greater part of this, Hero had returned and the superintendent dragged him unwillingly into the car.

When they reached the school, Armstrong drew Nigel aside and asked him if he would be present at the interview with Rosa. The maid was sent for. Nigel eyed her curiously as she came into the morning-room. She was still in the red dress, that showed the division of her breasts and the sleek contour of waist and thighs. She moved to a chair with a slinky, arrogant gait obviously modeled on that of her favorite film actress; a synthetic gentility sat strangely on her broad country face and body. As she passed Nigel she gave him the steady, challenging stare of the born wanton. Then she turned to the superintendent, a very different expression on her face. Nigel wondered what line of attack Armstrong would take up. He could feel the man's crude but powerful personality imposing itself upon the girl. Armstrong stared at her ruminatively for a moment or two.

"You know, a spell in prison would do you no harm, young woman," he began suddenly. Rosa started and relapsed again.

"Pardon?" she said in an offhand way, patting a curl into place.

"And I've a good mind to put you there, what's more."

Her eyes flickered. "Lord, what have I done now? Have you nothing better to do on a Sunday than to come bullying a harmless girl?"

"Just a little matter of giving false evidence to the police, that's all."

"I don't know what you mean, I'm sure."

The superintendent hunched himself together, like a rhinoceros about to charge, and said quietly, "You were telling the truth, then, when you said you were alone in your room from two till two-thirty on the day of the murder?" There was the faintest accent on the word "alone." Rosa twisted a handkerchief in her thick fingers. "Really, Mr. Armstrong, I don't know what–of course I was." Armstrong half raised himself from his chair and barked out, "Oho! So Mr. Wrench was not with you, *after all*."

"Yes. No. Oh, do leave me alone!" Rosa's self-possession had collapsed. Her lip trembled. The rouge, standing out on her pallid cheeks, made her look like a doll. The superintendent pressed home his attack.

"Yes? No? You must know if you were alone or not. Speak up, my girl."

"You make me so confused. Yes, I tell you, I *was* alone."

Armstrong sat back and threw a meaning glance at Nigel, saying mildly: "That looks bad for Mr. Wrench, don't it, sir?"

"Looks bad? Oh God, what do you mean, sir? You're not—"

"Well, if he wasn't in your room, we can make a very good guess where he was. That's all."

Rosa stifled a sob; clenched her fingers; said in a flat voice, "He *was* in my room," and burst out with hysterical weeping. Nigel felt ill at ease. He didn't much care for bull-baiting, even in the interests of justice; and he detected a kind of sadism beneath the superintendent's expression. Armstrong waited till the girl's outburst was over. Finally he said, "So Wrench was in your room, was he? What makes you change your mind about that all of a sudden?"

"Oh, sir, don't go on at me so! Cyril–Mr. Wrench said I was not to tell you, unless—"

"Unless?"

The girl buried her face in her hands. They could hardly hear her next statement.

"Unless he–unless you suspected him of having something to do with the murder."

"And how am I to know you're telling the truth this time?" asked Armstrong bluntly. "How am I to know you've not cooked up this story between you to conceal the fact that Wrench really was—?"

"You must believe me! You must! I swear it's the truth!" Rosa sprang up wildly. Her face was burning. Her body trembled as though an electric current was passing through it. She looked very handsome now, as she turned to Nigel with a tense, unstudied movement of the hands, and cried, "Please, sir, please make him believe me!"

"Well, well," remarked the superintendent, "if you want us to believe you, you must tell us all the facts–the truth this time. When did he come up to you?"

"Just after I went up. We'd arranged it. I pretended I was feeling ill."

"And he left you at two-thirty?"

"I don't know the exact time. A pistol went off outside, and Cyril said, 'Good Lord, that's the first race starting. I shall be late,' and he ran downstairs."

"He was in your room all the time?"

"Yes, haven't I just told you?"

"Describe the clothes he was wearing."

"Reely, I don't know if I can remember. He had a blue suit on, I think, and that pink tie of his, I remember that."

"Now, think carefully. What exactly did he do when he came into your room?"

"Why, I scarcely like to tell you, sir," said Rosa, with a faint return of her coquettish expression.

"We'll take all that for granted. But, besides making love to you, did he say or do anything–something he might remember which would prove that he was with you?"

"Well, he went to the mantelpiece and took up a photograph of my brother and asked who it was. And he kept on saying how dangerous it was for him to be in my room–in a fair panic he was, half the time."

"Very well. That is all I want from you just now."

The girl got up and moved hurriedly to the door. "Not so fast, not so fast," said Armstrong. He rang the bell and sent for the constable, whom he ordered to keep Rosa under his eye for the next five minutes. "We'll just go and see what Mr. Wrench has to say about all this." As they went along the passage and up the stairs Armstrong said, "They seem to have got their story pretty pat, eh?"

"You mean, you believe it?"

"Either it's true or that girl's a damn good actress, sir."

"And if she's telling the truth, Mrs. Vale must be a damn good actress?" The superintendent shrugged his shoulders.

Wrench received them with his usual half-defensive, half-aggressive manner. While Armstrong indulged in a little light conversational skirmishing, Nigel took mental impressions of the room. It was the ordinary schoolmaster's sanctum, overlaid with a thin veneer of estheticism. He strolled idly over to the bookcase: French novels; the brighter young poets; left wing, but not too extreme, political writers; and a number of educational treatises, which had clearly seen more service than their companions. Nigel suspected that Wrench's esthetic and political extravagances were little more than exhibitions to assert his personality amongst his colleagues—a common enough manifestation of inferiority feeling: the main current of his vitality ran through his schoolwork, his career. Nigel went back to his chair and looked noncommittally down his nose. Wrench was saying:

"… But I don't suppose you've visited me just for a spot of light conversation."

The superintendent took the hint and proceeded to ask Wrench about the Black Spot note which Sims had confiscated. Oh, yes, he remembered the occurrence and the contents of the note. Yes, Evans had also been present and suggested that no official notice should be taken of it. But what connection had this with the case? Armstrong explained Nigel's theory; Wrench's eyes widened and he whistled between his teeth. The superintendent then unmasked his heaviest battery. "Now, sir," he said, his voice grown suddenly harsh and unfriendly, "perhaps you will explain what you meant by giving me an entirely false account of your movements about the time of the murder?"

A spasm contorted Wrench's face, but he said coolly enough, "So you've been third-degreeing Rosa, have you? Well, you can't do that sort of thing to me. I shall consult a solicitor. Do I have to remind you of the judge's rules?"

"Don't talk to me like that, young man! If you don't come out with your new story pretty quick I shall hold you on a charge of obstructing the police." Armstrong's emphasis of the "new" was not lost on Wrench. "Oh, very well," he said. "I couldn't bear to obstruct you any longer. What *did* Rosa say?"

"Now, now, now, Mr. Wrench; don't try and put that stuff across on me. *I'm* asking *you* for your movements between one-thirty and two-thirty on the day of the sports."

"As I originally told you, except that I was in Rosa's room from two till two-thirty. Shocking, isn't it?" Wrench's tone rasped on Nigel's nerves.

"Two-thirty? You were on the field for the first race, were you?"

Wrench's eyes narrowed. After a pause he said, "Not exactly. The pistol went off when I was in her room. I ran downstairs at once and was on the field by the end of the race."

"And what was the point of your story about talking to a parent. Why not have said that you were reading in your room till two-thirty?"

"I had intended to, but during the sports a boy—Smithers—told me that he'd gone up to my room a minute or two before the sports began to bring me an impot, and hadn't found me there, so I thought it safer to invent the man in a brown suit."

"And you expect us to believe all this?" said Armstrong heavily.

"Well, of course; hasn't Rosa told you the same? You couldn't expect me to admit what I'd really been doing. It's the end of me, as it is—look here, superintendent, you don't need to come out with all this to the headmaster, do you?"

"You mistake me, sir. I'm asking how you expect us to believe this new story when your original one was just a pack of lies. How do I know that you and Rosa have not made it up between you?"

"Why on earth should we make it up? Do you think I want to ruin my career?"

"Under some circumstances, you might."

"What is the man driving at now?" said Wrench, turning with a nervous smile to Nigel. The latter was getting rather tired of Armstrong's delayed action tactics and spoke abruptly, not looking at Wrench: "He wants just to be sure you weren't compassing the sheer doom of young Wemyss, that's all."

Wrench started; his next words sounded indignant and alarmed. But Nigel felt that the start, the indignation and the alarm were forced; Wrench knew all along what the conversation was leading up to. Armstrong let him cool down and then asked him what confirmation he had of Rosa's story. None, he said at first. But by judicious questioning the superintendent elicited the details already given by Rosa about his clothing and the photograph on the mantelpiece. They left him, still retaining his assumed jauntiness, but looking decidedly the worse for wear. The superintendent was obviously put out by Nigel's intervention and pointedly refrained from asking his company on his next visit, which was to Sims. Nigel, too, had had enough of Armstrong's company; he was impatient to have a talk with Michael. That notion which Armstrong had put into his head—it all fitted in—yes, he must verify it at once.

Michael looked up at his friend with unconcealed eagerness as he entered the room. "And where have *you* been all the day?" he asked, "riding about chalking pornograms on the roads?"

"Worse. I have been making myself eligible for the Black Spot."

"The Black Spot? Oh, yes; the Black Spot; that's still going, is it? I'm glad. Stevens II is a natural leader. You get one every ten years or so in a school, and every hundred years in a country, if you're lucky. What happens to all the others I don't know. Go into an office, or get ruined at their public school, I suppose. But, I say, what are you doing in that gallery?"

"We of the Black Spot do not betray our secrets. But I've been mopping up information today. Today, in fact, may be described as the beginning of the end, the thin end of the wedge, or what you will."

"You mean, you're on to the criminal?" said Michael excitedly; "do we cease to be under suspicion?"

"You never were, as far as I'm concerned. But I'm afraid the superintendent is still unconvinced. Of course, he's felt different towards you since that joyride after the late James Urquhart—one can't share that sort of experience with a person without it affecting one's attitude towards him, but what facts Armstrong has point to you and Hero; it's only because they've so few of them that he doesn't arrest you."

The strained look that had been in Michael's eyes for several days returned to them. "Well, I did think the worst was over. It seems I've just been creating a sort of fool's paradise," he said bitterly. "I'm sorry. That sounds ungrateful. Tell me what you've found out today."

"Can I have some tea first?"

"Haven't you had it yet?"

"Yes. I want some more."

"Oh, God, I wish you'd take to a hypodermic syringe instead. It would save a lot of trouble."

While his friend boiled water and got out the tea, Nigel gave a series of extracts from the information he had collected, omitting the conversation in the wood. Michael was amazed that he had not seen before the connection between Wemyss' disappearance and the confiscated Black Spot instructions.

"And now to business," said Nigel, peering anxiously into the depleted pot. "I want to ask you some questions. We'll get over the most embarrassing ones first."

"Shoot, mister. We are never embarrassed."

"How did you and Hero arrange your meetings? Word of mouth?"

"Sometimes. But lately she took to putting notes behind a loose brick in the garden wall. Romantic."

"Did you ever miss any of them?"

"No—not as far as I know."

"Mm. You probably wouldn't. Where did you two meet? I mean, wasn't it frightfully dangerous?"

"Frightfully. But, you see, one gets so reckless. It was because we really half wanted to be found out and bring things to a crisis, I suppose. We met once or twice in the thicket early this term—the affair only started then—but that was going it a bit too much even for Hero; after that, it was generally somewhere out in the country. We never went to each other's rooms."

"And as far as you know, you were never seen?"

"We couldn't have been. The balloon would have gone up long ago, otherwise. Every one in the country round about knows Hero by sight; and nearer home, well—schoolmasters are about on a level with parsons where scandal is concerned. You can't conceive what the gossip of a common room is like. I suppose it's because we were so reckless that we never were found out—like chaps in the war who wanted to be killed and never got a scratch."

"This meeting in the haystack—how was it arranged?"

"A note in the garden wall. Hero put it there after dinner the night before, actually, and I fetched it in the morning. I had the second period off."

"You destroyed it, presumably."

"Oh, yes. What is the point of all this, by the way?"

"I can't tell you yet. But it's very satisfactory so far. You know, what worried me all along is why the murderer chose such an odd place to stage his act." Nigel cocked an inquisitive eye at his friend. Michael looked puzzled.

"Well?"

"Well to you," said Nigel. "You have all the facts. It'll give you something to think about."

"The mantle of Holmes sits very ill upon you, I may say," remarked Michael acidly.

"And now," said Nigel, waving off this unseemly petulance, "we come to our second head. I want you to try to remember everything that was done or said in your presence by any of the masters on the day of the sports. We'll take the rest of the week later."

"Look here. What do you think I am? A dictaphone?"

"Not so accurate, unfortunately. But we'll have to make the best of it."

It turned out to be a less superhuman task than Michael had feared. Stimulated by his friend's skilful questioning, he reconstructed that ill-starred day piece by piece. The conversations at breakfast, during recess, after lunch on the field, and later, in the common room; the remarks of Sims and Wrench beside the haystack—practically nothing was missed, however irrelevant it seemed. From this, Nigel led him through the succeeding days; he seemed particularly interested in the atmosphere that had prevailed in the common room, and took the greatest pains to get clear the details of the scene between Gadsby and Wrench. When it was all finished, he leaned back for a moment with his eyes closed. Then, "Tiverton seems to have brains," he said, half to himself; "spotted the key point of the problem at once. That pencil of yours–I wonder." Then he opened his eyes; Michael was astonished to see something very like fear in them. "You know, I don't like this at all. This murderer of yours is worse than clever; he's–oh, well—"

"Do you mean–you know who the murderer is?" asked Michael, feeling a flutter of apprehension in his heart.

"Yes," said Nigel gravely. "I think I know who the murderer is. But I doubt if I can ever prove it. A question of proof–that's a good title for a detective story, if you ever write one–and I've not got enough proof to fill an acorn. One wouldn't mind so much if there wasn't the danger that he—" Nigel broke off and shook himself. "Your Mr. Gadsby seems an efficient broadcaster. Would you mind telling him–at once, and in strict confidence–that you are under the gravest suspicion of this crime."

"Gadsby is far from accustomed to being the recipient of my maiden confidences."

"Never mind. He's not nearly critical enough to notice that. Run along, old boy, and pull your stuff. It will be safer for you to be published abroad as a prime suspect, just at present."

" 'Safer'?"

" 'Safer' was the word."

It is five minutes to eight–five minutes before that rather grisly cold supper which is the sole social contact between the Rev. Mr. Vale and his staff. Michael has spilled the beans to Gadsby, who is even now distributing them (in the strictest confidence) to his colleagues. Michael hastens into the drawing room, hoping to have Hero alone for a few minutes before the others come in.

She was there, waiting for him; her body, in its black dress, moved subtly as the wind; the incredible fairy gold of her hair glimmered through the twilight, and her living arms stretched out to him. The sun, hurrying to its rest, stood still while they kissed.

"Hero, my sweet love. You are so beautiful. You are the spring of water and the blossom in the wilderness. My dear, I can't live without you any longer."

She bent her head back from him, her body sweetly curving. The electric storms of love passed through them and they kissed again. Her mouth was lovely from his kiss; she gazed at him, her eyes bewildered with love. Then she caught her breath–a little sob like a wind dying among pine-tops, and her mouth drooped like a bough when the wind has died. "Oh, Michael, I can't," she sighed. "I love you so much. I would give all my mind and body to save you from a minute's pain or sadness. Yet I can't. They're not all mine to give. Michael, you must try to understand me. And don't be angry with me now–afterwards, if you like; but not now. I think I should die if you were. Promise not to be angry with me."

"I promise." Michael heard his voice coming as it were from a great distance, a great height or depth of tenderness.

"Michael, you are so good. Listen. These things that have happened have made me different. I love you infinitely more than I did before, but– I would have left Percy then with scarcely a thought, and now I cannot. Oh, my sweet, don't look as if I'd hit you. I feel towards you now as I never felt before, and that's why I have begun to feel the ties between myself and Percy too. You see–I just can't help myself–a part of me is bound to him and I can't get it away."

"You want me not to tell him, then?"

"Not yet. While he's in trouble I am not free not all of me. And when I come to you, it must be for ever and it must be all of me."

There was a deep and melancholy acquiescence in Michael's words. "Yes, Hero, you are right. And will you ever be really free, now, all of you, till–he is dead?"

"Oh, my heart's darling, I don't know–I don't know." The wild despair of her voice made Michael forget his own pain. He was going to kiss her, for the last time perhaps, when they heard voices in the passage.

"Hullo, superintendent, you still here? Hard at it? Nose down to the trail?" came Gadsby's hearty tones.

"Poking about, sir, just poking about."

Mr. and Mrs. Vale, Nigel Strangeways and the staff are sitting round the supper table. Gadsby, on a glass of insipid Graves plus something a good deal more potent laid in beforehand, is fancying himself the life and soul of the party. Nigel glances at Hero and almost cries out in amazement. There is an unearthly brooding light in her face, an expression of final sorrow almost intolerable to behold. He looks towards Michael; his face, too, bears the same unutterable sadness; it seems cut from rock, Nigel thinks, a rock at the edge of the world with the sunlight of the world's last evening dying upon it. His winged fancy was brought down stone dead by a particularly uproarious explosion of laughter from Gadsby, heralding the conclusion of one of his own jokes, "... and she said, 'but that's not my ticket–it's my sister's,' ha! ha! ha! It was her sister's, you see." A faint echo of Gadsby's hilarity went round the table. He showed his teeth all round, like a prima donna acknowledging an ovation; then, tuning his voice to a suitable minor key, remarked: "Well, headmaster, I suppose we shall have to give the parents' match a miss this year–er–after what has happened." Vale took a sip of water–the gesture was a dignified rebuke in itself–before replying.

"On the contrary, Mr. Gadsby. I have given the matter serious thought, and decided that it would not be in the interests of the school to forgo the fixture. Mrs. Vale entirely agrees with me, and since we were the nearest relatives of the unfortunate lad–in short, the match will take place on Tuesday, as originally arranged."

Sims rubbed his hands. "Good! Excellent! I'm sure you're right, headmaster. It is such a popular event, both with the boys and their parents. It would be a thousand pities to miss it."

Mr. Vale inclined his head in gracious acceptance of his subordinate's approval, took another sip of water, and gave a short, dry cough.

"If you will be so good, Mr. Tiverton, as to supervise Strang's men when they come to put up the marquee tomorrow. I have already informed the firm." Vale was one of those men who must always be standing over their work-people, either in person or by proxy. He proceeded on his stately way: "I have sent out invitations, and Major Fairweather has consented to select and lead the fathers' team."

"What's the idea of the marquee?" came an audible whisper from Wrench.

"Tea," said Michael.

Mr. Vale fastened a frosty eye upon the interrupter. "Our own eleven is doubtless decided upon, Mr. Griffin?"

"Yes," replied the gamesmaster, adding in a low, rumbling aside to Michael, "and if that old fool Fairweather potters about at the wicket for more than five minutes, I shall tell Stevens to adopt bodyline tactics."

Chapter X

Annihilation of a Schoolmaster

The next morning, Monday, at exactly seven-eighteen o'clock, Nigel Strangeways came wide awake, with the word "haystack" on his tongue. He sat up in bed, under a mountain of blankets and eiderdowns, and reviewed the problem. Yes, his instinct had been right: the haystack was the nub and center of the mystery. As Armstrong had said, it was too much of a coincidence altogether; either Michael and Hero had committed the murder, or the murder had been committed there to incriminate them; therefore, by elimination— He was pretty sure, too, of the murderer's motive in seeking to incriminate them, and thence, by psychological elimination, of the murderer. But that seemed to be a dead stop. The motive he suspected would not impress the superintendent, and any able barrister could laugh it out of court in half a minute. Yet something must be done; one simply couldn't have a murderer about the place; one had no particular liking for the legalized revenges of justice, it was simply that one preferred not to have a murderer walking around–so many temptations for the poor fellow. He might, of course, having erupted to his own satisfaction, become extinct; but volcanoes, fondly imagined to be extinct, have a nasty way of bursting out again, just when the local inhabitants have begun to feel thoroughly secure. No, proof one must have–visible, tangible, matter-of-fact proof; and that was the kind of proof which he despaired ever of getting. The haystack. Had he, so to speak, sucked it dry? If one can suck a straw, one could presumably, given time, suck a haystack. Leaving that academic point aside, however, had the haystack any more secrets to yield? All very well to say it was used to incriminate Hero and Michael. But surely a murderer of such unpleasant ability could have found safer means of incriminating them. After all, it was he who had to do the murder. Why choose such a public place? And when, *when* had he done it? There must be some logical connection between time and place. Nigel lit a cigarette and went over Michael's account of the Sports Day, detail by detail. Suddenly he threw his head up, extinguished his cigarette disastrously upon the topmost eiderdown and exclaimed, "Good God! Yes. Yes. It must be. Well, I'll be damned!"

After breakfast Nigel set himself to clearing the ground. There were a number of loose ends still lying about, and he felt that no advance could be made till they were out of the way. He went first to Mrs. Vale.

"Things are beginning to move," he said, in answer to her unspoken question. "I just want three things–a request and two questions. The request is this: will you tell anyone who happens to ask you that Michael is under strong police suspicion."

"But surely he isn't still, is he?"

"Yes. I'm sorry. So are you. But it shouldn't last much longer. Were any of the staff intimate with Urquhart?"

"They all knew him–Tiverton best, I think. But he made a habit of inviting each master to dinner at least once a year."

"What about Wrench?"

"He had dinner with James last month. James used to invite new masters their first term."

"Third, can you tell me what your husband was doing all the time he said he was changing?"

Hero gave him a quizzical look, and seemed to be debating in her mind. "Is it absolutely necessary for you to know? Percy'll probably divorce me if I tell you."

"I do want to know very much. As long as he wasn't committing murder or anything, I'll see it's not made public."

"Very well, then, he was changing."

"What? What?" stuttered Nigel, quite flabbergasted.

"Changing. Trying on different suits and things, and studying the effect in the glass. The parents were coming, you see. He doesn't know I know it, of course, but, well, I suppose every one has to have a vice, and vanity is Percy's."

Nigel thanked her and walked away, meditating the curiosities of human nature, particularly as exhibited by the Rev. Percival Vale. He routed out Stevens II and gave him certain instructions. His next port of call was Griffin. He asked him to come out in the field, and there they reconstructed Griffin's movements between one-forty-five and two-thirty on the day of the crime. They were in the middle of this when the gamesmaster suddenly bellowed out, "Hi, what the dickens are you doing over there, Stevens? Don't you know you're not allowed out now?" He was beginning to make tracks towards the offender, when Nigel laid a restraining hand upon him.

"It's all right. I told him to. I wanted to see if the murderer could have got to the haystack without attracting your attention. If Stevens couldn't do it, I bet the murderer couldn't."

As they reentered the buildings a small and dirty hand tugged at

Nigel's sleeve. It was Ponsonby. The boy drew him aside and muttered darkly:

"Promise you won't tell anyone, not even the dictator."

"Yes."

"Well, he knows who the murderer is–at least, he said he did, but he won't tell even me. S'pose he thinks he can track him down by himself." The mutinous lieutenant took himself off, not without several sinister glances over his shoulder at Nigel.

There was probably nothing in it, Nigel reflected; one couldn't hope for all that luck, but stones, however small, cannot be left unturned by the detective, so he went after Stevens again. A certain amount of tact had to be employed in order not to betray Ponsonby, but the information was obtained without much difficulty. Stevens II had not wanted to sneak on what the superintendent had called a "playmate," even to his friend, the great detective. "But," he said, "I've got my suspicions about that oaf, Smithers. You see, at breakfast that day, apparently Wemyss had been ragging him. Every one does, of course. Anyway, I heard Smithers say to him in recess, 'I'll kill you.' He looked jolly bloodthirsty too, sir. And he's been awfully funny lately–since the murder, I mean. I suppose I ought to have told you before, but it didn't seem fair, somehow, though Smithers is such a oick."

Nigel reassured him and made a mental note to interview the underbred Smithers in recess. The bell for first period now rang. Nigel strolled into the common room, where Tiverton was sitting with a pile of exercise books before him. He had this hour off. "I hope I'm not interrupting," said Nigel.

"Not a bit. I can do this any time. I say, is it true that the police suspect Evans still?"

"I'm afraid so. In fact, he's in a very awkward position. That pencil, you know—" Nigel added.

"But I thought that was disposed of. He told us he'd lost it during the hay battle."

"Yes. But the superintendent seems to have got an idea that he had it the next day–the day of the murder."

"Well, I must admit I thought myself I'd seen him using it that morning. I say, good Lord, I hope I haven't been making things difficult for him. No, it couldn't be. There were only Griffin and Evans himself in the room then."

Nigel gave him an inquiring look.

"When I happened to mention that I thought I'd seen him using the pencil on the day after the hay battle," explained Tiverton.

There was a little desultory conversation, then Nigel strolled out and made for the telephone in the private side of the house. He rang up the Staverton police station.

"Is that Superintendent Armstrong.... Oh, right, I'll hold the line.... Morning, Armstrong–this is Strangeways. Sorry to bother you. Would you mind telling me again about Evans' pencil that you found in the haystack? His fingerprints only? Mm. On the ground, you said, didn't you? Said he must have dropped it during the hay battle? Well, why not? ... Yes, exactly, no proof to the contrary? ... Very awkward for you, as you say. I take it no one but the police and his friends know about it? ... By the way, are you coming up today? ... This afternoon? Good. Yes, I may have something for you. Oh, I forgot to tell you–I know who the murderer is. Au revoir, then."

Nigel rang off, leaving the superintendent dancing with rage and baffled curiosity at the other end of the telephone. Sims' classroom, as Nigel entered it, presented an unusually orderly aspect; it may be that the repercussions of the headmaster's last visit had not yet died away, or perhaps Nigel's tacit disapproval of their treatment of the little man had percolated through Stevens II and Ponsonby to the rest. These two young gentlemen were sitting, for them, quite still, and when the form rose to their feet at Nigel's entry, they returned their fellow conspirator's glance with an expression so excessively wooden as to have aroused the deepest suspicions in any unbiased observer. Nigel advanced to the master's desk, peered vaguely at the books lying upon it. Sims made a fidgeting gesture towards the books. Nigel asked if he could have a word with Sims outside. The door was, fortunately, fairly thick, so neither of them heard a hissing stage-whisper from Ponsonby, "I say, he's going to arrest old Simmie," and another from Stevens II, "Go down the next street! He hadn't got any handcuffs–they'd bulge in his pocket."

"Terribly sorry to interrupt you like this, but it's rather urgent. The police, perhaps you've heard, have got some ridiculous idea that Evans is mixed up with this murder. We've got to clear him soon or they may take action. That pencil of his is the difficulty, of course."

Sims looked puzzled. "Pencil?"

"Oh, yes; didn't you know? They found his silver pencil in the haystack. Actually he dropped it there ragging about on the day before, but he can't prove that, you see. I suppose you didn't notice whether he had it on the morning of the murder, did you?"

"No. I couldn't be sure–that is. I didn't see him using it, as far as I remember. But I'm afraid that's not much use."

"Well, it can't be helped. Thanks."

Nigel wandered off again and read the papers in the common room. The Sudeley Hall murder occupied no space in them now; for two or three days their editors had announced that the police were making progress and shown the conventional optimism about an imminent arrest; the adjourned inquest had been reported, and there had been accounts in one or two papers of the boy's funeral, pulsating with that ghoulish sentimentality for which editors have coined the phrase "human interest." Even the echoes of the belaboring of that very dead donkey–police inefficiency– had died away. And what, after all, reflected Nigel, could Armstrong do? Police investigation lives by facts alone, and quite right too; facts are sometimes misleading, but at least they are safer than amateur psychological theorizing or confessions induced by rubber truncheons and dentists' drills. The superintendent had interviewed every one who could possibly be concerned, and he was clever enough to deal with any ordinary murder. But this was no ordinary murder; which accounted, amongst other things, for the dearth of facts, of material clues.

When the bell rang for recess, Nigel went out into the yard and inquired for Smithers. He was pointed out a yelling ring of boys. They were engaged in a local form of bear-baiting known as "chub-chub"; this consisted of darting in at the victim, giving his cheek a violent tug, and melting again into the crowd of the oppressors. The victim, needless to say, was Smithers. He was red in the face and his eyes were strained with pain and humiliation; he backed slowly away from his tormentors, swinging wildly at them with the flat of his hands–he had once hit someone with a fist, and had not been allowed to forget such a violation of the code of sportsmanship. As he backed, malicious feet swung at him from behind and pushed him into the middle of the ring again. Nigel approached the group. He was glad to see that Stevens II and Ponsonby were not among them. He felt furiously angry. The boys stopped and stood sheepishly when they saw him. He whipped them soundly with his tongue for a minute–Nigel could be devastating when he wished. He made more impression than he realized at the time, for he knew the insensitiveness to rebuke of boys in the mass. Several masters had from time to time given tongue publicly on the subject of the bullying of Smithers, but it had had little effect; the boys knew that one must expect that sort of thing from masters, it was what they were paid for. But this intervention of a disinterested party, so to speak, and the heroic detective at that, was a different matter. It gave them a shock; and life was much easier for Smithers from that moment.

If Nigel had made an impression on these tough eggs, Smithers' tormentors, the effect of his action on Smithers himself was enormous. The boy was a little dazed at first by the sudden relief; a little suspicious, too, as a trapped animal is suspicious of its rescuer. But soon enough, to continue the metaphor, he was ready to eat out of his hand. He found himself walking towards the field at the side of this kind and godlike man, a man who was talking to him as no one seemed to have talked to him for years. Nigel was wiser than to make any reference to the scene which had just taken place or to the dead Wemyss. This boy was no murderer, and anything he had to say could well wait for a few hours, till he had calmed down a bit inside. So he was content to draw the boy out about his home and his interests; it was easy enough, because Smithers turned out to be an authority on the beasts and birds of the countryside, and Nigel never had need to pretend interest in any subject of which he was ignorant. They had been talking for nearly a quarter of an hour when there was a pause and the boy gave him a look which he could not quite fathom; he imagined, however, that Smithers was going to try to express his gratitude, so he said quickly:

"Don't you bother about that. Come and have tea with me–to-day or to-morrow–I'll tell you later. And, of course, if ever there's anything particular you want to talk about, I'm always here."

Smithers opened his mouth, but the bell rang for school, and Nigel was spared any display of gratitude which may have been coming to him. He had scarcely got indoors again when he received a message–Superintendent Armstrong was in the morning room and would like to see him. Nigel smiled ruefully. Armstrong certainly did not let the grass grow under his feet. He had been a fool, indulging in that piece of rodomontade over the telephone. And the superintendent soon let him know it.

"Now, sir, what's all this about your knowing who the murderer is?" Nigel was a little nettled by the aggressive manner of the question.

"Just that," he said, "but it's not for publication yet."

"Come, come, Mr. Strangeways. My time is valuable. I take it this is not a practical joke. If you have proof about the murderer, I must ask you to hand it over to me at once."

"I never said I had proof. I said I knew who the murderer was. You have all the facts in your possession that I have. We agreed not to bother each other with theories until either of us had a fairly watertight case."

"I'm afraid I don't understand you, sir. You say you know who did the murder, but have no proofs. It sounds silly to me."

"Not the sort of proofs that would satisfy you; or a court of law," added Nigel hastily. "I've not found an eyewitness, or a signed confession or any hot news like that. My clues are of the invisible, intangible sort."

"Oh Lord," snorted the superintendent, "what they call psychological induction: or have you been consulting a medium?"

Nigel grinned patiently. "No, I've been talking to one of your suspects–by the way, Mr. Evans is not the murderer; I'll give you the significant extracts and you can go home and chew on them."

He proceeded to relate some of Michael's reminiscences and certain conversations at which he himself had been present. As these have all been recorded already, there is no need to repeat them. When he had finished, Armstrong remarked irritably:

"Well, really, sir, if I didn't know of your reputation, I should be inclined to say—"

"Don't say it! Let us rise above personal abuse."

"And you don't propose to tell me the name of this"–the superintendent choked–"this psychic suspect of yours?"

"No. Not at present. What'd be the use? You go the high road and I'll go the low road–and I'll see you in Scotland if you ever get there."

"I'll see you in—" remarked the superintendent with the beginnings of a grin.

"Now, now! No recriminations! But, seriously, give me another day. Come up tomorrow afternoon, there's going to be an exciting cricket match; either I'll have something more solid for you by then, or I'll give you my theory, for what it's worth."

Armstrong had to be content with this. But he felt vexed; what on earth did Strangeways see in those conversations that he couldn't? And to discharge some of this vexation he proceeded to take the high road with a vengeance, as was testified in the course of the day by the faces of Hero and Michael, Wrench and Rosa–those oddly juxtaposed pairs of lovers. But their stories remained unshaken. The high road didn't seem to lead anywhere.

"It's a gesture, certainly, but pretty safe from Percy's point of view," Michael replied. It was Tuesday afternoon. He and Nigel were sauntering out onto the field, where already a few fathers were getting their eyes in at the nets. "After all," he continued, "the business-as-usual slogan gets the British middle class where they live–it has just the right combination of backs-to-the-wall bulldog courage and commercial *savoir-faire*. In this case it will leave its only rival–the respect-for-the-dead ballyhoo–at the post. Those parents who are shortly going to take the field will get quite a kick out of feeling that they are carrying on; just like the old days–the General Strike and the Great War. I gave my sons and kept the home fires burning, only in this case it's Percy giving his nephew. Thank God the boys don't think like that. Two teams demonstrating the middle class's capacity for carrying on would be more than I could bear." Michael was trembling all over, as he always did when engaged in controversial statement.

"You take things too much to heart," said Nigel lightly. "Admittedly most of this business-as-usual stuff is hypocrisy. But a certain amount of hypocrisy is necessary to oil the wheels of society. Very few people have either the ability or the training to understand their own motives–and a good thing too. It's all very well for the philosopher, but it's no use for the practical man; he'd never get anything done if he appreciated his motives for action. Only a great man can be a consistent protestant, and the rest of us must have our external sanctions–slogans if you like–and live under authority. It seems to me the real job of you schoolmasters is to train boys in the choosing of the best slogans to obey."

"And if I did, I should be chucked out of here soon enough. The best slogans I know are the ones in the Sermon on the Mount and 'to each according to his need, from each according to his ability.' As a matter of fact I shall probably be in prison before I have time to do any proselytizing. That blasted superintendent put me through the hoops again yesterday. Oh, there he is. I wish he'd get out the handcuffs and have done with it."

Armstrong came up and greeted them; Michael impassively, and Nigel with ill-concealed impatience.

"Not till after the match," remarked Nigel in answer to his unspoken appeal; "don't let's mix up business and pleasure. The murderer can't get away." He glanced significantly to where the plainclothes constable lounged near the gate, a substantial skeleton-at-the-feast.

They strolled once or twice round the boundary line. The boys were taking their places on benches or the grass on the far side of the field. On the other side, between the school building and the boundary line, were deck chairs for the more privileged spectators, with the tea tent immediately behind them. On the right-hand side of the field, looking from the school, was the pavilion, the nets beyond it. Michael could see Major Fairweather tossing up with Anstruther; it was evident, from the jocular backslappings which followed, that the fathers had won. Nigel invited the superintendent to occupy one of the benches with him; he wanted to watch the cricket and not to have his attention distracted by the restlessness and amateur comment of proud mothers. Michael hurried across to the other side of the ground; of two evils he would prefer hobnobbing with the parents to hobnobbing with the superintendent; also, Hero was there. She was sitting beside the headmaster, and gave Michael a sad, caressing look as he approached. Then some parents came up to her, and Michael set himself to be sociable.

The umpires came out; Griffin with his rolling gait, and Tiverton looking trim and professional. They were followed by a lanky bespectacled parent, and the Vicar of Sudeley, an old Cambridge blue. There was a tradition handed down among parents of the better sort that in this match one did not make more than twenty-five, and made it as quickly as possible. Unfortunately, there always seemed to be one or two parents more interested in their average than in tradition and a jolly game. A sensible captain generally ran these out, or told someone else to. But Major Fairweather was not this type of captain. Michael felt uneasy. And his uneasiness was justified when the innings were brought to a close, but the fathers had scored two hundred and three. The boys straggled in to tea, looking disconsolate.

Events after tea seemed at first to justify their worst forebodings. Griffin was still umpiring at one end, but Tiverton had been relieved by one of the parents. Off the second ball, Major Fairweather at square leg held a low, hard catch–a shot which any right-thinking father would have allowed to pass to the boundary. Stevens I, the other opening batsman, overawed by this reverse, allowed himself to be bowled shortly after by a rank bad ball. Then the score crept up and up; one hundred and twenty-one for four; one hundred and fifty for five; one hundred and fifty-eight for six; one hundred and seventy for seven; one hundred and eighty-four for eight; one hundred and ninety-four for nine. The fathers were all on their toes now; they meant to win.

The spectators ceased to be bored or mildly interested. Every ball was preceded by nervous suspense and followed with signs of relief or wild applause. "That's the idee! That's the idee!" yelled the school–a catchword of the moment–as each run was scored. Even the little boys, who had spent most of the match tumbling over each other on the boundary, stopped their antics and mingled their batlike shrieks in the applause. It was a regular school-story finish; the sort of finish that does, as a matter of fact, occur quite frequently in prep-school matches.

Chapter XI

"I Have Thee Not ..."

"This is going to be a good finish, Hero," said Mr. Vale.

"Yes, it's frightfully exciting, isn't it."

Hero leaned forward. The first ball of a new over. Giffard could never do it. She saw the ball miss stumps and wicket-keeper, and long legs tearing round to cut it off from the boundary. Anstruther turned and leaped forward for the third run. "He'll never do it," she cried. There was a grunt from her husband. Anstruther got home. "Hooray, he's done it." Hero turned to Vale, eyes sparkling with enthusiasm. "Isn't it—? Wake up, Percy! Are you feeling ill?" She shook him. As he slumped slowly sideways, and on to the ground, she saw a tiny hole, a tiny ooze of blood through the coat on his back. It was too much. Hero moaned and fainted away.

Michael heard that little moan. It almost broke his heart. He ran to Hero and laid her on the ground and took her head on his lap. A crowd gathered round. Tiverton and Sims were bending over the headmaster. Wrench, pale as death, stood a little aside. The superintendent and Nigel came pounding across the field, scattering the players. "She's fainted. Run and get her some water!" somebody said. Michael was off like a flash, making for the school; he heard, as in a dream, an angry shout from the superintendent, ordering him to stop. It would have taken an electrified fence to stop him. Armstrong shouldered his way through the throng, gave one look at the body, and shouted for the plainclothes man. He ordered him to ring up first Dr. Maddox and then the police headquarters at Staverton. While he was giving directions his eyes were not on his subordinate; they wandered vigilantly from side to side of the field. "No one passed into the school just now, Jones?"

"Only Mr. Evans, sir. Said he was getting water for Mrs. Vale, so I let him pass."

"All right. Off you go! Mr. Strangeways, will you please stand at the school gate and allow no one to pass in on any pretext whatsoever. You there, Mr. Griffin? Right. I want you to station yourself at the end of the path leading to the wood. If anyone tries to get away through the wood or over the hayfield, jump on him." The superintendent posted two of the most stalwart parents, who had been taking part in the match, at other strategic points. He was now certain that no one could leave the field, and he was pretty certain that no one but Evans had left it since the murder. Armstrong next turned to the bystanders and began shouting an order. But there was a hum of conversation around, and a number of people were standing at some distance out of earshot. "I'll get the megaphone," said Wrench, and walked quickly over towards the pavilion. Armstrong had raised his hand, then dropped it; but he followed Wrench with his eyes till he saw him emerge from the pavilion carrying the megaphone and start walking back. Meanwhile Evans had arrived with a tumbler of water. Hero's clothing had been loosened and she had been made more comfortable. Michael propped her head up, sprinkled water on her forehead, and as she rose up into consciousness again, held the glass to her lips. Armstrong gave him a searching look, then he raised the megaphone and bellowed: "Ladies and gentlemen, no one is to leave the field. Mr. Vale has met with an accident, and the doctor has been sent for. Mr. Tiverton there? I want all the boys collected by those benches on the far side and kept there. Will those gentlemen who were playing in the match stay just outside the pavilion." He lowered the megaphone and addressed the parents and masters standing nearby. "Will you gentlemen move these chairs further away; the ladies can sit down; we shall have some time to wait. No one must go near Mr. Vale."

The plainclothes man returned and reported that the doctor and the police reinforcements were on their way. Armstrong sent him to relieve Strangeways at the gate, and when the latter returned began questioning those who stood nearest. "Did any of you see what happened? Which of you were closest to Mr. Vale when the—er—accident occurred?" Sims, Wrench and Gadsby stepped forward. Sims, it appeared, had been standing a yard or so to the right of the headmaster's chair, behind it; Wrench and Gadsby behind it to the left. Gadsby said that Tiverton had passed a remark with him about half a minute before Mrs. Vale fainted and had then moved away. The visitors sitting on the chairs on either side of Mr. and Mrs. Vale had not moved during the fatal minute. Indeed, from the moment the bowler had begun his run for the first ball of that last over till Mrs. Vale had fainted, no one had had eyes for anything but the game. "And you, Mr. Evans?" Armstrong repeated the question rather sharply. Michael, who had turned Hero's chair with its back to the huddled body on the ground and lifted her gently into it, was stroking her hand, oblivious to the crowd's gaze and the superintendent's words.

He looked up vaguely, jerked his hand over his shoulder, and said,

"Me? I was standing over there."

"Come, sir, please be a little more explicit."

"Over there, I tell you. Near Sims."

"That's right, superintendent. He was standing beside me at the end of the last over," said Sims, gratified at his brief moment in the limelight.

"And then?"

"Then? Oh, I see. W-well, I m-mean I didn't n-n-notice anything once the over b-began," stuttered Sims.

Armstrong motioned the bystanders, whose curiosity had led them to draw nearer the protagonists, to move back. He then approached Mrs. Vale. She looked up at him, horror still close beneath the surface of her eyes.

"Now, madam, I'm very sorry to have to trouble you just now. But you realize that the sooner I get all the facts, the quicker we shall find your husband's–murderer." He raised his voice slightly on the last word and glanced keenly about him. The faces were rigid and white, immobile with shock. Like a breeze rippling over a field of corn and dying at its farthest limit, the word "murder" rustled through the crowd, causing a visible tremor in its mass, and communicating itself even to those who waited on the other side of the ground.

Hero moistened her bloodless lips. "I don't know. He spoke to me just before the over began. And when we had won the match I turned to him again. I thought he'd gone to sleep. So I shook him, and he fell off the seat, and I saw—" Her voice shuddered and broke.

"Are you quite certain you heard or saw nothing else? I'm sorry, Mrs. Vale, but I must ask you this. Nothing, however unimportant?"

"When they were running I said, 'He'll never do it' or something, and my husband gave a sort of grunt–answering me. Oh, God, he wasn't answering me. He was—" Hero had been speaking in a tense whisper, but such was the concentrated silence of the onlookers that every word reached them. Hero's body straightened, then collapsed into the arms of Michael standing beside her chair. He held her there, tight, stroking her golden hair.

Armstrong raised the megaphone to his lips and shouted: "If anyone saw anything unusual happening here after the beginning of the last over, will he kindly report it to me at once." Again the crowd stirred and heaved uneasily, but no one stepped forward. "Did any of you touch the body before we came over?" Nigel asked of the group standing nearest. There was a brief silence, then Sims volunteered: "Tiverton and I turned him–it–over, to see if—" his voice trailed away. "And who reached it first?" "Tiverton. I was j-just behind him." The superintendent broke in brusquely. "And why did you or he remove the weapon? Don't you know that you should never—" "Oh, but we didn't. Really, we didn't. I mean to say, there was no weapon there," interrupted Sims, looking bewildered. The superintendent gave Nigel an enigmatic look, then he turned to Evans and said, "Would you mind asking Mrs. Vale whether there was a weapon in the body when she saw it fall to the ground." Nigel reflected that, though Armstrong was putting up a show of tact and consideration, he seemed to be listening very carefully to the whispered colloquy between Michael and Hero.

"She says she is certain there was no weapon," Michael finally informed the superintendent, then, with a spurt of indignation, he added, "If you've finished your badgering, perhaps you'll let her go indoors where these human sheep can't stare at her any longer."

"No one may leave the field till he has been searched. You can take her into the tent there, if you like."

Michael carried Hero into the tent, in full view of two hundred eyes. He could see nothing but her desperate tears, hear nothing but the sobbing of her breath. The tent was empty; the tea had been cleared half an hour ago. Hero clung to Michael like a child; over her shoulder he could see a section of the crowd, waiting, white and silent; he could not see the superintendent, who was standing close to the outside wall of the tent—listening.

Whatever Armstrong may have hoped to hear, he was not given much time for listening. Dr. Maddox arrived, his jaunty walk sobered to the occasion. He nodded to Armstrong and bent over the remains of Percival Vale. "Dead, of course. Instantaneous. Can he be moved?" "Yes; it can't make any difference. Will some of you gentlemen help me to carry him behind the tent."

The remains of Percival Vale were taken up and put down again. Dr. Maddox bent over the body. After a minute or two he stood up and brushed his knees. "Well, sir?" said Armstrong eagerly.

"He was stabbed. Some very thin weapon, like a stiletto, for instance. The point entered the body below the left shoulder blade and pierced the heart. I should say it was delivered a little from the left; the post-mortem will verify that. Death, as I say, was instantaneous. There was practically no bleeding."

Nigel glanced at the superintendent. It was easy to imagine which way his thoughts were tending. Hero had been sitting on the left of her husband. He strolled round and inspected the chair on which Vale had been sitting; the canvas was pierced at the back, just below the bar. A group of masters were standing near, speaking in undertones.

"God!" Gadsby was saying, "it's amazing–incredible. Killed in full view of every one. Why, damn it, it's impossible."

"Well, it's been done, anyway," said Wrench. "I guess the murderer's feeling pretty sick, too."

"What do you mean?" asked Sims.

"The police are going to search every one. And presumably he's still got the gory blade concealed amongst his underwear."

"Really, Wrench," protested Gadsby, "this is not the time or place for your rotten cynicism."

"Nor the time or place for a murder," returned Wrench: "damned bad form, I call it–in front of all the parents."

It was not long now before the police from Staverton arrived. Sergeant Pearson, several constables, a police matron, and with them the chief constable, looking flustered and ill at ease. Armstrong went straight up to the latter, saluted and spoke quickly. Nigel edged nearer; he was only able to catch the last words, but these were quite enough:

"… search warrant for Evans' rooms, sir."

"Are you sure it's absolutely necessary. I mean—"

"It's essential, sir, and the sooner the better."

"Very well, Armstrong."

The superintendent sent constables to relieve the plainclothes man and the amateur sentries. As the former came over he whispered to him, "Was Mr. Evans carrying anything?"

"Yes, sir, a tumbler of water."

"Don't be a damned fool. When he left the field, I mean."

"Sorry, sir. No, sir, he didn't appear to be."

Armstrong now summoned the sergeant and the police matron. He addressed the latter first: "I want you to search all the women, in that tent. You can start off with Mrs. Vale; she's there already. You're looking for some kind of very thin pointed blade. You will also, in Mrs. Vale's case only, examine the clothing carefully for bloodstains." He turned to the sergeant. "Pearson, your job is to search all the boys and the gentlemen who were playing in the match. You won't find anything but it must be done. Take the visitors' room in the pavilion. I shall do the rest of the men myself." Armstrong moved towards the crowd and bellowed the necessary directions through his megaphone. The crowd began to break up into two streams, the women moving towards the tent and the men over to the pavilion. Many of them were too dazed by the tragedy to protest, but there were a good number who stuck in their heels and made scenes. The chief constable nibbled his mustache uneasily in the background; he foresaw an unpleasant correspondence on his breakfast table tomorrow. Armstrong, however, like a large sheepdog, barked and maneuvered and threatened to bite, rounding up the recalcitrants and putting them in their place.

A constable was left to picket the actual site of the crime, and Armstrong began his search. "Mr. Evans, please." Michael came into the room in the pavilion and Nigel entered uninvited with him, looking faintly puzzled. "Will you please undress, sir." Michael lifted one eyebrow, but obeyed; a curious use this changing room is being put to, he thought. The superintendent minutely examined each article of clothing as it was removed. His expression at the end of this was far from pleasant. "No blood-stains, after all?" said Nigel mildly. Armstrong glowered at him and paced once or twice across the room. "Just a minute, Mr. Evans," he said, as Michael was about to depart, "you took a long time about that glass of water, didn't you?"

"No longer than I could help."

"Hm. Where did you get it?"

"My bedroom."

"Do you mean to say there's no tap nearer than that?"

"No, there are lots. But not glasses."

"Wouldn't it have been quicker for you to get a glass from the kitchen?"

"I don't think so. It might, perhaps. But I knew there was one in my bedroom; I went there naturally."

"That will be all, then, for the present. I must ask you, though, not to return to your rooms till I give you permission."

Michael looked inquiringly at him; he had no idea what all the fuss was about, which was fortunate for his peace of mind. The moment he went out Armstrong signaled to a policeman and told him not to let Evans leave the field till further orders. Armstrong now began the tedious business of searching the rest of the men. He started with the masters who had been standing near the victim; their clothing, too, was searched for blood as well as for a weapon. Nigel stood unnaturally still during these operations. It was too much to hope for, he thought. God knows what the murderer has done with it, but he's a sight too clever to be found with any traces of the crime on him. And Nigel was right. After what seemed an interminable period, the last person was searched and dismissed. Not an inch of steel, not a drop of blood had been discovered. The police matron entered and informed Armstrong that she had found nothing. "Mrs. Vale?" he said sharply. The woman shook her head. "Very well," said Armstrong, "we can't keep her out here any longer. Will you take her into the house, Miss Gilray, and don't let her out of your sight." Sergeant Pearson came in to report. "Nothing?" said Armstrong. "Take Jones and search Mr. Evans' rooms. Colonel Humphries will give you the warrant; you may find a bloodstained handkerchief or something as well; he must have contrived somehow to keep the blood off his clothes." Nigel raised his eyebrows, but said nothing. He was busy with his own thoughts. Michael and Hero had not done this–that was his major premise–therefore the weapon could not have been taken off the field. The weapon had not been found on anybody, therefore it must have been hidden on the field. They would have to search there in the end, for it would not be found in Michael's rooms, but the delay was intolerable.

He stepped out of the pavilion. The superintendent had given his orders. The boys had been sent in with Griffin. The visitors were straggling off the field in a mute, funeral sort of procession, the fine feathers of the women seeming to droop upon them. The masters had been told not to leave the ground yet; they were collected in a group around Tiverton, upon whose shoulders the responsibility for carrying on the school had presumably fallen. Somewhere in that bleak great building its late lord and master was lying; no longer a scholar, a gentleman, an absolute ruler: only a body with a hole in it.

It was not long before Sergeant Pearson came out. There are few possible hiding places in the bare rooms of masters. He had ransacked Evans', and there was nothing to be found. The superintendent bit his lip, but he was not beaten yet. He divided up his little force and sent one half to search the school. "The common room first, Pearson; when you've done that, let me know and I'll send these gentlemen in there. See that they stay there, too. Then go over the whole blasted building; that weapon can't have vanished. Interview the servants yourself, and find out if any of them saw Mr. Evans after he went in for that glass of water or knew anything at all about the murder. Not much hope of their having seen anything; that infernal tent stands right between the windows and the place where Mr. Vale was sitting. Off you go!"

As Armstrong turned aside to give his own men their orders, Nigel spoke to him in a low voice, "There's always Wrench and the megaphone."

"I've not forgotten that, Mr. Strangeways. Like to help me search the pavilion?" The other men received their instructions and began moving slowly about the field, radiating from the place where the body had lain. It did not look as if a pin could escape them. Nigel and the superintendent crossed the deserted pitch and entered the pavilion. Nigel left the burden and heat of the search to his companion. Armstrong was a thorough man, he reflected; he might jump too quickly to conclusions, but he gave every possibility a good run for its money. After quarter of an hour the pavilion had been turned inside out, and there was nothing to show for it.

"I suppose he couldn't have hidden it here and taken it away again after you'd searched him?" Nigel suggested tentatively.

"Not he. I had a man watching every one as they left the changing-room. They had to move off double quick."

"You think of everything," said Nigel, not without admiration.

At this moment Sergeant Pearson came up. "We've been over the common room, sir. No good." Armstrong frowned. "Very well, the school next. I'll come across and help in a minute." Pearson doubled off and Armstrong approached the little group of masters.

"You gentlemen may go in now. But I'm afraid I must ask you all to stay in the common room for the present. We've searched that and there only remains the rest of the building to do."

The masters presented a woebegone and shattered appearance. Tiverton's lean, sunburnt face was twitching spasmodically; Evans stood by himself, gazing over towards the school as though he expected any moment to hear another call for help from Hero; Gadsby, Sims and Wrench were clustered together, conversing in jerky undertones; Gadsby's face was mottled; Sims and Wrench looked white and sick.

"S-searched the common room?" repeated Sims dully.

"Yes, sir. The weapon must be hidden somewhere. But we've found nothing so far."

Sims moistened his lips and stared uncomprehendingly at the superintendent. "Nothing so far," he repeated. Armstrong thought he was going to collapse, and put a hand under his elbow, saying, "Hold up, sir. This tragedy has been too much of a shock for you. Just you go indoors and I'll send in some whisky for you. Perhaps one of you gentlemen would be so kind as to—"

"There's sure to be a bottle under Gadsby's bed. I'll fetch it down," muttered Wrench.

Gadsby's face became more mottled than ever. "Wrench, you little tick, can't you ever do anything but try to be clever? If you were a gentleman, you'd know that there are occasions when one tries to show a little self-restraint."

Wrench grew red as fire and glared at him furiously. "When you've all finished blackguarding each other, perhaps we might go in," remarked Tiverton in a voice not quite so bored and detached as he tried to make it.

"If you have some whisky, sir, by any chance, I think it would do none of us any harm," said Armstrong smoothly to Gadsby. "I'll fetch it myself."

"You'll find a bottle in the cupboard," said Gadsby.

"Empty," said Wrench.

An hour later. Nigel and the superintendent are sitting in the morning-room. A very stiff tot of whisky indeed is in front of the superintendent. Nigel has somehow conjured up a pot of tea, and as they talk he moves restlessly from one part of the room to another, carrying his cup and saucer with him and putting them down precariously whenever he comes to a halt.

"Well, this fair beats me," groaned Armstrong, clapping his hand to his forehead. "The field, the tent, the pavilion, the path into the school, and the school itself; we've been over the whole ruddy caboodle with a fine-tooth comb, and not a smell of that bleeding dagger–nothing even that begins to look like a dagger."

"I have thee not, and yet I see thee still," quoted Nigel, "only we don't see thee."

"Whassat?"

"Poetry. The Bard."

Armstrong beat his clenched fist again and again upon the table. "Am I going batty or am I not? A man is stabbed. Every one and everything within a hundred yards of him is searched–no one could possibly have got away–but, hey presto! the weapon is gone."

Nigel loped over to another corner of the room and balanced his teacup on the edge of a pouffe. "We ought to have found out if anyone here is a sword-swallower. He may be coughing it up privily at this very moment."

"Ah, t'chah!"

"Well, produce something better."

"Why, it's as plain as my foot–or should be," the superintendent's feet did certainly obtrude themselves upon one's notice. "Mrs. Vale carries the stiletto in her clothing, waits for a moment when every one's eyes are glued on the game, stabs him in the back. Quite easy from where she was sitting; weapon entered the body rather from the left; it all fits in. Then she gives him a push and pretends to faint. That is the signal preconcerted with Evans. He runs up, cuddles her a bit, and she passes the weapon to him. He puts it inside his coat, goes off for water, and hides it somewhere in the school. Damn it, it must be right. There must be some hiding place we've missed."

"Blood, old boy, blood. There'd be bound to be some on her clothing or his."

Armstrong lowered an eyelid ponderously. "That's all right, sir. I forgot to tell you, there was so much to do. After you'd gone in with the masters just now I took another squint at the ground by the tent. Two smears of blood on the grass, quite close where Mrs. Vale fainted. One of 'em must have wiped the blade."

"That's certainly a point to you. But, look here, what was the point of Mrs. Vale's pretending to faint? Surely she would want all eyes concentrated on Vale while she transferred the weapon to Evans. Fainting would distract some attention to herself."

"That's true, sir. But there had to be some pretext for Evans' going so close to her."

"And the motive? On your theory Evans murdered Wemyss to prevent his intrigue with Mrs. Vale coming to her husband's ears. That seemed to me thin enough. And now Mrs. Vale murders her husband, although she knows she and Michael are under suspicion of the first crime–what for? To get a separation? She'd only to ask Vale for a divorce, hadn't she? One might conceivably murder a person if that was the only way out, but she hadn't even asked her husband for a divorce yet."

"Can you prove that?"

Nigel was taken rather aback. "Prove it? No. But one of them would have told me if they'd decided to take the step."

"I'm sorry, sir, but I can't take that as evidence. You see, I happened to be passing the drawing-room door on Sunday evening before supper, and I heard Mr. Evans ask Mrs. Vale whether she would ever be really free of her husband till he was dead. I'm afraid that will sound more convincing in court than something which one of them would have told you."

" 'Happened' is good."

Armstrong shifted in his chair and said stiffly, "This is not a game of cricket; it's a murder investigation. Someone's got to do the dirty work."

"So you're really going to arrest them this time."

"We'll have another look for that weapon tomorrow morning. If we find it, I shall arrest them. If not, I shall ask the chief constable to call in the Yard."

"Yes, you'd certainly have a pretty good case. But just think a minute. A woman might use that sort of weapon. But I ask you, would anyone in their senses go and commit a crime in full view of two hundred people, when there were a thousand opportunities for doing it on the quiet, and quite enough brains to think out any number of safer methods if, as you hold, they had enough brains to think out the first murder."

"Hmph. It took some brains to get rid of the weapon like that. It seems to me there's a remarkable similarity between the two murders. In each case the criminals deliberately put themselves under suspicion, first by admitting that they were in the haystack and then by being in the obvious proximity to Mr. Vale when he is murdered, and in each case they arrange it so that there shall be no proof. I tell you, sir, it's a double bluff. And damned clever too. Surely you're not suggesting that there's no connection between the two murders?"

"Far from it. I suggest that there's even more connection than meets your eagle eye. Hasn't it occurred to you that there's at least just as much likelihood of the murders having been done like this by *somebody else* in order to incriminate Evans and Mrs. Vale as of having been done by them so as to incriminate themselves?"

Armstrong started and fingered his top button uneasily.

"And secondly," pursued Nigel, "doesn't the highly *public* nature of both crimes suggest anything to you?"

Armstrong looked puzzled. "I don't see what you mean. This last crime was public enough. But the murder of Wemyss? Well, the haystack was in rather a prominent position, I grant you. Still, I don't see how you could call the murder itself 'public.' "

"No…. No. Of course not," said Nigel, looking at Armstrong quizzically.

"Look here, sir, what is it? You've got something on your mind. What's this new theory of yours? You told me you'd come across with it this afternoon, one way or another."

"Yes, I know. But things have happened since that. This Vale business complicates matters. Hell and damnation," he went on, talking almost to himself, "and I could have stopped it. I had all the facts. I might have known–oh well, spilt milk and all that. I want a day more. They can't get away, can they? Let me know, by the way, when you're going to arrest them, and we'll see what your humble servant can do." Nigel rose wearily. As he was opening the door he turned and said over his shoulder, "And, incidentally, Armstrong, I'm prepared to lay twenty to one that you find the weapon in Evans' room tomorrow."

"Wh-wh-what?" gurgled the superintendent, but the only reply was a squeak from the closing door. "For all that," Nigel was saying to himself on the other side, "I wish I knew where it is now."

Chapter XII

Shocks All Round

The next day was perhaps the busiest and most eventful in Nigel Strangeways' life. Before twelve hours of it had elapsed, the whole structure of deceit and misrepresentation which the murderer had erected had fallen in like a house of cards. It was a terrible day for Michael and Hero. Michael, waking early after fitful sleep, felt a vague nightmare weigh upon his heart; he remembered that it was exactly a week since he had woken up in sunlight and kissed Hero in the haystack–a week since someone had tied a piece of string round a boy's neck. But it was not this that oppressed him. Then he remembered; he had started from sleep in the middle of the night and suddenly realized the full meaning of the superintendent's activities that evening. They suspected Hero of killing her husband, and himself of hiding the weapon. So obvious, when one came to think of it. Hero's face, lovely and forlorn, rose up before his eyes; then the mists of fear came down, blotting out everything but the difficult and treacherous path beneath his feet–a path, he reflected grimly, so likely to end now in a sheer drop. Nigel said he knew–that was his last hope. Hero herself lay in bed, wan and wide-eyed. Wherever she turned she could see nothing but a body with a tiny hole in the back and a tiny ooze of blood on the gray coat. That she was free at last, free to marry Michael; that at least one person believed her to be the murderess of her husband–these things did not enter her mind. The darkness of physical horror still enveloped it too closely. It was an exciting day for Superintendent Armstrong and more than one of the staff. It was a day notable, moreover, for perhaps the only triumph in the drab life of Hugo Sims.

Michael got out of bed and studied his face curiously in the glass. It looked exactly the same as it had looked a week ago. No pallor, no dark pouches, none of the conventional imprints of mental anguish. He felt vaguely resentful; one might at least have something to show for it. He dressed and opened the door to go downstairs. As he closed it behind him another memory started up out of his unconscious. Sometime last night, in the shadowy gulf between waking and sleeping, he had heard that same sound, seeming to come from a great distance. It couldn't really have come from a great distance, of course, or he wouldn't have heard it. It was probably part of a dream, anyway. He dismissed it from his mind.

Michael took out pencil and paper, and wrote a little note. "Darling Hero, I love you. Remember, I shall love you always and whatever happens. When you want me, I will come. Be brave. Michael." He folded it up, knocked on Hero's door and slipped it underneath. Then he went down to breakfast. They were all there, Nigel too. He saw Nigel's lips moving, "It'll be all right, don't worry," he seemed to be saying. The masters treated him with a strange blend of awe and pity and embarrassment, as though he were dying of a plague. Of course, they had seen him and Hero. Every one must know about that now, and every one must be thinking the same as the superintendent. Only Griffin remained constant in friendship. Michael felt nothing but love and fidelity in his attitude. Having paid their respects to the dying man, so to speak, the masters returned to the topic they had been discussing before his entry.

"No, no," Tiverton was saying, "even supposing any of us had the money to buy the place, we'd not get the boys. Do you suppose the parents will send their children to a place where two murders have been committed?"

"Good-bye to our little bread-and-butters, eh, Tiverton?" said Gadsby. "I think you are taking too pessimistic a view of things. We don't know, of course,"–here he lowered his voice discreetly and gave a wary glance in Michael's direction, a perfect example of tactless tact–"what Mrs. Vale's plans are, but I imagine she would be only too glad to get rid of the school. My advice to you, Tiverton, is to sound the parents and see how many would continue to send their boys to us if we moved to some other part of the country. There's nothing like trying, is there?"

Sims leaned across to Tiverton with a worried expression. "I agree with Gadsby. I mean, it's very awkward for some of us. There are so few jobs going nowadays, especially for older men. I'm sure the parents would be sympathetic. After all, it's not our fault that all this has happened."

"Not *our* fault," said Wrench, "but the fault of one of us. Or do you attribute these murders to some outside agency?"

There was a frozen and scandalized silence; the kind of silence that obtained in the common room when someone had the bad taste to bring Russia or religion into the conversation, Michael noticed. He glanced across at Nigel. His friend was sitting quite still, staring noncommittally down his nose and listening far harder than anyone would have supposed. He looked just like a junior master, listening respectfully to his seniors. Griffin broke the silence. "I'm all for the idea. Let things calm down a bit, and then start off somewhere else. I rather fancy you as a head beak, Tiverton."

"Yes," said Wrench enthusiastically, "we could have something like a school. Do away with all these ridiculous petty restrictions and teach boys to think in English instead of Latin."

Wrench was going down badly this morning. His last remark was an implied criticism, not only of the late headmaster, but of the whole school. And the first thing a schoolmaster must learn is to venture no criticism of a school till he has been there at least two years. However much masters may dislike each other or the system under which they are working, the fact of working together in a group unites them in opposition to the criticisms of any newcomer. It was Sims this time who broke the hostile silence. "I know. We could do an awful lot, couldn't we?" he said, his eyes shining. Every one was taken rather aback. Then Tiverton remarked, in the encouraging, slightly patronizing tones which every one seemed to use towards Sims when they were not snubbing or ignoring him, "Well, what would you suggest?"

Blushing and stuttering, the little man proceeded to give a lecture on how he would run a school. It was really very good, Michael said to himself. Sims had evidently given a great deal of thought to the subject; it was a pity he was such a failure in practice. Sims suddenly realized the attention which was being given to his remarks, and trailed off into silence, blushing more furiously than ever. Wrench was looking sulky at this stealing of his thunder. Gadsby patted Sims on the back. "Well done, old man," he said effusively; then, collecting eyes and showing Sims, as it were, like an infant prodigy, "He's got quite a lot under his bald patch, has old Simmie. Ought to be a headmaster. I always say, you never know what there is in a fullah till—"

"Last time you treated us to that observation it referred to a capacity for murder," Wrench pointed out sourly. Every one began simultaneously talking about something else, and breakfast was finished to an accompaniment of inconsequential chatter. When it was over, Nigel drew Griffin and Evans aside. "There are one or two things I want to get clear about yesterday. You'll be able to tell me, Griffin, how is the umpiring arranged–I mean, is it the regular thing for umpires to change in the middle of the game?"

Griffin gave him a long, steady look. "I see.... Yes. We generally do as we did yesterday; take it in spells."

"When did Tiverton ask to be relieved?"

"He didn't. I suggested it at tea. He's got a bit of a gammy leg–the war, you know–and can't do with standing about for too long."

"Was it your own idea to run in for water when Mrs. Vale fainted, Michael?"

"Of course, what else could I do? They'd removed all the tea things from the tent."

"Nobody else suggested it too, I mean?"

"Well, I think somebody did say 'fetch her some water,' as a matter of fact. But I should have gone anyway."

"Who was it?"

"I really have no idea. I was not in a state to notice."

Nigel left them and went into the common room. Tiverton, Wrench and Sims were there. "I want to get it quite clear what every one's position was immediately after the murder," Nigel said. Each of them explained. "And it was when you were bending over Mr. Vale that you noticed Mrs. Vale had fainted and told Evans to get some water?" Nigel was looking impartially at the three of them; it was difficult to know to whom the question was addressed.

"*I* never said that," said Tiverton at once.

"I thought it was you who made the suggestion, Sims," said Wrench.

"I don't think so. I may have, of course. I mean, it's the natural thing to say. Perhaps I did. Everything happened so suddenly. Yet, I don't seem to remember." Sims shook his head in a puzzled way.

Nigel asked a few more questions, then left them. He next walked into the day room, detached Stevens II from a circle of boys loudly discussing the demise of their late headmaster, and brought him out on to the field.

"Stevens," he said, "are there any hiding places in the school which no one would be likely to know about?"

"I say, sir, do you want to hide somewhere?"

"No; I mean places where you could hide a thing, quite a small thing?"

Stevens considered. "Well, sir, I suppose there are some. But I think they'd be pretty easy to find. We've played that game sometimes, but we always found the thing very quickly. It's a bare sort of place. I wish there were some secret passages or something."

"Mm. I was afraid so. By the way, do you ever have fire alarms here–practice ones?"

"Rather. Jolly good sport. There's a whopping great bell, just outside No. 1 dormitory. When it rings every one has to hurry out of school and form up in the yard–that's in the daytime. At night we form up in the dormies instead, and the masters come in and we slide down those chute things. We made somebody ring it once as a test for the Black Spot, but there was a frightful row; he got tanned, and Percy said anyone who did it again would be expelled because if people kept on doing it there might be a fire one day and no one would take any notice because they'd think it was another joke and every one would be burnt to a crisp," Stevens recited breathlessly.

"That's rather a pity," said Nigel slowly, "you see I wanted it rung today. Oh well, it can't be helped."

Stevens' eyes twinkled. "I'll ring it, sir."

"Will you really? That's awfully decent of you. I want it done five minutes before lunch. And you're going to be caught."

Stevens stared at him. "Caught? What do you mean, sir?"

"Mr. Griffin is going to catch you. That's part of the plot. But don't worry about that. I'll see it's all right. And don't tell anyone. You must swear not to tell anyone until Mr. Griffin catches you."

Stevens bound himself by the most bloodcurdling of the Black Spot oaths, and was then sent in to fetch Smithers. Nigel did not expect that the boy would be able to tell him anything very important, but he wanted to clear up loose ends before making his dispositions for the final attack. He was more certain than ever that his theory of the case was the only possible one, but he had no more material proof of it than when he first formed the theory. There was just the chance, a hundred to one chance, a very long shot indeed.... But then, the weapon. It made no difference to his theory where it was found or indeed whether it was found at all, but it piqued him; his total and abject failure to imagine how the murderer had disposed of it. Smithers aroused him from his reverie.

Michael and Griffin, strolling towards school from the far side of the field, saw the meeting between Nigel and Smithers. They saw the two walking slowly along the path towards them, the boy talking up into the man's face and holding with shy affection on to his sleeve. They saw Nigel walk slower, and then suddenly stop quite dead as though he had seen a cobra in front of him; his head jerked forward; Michael was near enough to see that his face was lit up. It did not look like astonishment or satisfaction; it seemed to be a mixture of the two. Michael hurried towards them. He felt certain that something very important had happened; also, he had just remembered again the noise he had heard in the night, and thought Nigel might as well know about it. As he approached, he heard Nigel saying, "... tell the superintendent. It's all right. I'll explain to him."

Smithers moved away. "You look as if the angel Gabriel had appeared in person to you," Michael said.

"An angel in disguise, as they say. I've just been getting the inside dope on the Wemyss killing. This is going to make Armstrong look pretty blue. The trouble is, he'll never believe that I had guessed it long ago—"

"Good Lord, you don't mean that Smithers—?" interrupted Michael.

"Oh no, he is not the perpetrator of the dastardly outrage. It took a good deal more brains than that poor lad is blessed with. Well, I must run along and tell the superintendent that this is where he gets off."

"Just a minute. It's probably unimportant, but something happened last night—"

It was Nigel's turn to interrupt, "You heard the door of your sitting-room open, perhaps."

"Oh, it was *you*, was it?"

"No. Unless I walk in my sleep."

"Then how the deuce—?"

"Elementary, my dear Watson. I'll explain later. By the way, Armstrong may conceivably arrest you and Hero this morning. But don't let it impair your appetite. We'll have you out again before the evening."

Nigel walked off towards the school, leaving Michael gaping in an unbecoming manner. "Your friend seems in good spirits," said Griffin, who had just come up. "Yes, he's just told me that I shall probably be arrested before lunch." It was Griffin who gaped now. After a bit, he said wistfully, "I suppose you wouldn't like someone to give that policeman a sock in the jaw, would you?"

"Not just at present, thanks very much all the same...."

Nigel went through into the private side of the house and discovered Armstrong in the morning-room, gazing complacently at an object laid before him on the table. Nigel moved closer to inspect it. It was a thin length of steel, which had been filed to a point at one end.

"Is this a dagger that I see before me?" he asked.

"That's right, Mr. Strangeways." The superintendent beamed. "Found it in Mr. Evans' room, resting on top of the picture rail. Pearson swore it wasn't there last night. Reckon he didn't look properly, myself. I didn't half tell him off. That was a good guess of yours, sir."

"Pretty obvious. The murderer has been trying to incriminate Evans all along. He fetched the thing in the night from wherever he'd hidden it and stuck it up there."

An almost theatrical expression of skepticism appeared on Armstrong's face.

"Evans thought he heard his sitting-room door being opened last night," continued Nigel.

"Sez he!"

"You're very skittish this morning, superintendent. I shall always know now what the early bird looks like when he has caught the worm."

"Well, sir, mustn't waste any more time. I'm sorry; very painful for you, sir. Got the warrant here," he tapped his side pocket, "going to arrest them now and get it over."

"Sez you."

The superintendent, who had half risen from his chair, lowered himself back into it with great deliberation.

"Now what *is* it, Mr. Strangeways? Here am I just about to arrest a friend of yours for murder, and there are you grinning fit to split your face. If you've really got something, hadn't you better come across with it?"

"I'm going to bring in a boy called Smithers, and I want you to promise not to ballyrag him. He's been withholding valuable information, but quite unintentionally. If you start blustering at him, he'll probably dry up altogether. He's very sensitive, though he doesn't look it."

Armstrong tried to look hurt. "Come sir, you know I never bully witnesses."

Nigel rolled his eyes mutely up to heaven. Then he went out and returned with Smithers. The boy sat down stiffly in a straight-backed chair, casting an apprehensive glance at the superintendent.

"All right," said Nigel, "he won't eat you; he's quite a nice man really." Armstrong passed his finger round the inside of his collar. "Now then," Nigel went on, "the superintendent would like to know what you told me just now. Start where you went upstairs."

"Well, sir, just before the sports I went up to see Mr. Wrench. I'd just finished an impot, you see. He wasn't in his room, so I waited a minute or two."

"And then?" said Nigel encouragingly.

"I looked out of the window. You can see the hayfield from it. I saw Wemyss in the haystack," he broke off lamely.

"Well, what about it? We all know he was in the haystack then. He'd just been murdered," said Armstrong impatiently.

"Oh, n-no," stammered the boy. "I mean he was there, of course. You see he waved to me."

"He WHAT?" bellowed the superintendent, starting out of his chair.

Smithers bit his lip. He looked as if he were going to cry.

"That's all right, old man," said Nigel. "Mr. Armstrong is just a little surprised, that's all."

"Did I hear you say he WAVED to you?" asked the superintendent, making a herculean effort to control his seething emotions.

"Yes, sir. I s'pose he heard me opening the window or something. He was sitting up against the side of the haystack, and he waved his hand."

"Just after morning school Wemyss hinted to Smithers that he was going to be tried for the Black Spot Society–a gross breach of confidence by the way, but Wemyss wanted to crow over Smithers. Smithers said he didn't believe the Black Spot would ever think of having a worm like Wemyss for a member, or words to that effect. So Wemyss told him it was a deadly secret, and he (Smithers) would be murdered if he let out anything about it. That's why Smithers held his tongue when you asked if any boy knew what Wemyss was doing after school," amplified Nigel.

"And when did you leave Mr. Wrench's rooms?" asked the superintendent, in an ominously quiet voice.

"Immediately after that, sir. I only got on to the field just in time for the first race."

Seeing that Armstrong was blowing up for a hurricane, Nigel dismissed the boy with a nod. Armstrong beat his clenched fist slowly against the table.

"That means Wemyss was not murdered till after two-thirty," he said incredulously.

"Your deduction is inexpugnable."

"Gawd! Now we've got to start all over again. Look here, sir, was this your great idea?" Armstrong said suspiciously.

"Yes; believe it or not, I'd decided some time ago that Wemyss hadn't been killed when you thought. But I had no proof till this morning."

"Well, hadn't you better tell me exactly when he was killed, and by whom?"

Nigel looked down his nose. "I think not. I need one thing to prove my case. If I don't get it, I shall have no more material proof than you have against Evans and Mrs. Vale–a sight less, in fact. We can do you a very nice variety of suspects, though. Wrench running out on to the field, so he says, when the pistol went off; he might have taken the haystack en route. All the masters were on the field during the sports and they've all got nice alibis for after the sports. All of them except Griffin were near enough to Vale to murder him during the cricket match. You're going to have a jolly morning's work."

The superintendent groaned. "For all that, sir, Mrs. Vale and Mr. Evans are my choice for the second murder. And if they did the second, one of them presumably did the first," he said doggedly.

"So you're going to arrest them still, are you?"

"Ah, that's another matter."

Nigel blinked at Armstrong in a friendly way. "You know, I wish you would. I half promised Evans you would, in fact."

Armstrong gaped.

"You see," Nigel went on, "the murderer wants them hung. Every one is expecting you to arrest them. If you don't, the murderer will know you've found some new evidence, and I'm rather afraid he may get impatient and have a shot at doing them in himself."

Armstrong hesitated. "That's only your theory, sir."

"Please. You can't do any harm by arresting them. And we don't want any more murders for a day or two." Nigel spoke lightly, but there was a strong compulsion in his look. "Don't you see," he added, "it will put the murderer off his guard too. Knowing they are in prison, he may get careless and give something away when you question him on your new lines."

Armstrong extricated his huge bulk from the chair. "Very well, sir, as you say, it can't do any harm."

"That stiletto affair, what do you make of it?" asked Nigel.

"It's queer, sir. An ordinary carpenter's tool, you can see for yourself, with the end filed to a point. Wiped clean, of course; no fingermarks or traces of blood. Pearson is inquiring which of the masters used the carpenter's shop here and whether any tools are missing. Anything strike you about it–the weapon, I mean?" Armstrong gave Nigel a sly look.

"Well, I don't know. Yes, of course, why has the handle been removed?"

"Exactly, sir. And I can tell you for why. It had to be removed in order that the weapon might be hidden. I've tried with a tool of the same size that had the handle, and you can see it just sticking out over the top of the picture rail. And, by Jove, sir! Look at it this way. If the murderer, as you suggest, put it there to incriminate Mr. Evans, he'd have left the handle on because he'd want it to be noticed. Therefore, I say it's Mr. Evans who put it there."

"Think again. It was mere chance that Evans didn't go into his sitting room before you this morning. If the murderer had any sense, he wouldn't leave the handle on, because Evans might notice it, and get rid of the weapon before you came. He was pretty sure you'd look again, so he arranged it that an expert search would find it, but a casual glance shouldn't."

"Umm. You've got a brain-box all right, Mr. Strangeways. Well, handle or no handle, I must be getting on with the job. See you later."

As Armstrong left the room, Nigel was muttering to himself, "The handle; the handle; why? There's more to it than that, I'm certain."

He went out and found Griffin. He told him about the false alarm of fire that was scheduled for twelve fifty-five. "Now, first, I want every one out of the school, boys and masters. If necessary, you must start a panic in the common room yourself. And second, when every one's been outside for about five minutes, you've got to catch Stevens II–he'll try to skulk out unnoticed–and make a great fuss about a practical joke. Get him to confess publicly, before all the masters."

"I'll see to all that."

"Good man. I'm hoping that that five minutes will give me the key to everything."

Nevertheless, sitting again with the superintendent at twelve-fifty, Nigel felt as nervous as a dramatist on the first night of his first play. It is one thing to make psychological deductions, and quite another to follow them blindfolded into the minefield of fact. He stirred uneasily and looked at his watch, and became aware that Armstrong was speaking.

"... Like a cat on hot bricks, as you might say. I don't believe you've been listening at all, Mr. Strangeways. Is the murderer late for his appointment, or what is it?"

"Listening? Oh yes, I've been listening–'the bell invites me. Hear it not, Duncan; for it is a knell that summons thee to heaven or to hell'; or shall we say, 'me to heaven and thee to hell.' You were saying—"

"An inch or two further. They were all at the sports. Can't swear to each other's presence for every minute of the time, of course. You can call it a perfect alibi or no alibi at all. But what does it signify? Who's going to commit a murder with all those people walking around?"

"He couldn't be seen in the haystack."

"He had to get to it, didn't he? And back? No, the only hope is tea time. I've had another talk with that Mould. He's a poor sort of witness, but he admits that he may not have had Griffin under his eye the whole time they were tidying up the field. I know four o'clock was fixed as the final limit, but I've just had a talk with Dr. Maddox on the phone and he says that rigor is often delayed by sudden death. Now supposing Wemyss—"

Armstrong's disquisition was cut short by a terrific clangor overhead. Stevens II was certainly doing himself proud. The tongue of the great fire bell hammered and yammered as though London Town was burning, filling their ears with harsh waves of sound. Armstrong looked startled for a moment, then he winked slyly at Nigel. "You mentioned a knell, didn't you, sir?"

"Yes. This is zero-hour. Just go and stimulate the panic, will you? I want the school to myself for a few minutes."

Nigel went and peeped through the door that divided the private side from the school. The pot seemed to be boiling admirably. Boys were scurrying out by the two main exits. A hum of wild surmise and several half-repressed female shrieks came from the kitchen and dining hall on his left. Masters began to emerge from the common room; Gadsby trying not to hurry; Sims almost scuttling at his side; Tiverton walking calmly to one of the doors and rebuking in sub-acid tones four boys who were trying to get through it simultaneously. Last came Griffin and Wrench. Griffin had a firm grip of the other's elbow. Nigel heard Wrench saying, "… fantastic! Who the hell would arrange a fire practice for today?" "Some ass probably set fire to the dinner. Come along, we're supposed to go outside."

Nigel waited till the sounds in the school had died down and he could hear Tiverton calling the roll on the field. Then he dashed into the common room, went up to one of the lockers, rummaged in it, withdrew something, studied it for half a minute, and ran out through the private side on to the field. It had been so much easier than he expected: and yet, no; it was all of a piece.

"What was all that din?" he said to the group of masters. "Sounded like the end of the world."

"Some ass rung the fire-alarm. Griffin's gone to investigate. Stevens II didn't answer his name, so I expect he's the culprit," said Tiverton.

"A queer day to choose for a practical joke," grumbled Wrench. "Oh, here he comes."

Griffin rolled on to the field, leading Stevens urgently by the ear. Tiverton stepped forward.

"Was it you who rang that bell?" His voice snapped like a whip.

Stevens II wriggled and cast a doubtful glance at Nigel, who did not return it.

"You don't deny it? You needn't look so proud of yourself." Stevens didn't, as a matter of fact, but Tiverton was "in a fair bate," as the boys put it, quite pale with anger. "It was a stupid, baby trick. Get inside and I'll deal with you after lunch."

The school trailed in again. Nigel and Armstrong remained behind for a moment.

"Well, are you happy now, sir?"

"Mm. So, so." Nigel looked, in point of fact, abstracted and rather melancholy. He fingered something that reposed in his capacious inside pocket. "And what are you going to do this afternoon, Armstrong?"

"Just keep on at it, sir, until the oracle sees fit to speak; just keep pegging away, that's how mysteries are solved, you know, sir."

"Yes. Pegging away. I wonder what the source of that metaphor is. Clothes-pegs, whisky-pegs, tent-pegs—" his eyes blazed up like a heath on fire. "Oh! oh, my holy heavens! What abysmal fools we are! Tent-pegs. Quick!" And he dragged the superintendent towards the place where Vale's body had died and fallen.

Chapter XIII

"Give Me Some Light: Away!"

The marquee had been taken away early that morning. But it was not, apparently, in the marquee that Nigel was interested. He went down on his knees, close to the spot where the body had lain, the superintendent watching him indulgently, like a bear the antics of its cub, and prodded a long stick into a hole in the ground; then he moved along a yard or two and prodded again; then he got on to his feet and beckoned to the superintendent.

"Look on this puncture and on this." Armstrong bent and peered into the second cavity. He shook his head, bewildered. He moved over to the first, peered, stiffened and pounced.

"Good Lord, Mr. Strangeways, you've got it! This hole goes down much deeper. It's–well, I'll be damned for a—" The superintendent made a number of discreditable reflections on his ancestry.

"I doubt if it's as bad as all that," Nigel said soothingly, "it would have taken in anyone. This murderer is infinitely subtle, but his nerve is greater even than his subtlety. It takes brains to think of how to hide the vital clues right under our noses, but it takes even more nerve to go and do it. The courage of despair," he went on, half to himself, "no, not quite 'despair'; call it—"

Armstrong interrupted, "That's all very well, sir, but I can't let myself off so easily. To think that that blasted dagger was sticking in the ground the whole time while we were turning every one and everything inside out. I swear I'll be glad to get the fellow hung," he said vindictively.

"It's an example of safety in numbers. One tent-peg would have attracted attention; but a dozen of 'em, all sitting round quietly, and pulling their weight and looking thoroughly respectable. No, you might as well have gone tearing up the bushes expecting to find a blade instead of a root."

"How do you figure out the details, Mr. Strangeways?"

"I imagine the murderer got hold of an ordinary tent-peg, sawed off the end and fitted that chisel thing into the top. Then he waited for his opportunity and substituted the contraption for one of the pegs that were already in the ground after the tent had been put up. The arrangements for these school functions are apt to be pretty identical from year to year, so he'd know exactly where Vale was likely to sit–the contiguity of the position to the tent probably gave him the idea to start off with–and chose the peg that would be nearest to his seat. Or he may have done it after the seats were arranged. You can ask Tiverton for times; he superintended the seating."

"Yes, by Gad," broke in Armstrong eagerly, "he had only to stand unobtrusively near Mr. Vale, wait till a crucial moment of the game, pull the tent-peg dagger out of the ground, stab him, and put it back. I dunno, it sounds so easy. It *was* easy, mechanically, as you might say. But, just think, sir, would you or I ever bring ourselves to do it? I mean, even at the most critical point of a game, you can't be certain that every one will have his eyes fastened on it."

"You or I, or most people, would certainly not bring ourselves to do it. But we are normal people. The murderer is abnormal or, shall we say, every one is abnormal when he commits murder. He is either blinded by the heat of the moment, or he has screwed himself slowly up to the state of mind in which one is automatically compelled, as it were, to take advantage of the occasion and one's own preparations. He was quite safe up till that point, too. You see, if no occasion had offered, he'd just have left the weapon in the ground and removed it at the first opportunity. That is another point of similarity between the murder and—" he broke off suddenly. But the superintendent was following out a private train of thought.

"That business of the seating, you know, sir, the murderer couldn't rely on Mr. Vale being near enough to that particular tent-peg to make it safe. And he doesn't seem the sort of cove who leaves much to chance. It was Mr. Tiverton, you say, who arranged the seating?" he continued after a pause, "and Mr. Tiverton stopped umpiring at the tea interval, and Mr. Tiverton was the first to be seen bending over the body. Mm."

Nigel eyed him speculatively. "Tiverton and Sims were the first, to be strictly accurate. By the way, did you find out anything about the weapon itself?"

"It comes from the school workshop all right–at least, Gadsby says there's an identical one missing; he's in charge of the workshop, you know. But all the masters had access to it."

"And your case against Evans and Mrs. Vale?"

"Well, that's about as it was, sir. She could easily have reached the tent-peg from where she was sitting. They could have done it, of course. But if they did, why leave the weapon in his room for us to find? The trouble in this case is the difficulty of establishing motive. Evans and

Mrs. Vale have a pretty clear one for the second murder and a conceivable one for the first. Wrench might have killed Wemyss because
the boy had found out about him and Rosa, but why should he kill Mr.
Vale?"

"His career. Vale might also have discovered his relations with the girl.
He'd never get taken on at any school if that became public."

"You may be right, sir. I must have another go at Rosa. Then there's
Sims. He had a grudge against Wemyss all right. But again, why Vale?"

"He had a first-class row with the headmaster the other day." Nigel
gave the details.

"Did he just? Excuse me, sir, but I thought we were to share all information," said Armstrong, looking rather aggrieved.

"I've not been double-crossing you. That fact could not be of any significance till Vale was murdered. It told us nothing about the Wemyss
affair."

"That's true enough, I suppose. Though it might have helped us to prevent the second murder. Still, motive again. We don't go killing our superior officers because they put us on the mat. Now take Tiverton. He might
have killed Wemyss, and he's still more suspect in the case of Vale. But
why should he?"

Nigel related some of the conversation at breakfast that morning. "So,
you see, he would have the good will of the masters and a fair number of
the parents at least. With Vale out of the way he stood a good chance of
being headmaster, supposing the school continued."

"But he'd no earthly reason, as far as we know, for murdering Wemyss.
Then there's Griffin. He looks more promising for the first murder, but
there's no motive; and he couldn't possibly have done the second. I suppose the two murders were committed by the same person." Armstrong
fingered his chin doubtfully.

"That's pretty evident, I think. What about Gadsby, by the way?"

Armstrong snorted. "That soaker! He'd not have the nerve. And what
motive had he got, anyway?"

Nigel looked down his nose. The superintendent kicked his heels irritably. "Here am I going on like a talkie, and all the time you know who
the murderer is. One would think you wanted him hushed up."

"I'm sorry, but it's been very difficult. I was certain in my own mind
that I knew, but I had no facts; and at any moment new facts might have
come to light which would have disproved my theory."

"Well, have they?"

Nigel ignored the question. "I've got hold of the key now, I think. But
I've not had time to–er–examine it properly yet. I want to have a reconstruction of the first crime at two-thirty this afternoon. I think I can prom-

ise that will give you the criminal. We don't need the boys, of course, just the masters. I'm going in to lunch now and I'll tell them."

"Do you want Mr. Evans?"

"No. No, we can do without him. In fact, he'd very much better not come."

"Very well, sir. I'll be back by two-fifteen. I must get on to the firm that supplied the tent first. Not that that will be any use. Presumably the murderer came out last night and substituted the tent-peg he'd originally removed for the doctored one, but I reckon he's not left any fingerprints about. Still, the men may have noticed Tiverton moving the chairs. Got to do something: I can't just stand about while you solve the problem."

The superintendent touched his cap and moved away. Nigel went slowly up to his room and, taking out the object which he had found in the common room, proceeded to make a thorough examination of it. Then he slipped it under his mattress: one could take no chances now; if its owner got it back again and destroyed it, he could snap his fingers in Nigel's face. He rather wished he had shown it to the superintendent. And yet, no, that would have deprived him of his triumph. Nigel had a weakness for consummating a case in the most spectacular way possible; it was a kind of extravagant repayment to himself for all the wearisome business that preceded. He thought again. Not this time; he must forgo part of his spectacle. Had one of those hypothetical observers, so dear to the heart of Thomas Hardy, been present in Nigel Strangeways's bedroom at that moment, he would have seen on his face emotions highly unsuited to a detective on the threshold of success—pity, regret, indecision, pensive brooding, determination. After a little he looked at his watch and went hurriedly downstairs. A short search in the school and he had found an object similar to the one removed from the common room and put it carefully back in the place of the other. Then he waited for the masters to come out from lunch.

When they entered, it became evident that there had been some controversy during lunch over the Stevens II outrage. "Tan the little blighter's hide for him," said Gadsby, "nothing like teaching 'em a lesson. But I should let it stop there, Tiverton, really I would."

"We can scarcely afford any more scandals just now, certainly," remarked Wrench.

Griffin turned rather distractedly to Nigel; he clearly did not know his cue. "Look here, Strangeways, you're not an interested party. Tiverton says Stevens ought to be kicked out because of this bogus fire-alarm business. It happened once before and Vale said if it happened again the offender would be expelled, but—"

"It seems awfully silly, making such a fuss over a trifling thing like this, when–well, I mean to say, murder rather puts everything else in the shade," stammered Sims.

"That is obvious enough," said Tiverton acidly, "but our job is to run this school and keep discipline; we can't let them get away with anything just because a murder's been committed."

"One merely suggests that it's a bit gratuitous expelling boys when half of them will be taken away by their parents anyhow," said Wrench in his most irritating voice.

"Like throwing the rats out of the sinking ship," smiled Griffin.

Nigel, gazing modestly down his nose, meditated on the curiosities of human nature. Here was a body of quite ordinary men, seriously discussing a boy's delinquency, with a fellow creature lying murdered, scarcely cold, as the papers would say, a few yards off. It was the normal working of their defense mechanism, of course. In proportion to the seriousness with which each of them was taking Stevens' escapade, one could estimate the depth of his reaction to the murder. Tiverton evidently felt it most acutely; Wrench, probably, next, for cynicism and flippancy were his type of protection against the stirrings of the heart. Nigel became aware that Gadsby was speaking to him. It was one of Gadsby's most irritating characteristics, to ask a rhetorical question and single out some individual for an answer.

"Well, I really am not qualified to express an opinion. But I think it might be allowed to wait over till this evening. You see, I want to have a reconstruction of the crime–the first crime–at two-thirty."

There was a sensible tightening of the atmosphere, a feeling as though the ghost they had been trying to exorcise was at the door again. Gadsby was the first to speak. "A reconstruction of the crime? You mean you've not found out yet—?"

"Don't be a fool," said Griffin, "you don't suppose Evans and Mrs. Vale really did it, do you?"

Gadsby bridled. "I never said I did. But, damn it all, somebody must have. And they *have* been arrested."

"It's just a blind, is it–their arrest?" said Tiverton slowly. His brown, tight-drawn face appeared expressionless.

"Not exactly that," said Nigel equivocally, "the police have a very good case against them, I'm afraid. They never take action unless they have, you know. Of course, it may be that Armstrong has been badgered into it. I imagine the chief constable has been getting pretty impatient."

Griffin laughed grimly. "I should think it's about as easy to badger Armstrong into doing anything against his will as to barrack a Lancashire opening batsman into scoring runs."

Wrench leaned forward. "What's this about a reconstruction of the crime?"

"I'm asking every one–all of you, that is–to go through the same actions as you did at the beginning of the sports."

"And what's the big idea?"

"Not a very big one, I fear," said Nigel mildly, "but I want to get the relative positions clear, and there's a chance that something may turn up, some loophole we've not noticed before."

"Is this a sort of Hamlet stunt, the murderer going to rush off calling for lights and so on?" said Wrench with a sneer. "You have a very ingenuous mind for a detective, Strangeways."

"Are the boys to take part in this–er–reconstruction?" said Sims.

"No. That will not be necessary."

"Which means," said Tiverton, "that you suspect one of us in this room to be the murderer."

Nigel looked him full in the eyes for a moment. "That is an unwarrantable inference. I hope to expose the method of the crime by my reconstruction. There's no doubt that the murderer was a person fully cognizant of the workings of the school. I can't go further than that at present."

There was an awkward silence, broken finally by Gadsby. "Aren't you rather frightened, then, rubbing shoulders all day with a murderer? I wonder he doesn't have a go with you," he said with gruesome jocularity.

"Perhaps he considers it unnecessary," said Wrench.

Nigel disregarded the impolite innuendo. "I can't say I'm terribly frightened, though I must admit I keep a revolver under my pillow. I've rubbed shoulders with criminals before, and it was generally they who suffered the most."

The mention of the revolver created a minor sensation. It brought home to them the state of spiritual blockade in which they had been living for a whole week. Though it was not before their eyes, it seemed more solid and vivid than had the body of Percival Vale with the little rivulet of crimson down the back. Gadsby, with his usual infelicity, put the general thought into words:

"Somehow brings the thing home to a fullah–that, don't it? I mean, about Strangeways' revolver—"

"We don't all inhabit fools' paradises," interrupted Wrench sharply.

Gadsby ignored him. "It's amazing how small things stick in one's head, don't you think, Tiverton? I remember—"

Wrench interrupted again. "Like fish bones in one's throat." He took out his watch. "Nearly two. Just about this time a week ago one of us was getting set to commit a murder. I wonder how he feels about it now."

Tiverton jerked in his chair and exclaimed, "For God's sake, Wrench, try to behave like a normal human being and not like a Greek chorus."

Nigel rose. "May I ask you all, then, from two-fifteen onward to go through exactly the same actions as you did last Wednesday." He looked impassively towards the corner where Wrench was sitting. "*Exactly* the same actions." Wrench turned his face away a little. "I shall take Evans' part myself. That reminds me. Will you give me the stopwatch he had, Griffin? What was the exact time the race took?"

Griffin told him the record and after a little fumbling in one of the lockers produced the watch. Nigel turned to Sims. "Could I have just a word with you?"

Four pairs of ears were strained to their uttermost as the two went out into the passage, but all they could hear was:

"Look here, Sims, I want you to—"

There was silence for a few moments after the voices had died away. Gadsby made one or two attempts to resuscitate the conversation, then he also went out, "to prime himself for the ordeal," Wrench said.

"What do you think of our private investigator now?" asked Griffin.

Tiverton considered. "Well, he doesn't seem to have done much so far; he's supposed to be examining the case in the interests of the school, yet here he is practically accusing us to our faces of harboring a murderer on the staff."

"You mean, if he has found the murderer here, he ought to drop the case and go away with the solution under his hat? A highly immoral suggestion to my mind," commented Griffin.

Wrench broke in. "I say, what is the superintendent driving at now? You know all those questions he's been asking this morning, about where we were standing during the sports and what we were doing after them. It's rather perplexity-making"–Griffin shuddered–"I mean, it was obvious, wasn't it, that the murder was committed before the sports."

"Apparently not," said Tiverton grimly, "otherwise, why this reconstruction of Strangeways'?"

"I wonder what he wants with that watch?" said Griffin.

"And with Sims?" said Wrench.

At about ten minutes after two Armstrong ran Nigel to earth on the hayfield. Armstrong was evidently boiling over with news, but he postponed it for a moment to ask, "What are you doing with all those deck chairs, Mr. Strangeways, sir? Going to set up as a Lido proprietor?"

Nigel acknowledged the jest politely. "No, I am building something to represent the haystack. You are looking very cheerful, aren't you?"

"Just been having another talk with our Rosa." He paused provocatively, but Nigel refused the gambit, so he continued in slightly deflated tones: "I went to Strang's first. No luck with the tent-pegs, of course, but one of their men noticed Tiverton move two of the chairs a bit nearer to the tent."

Nigel stopped working. "Which two chairs?"

"The ones Mr. and Mrs. Vale were to occupy, as far as I can gather from his description. He's coming up this afternoon to verify it."

"And Rosa?"

The superintendent rubbed his hands. "Ah, there, sir, I think I have the advantage of you. You may be able to get round these boys, Mr. Strangeways, sir, but that type of girl—why, I know 'em like I know the back of my hand."

"For shame, Mr. Armstrong, for shame."

Armstrong emitted a sound which, coming from anyone less elephantine, would be called a giggle. "Be that as it may, sir, she's come across with something now, all right."

"I trust you were not brutal to the poor little thing."

"No, no. She didn't need no pressing, as you might say. You see, I know that class of girl. I said to myself that young Wrench is probably getting tired of her, or else he'll be laying off her for other reasons, now's the time to find out how much she really knows. Spiteful she is, see, and she wouldn't mind what she said about Wrench if she thought he'd done with her."

"Can we cut the psychology? There's not much time."

"Well, I got it out of her that Wrench believed Wemyss knew about their affair, had seen him snooping about once just after he'd left her. A fair spitfire she is, Mr. Strangeways; as good as suggested that Wrench had done in young Wemyss to silence him. That's a pretty enough confirmation of motive, isn't it?"

"Hm. Doesn't sound a very reliable witness to me. Spite plus film-fed fantasy equals any amount of lies you like. However … I wonder what he's saying to her now."

Armstrong started.

"Yes. I told them all to go through exactly the same actions from two-fifteen that they went through on the day of the crime. Embarrassing for our Mr. Wrench when you come to think of it! Still, he may not take it literally. We shall see. Ah, things are beginning to start."

They could see Griffin, in the middle of the field, carrying a large revolver and going through a series of pantomime gestures over a row of imaginary hurdles. By his side, Mould, the groundsman, scratched alternately his head and the seat of his trousers. Nigel finished his business with the deck chairs, and walked with the superintendent towards the place where the race had started.

"Now, keep your eyes skinned," he said, "watch very carefully. You observe, I have nothing up my sleeve."

Armstrong made an offensive noise. "Watch? Who am I supposed to watch?"

"Every one."

Five minutes passed. Masters began to emerge from the school building. Griffin approached Nigel, looking expectant. "You're late on your lines," he said, "you've got to say 'Who were you thinking of shooting?' "

"Who were you thinking of shooting?"

"That moron Mouldy's gone and put out one too many sets of hurdles. Business with revolver. First juvenile lead and walking gentleman attempt to retire up left but are intercepted by Gadsby, comic relief. Where is Gadsby, by the way?"

"You've got a good memory. There he is, just coming out."

"He's missed his cue badly. You'd better cut that bit and go on to humorous dialogue with Tiverton, down right."

Nigel went.

"What do we call this in the profession, I wonder," said the irrepressible Griffin, "a post-mortem dress rehearsal. You know, it's rather an eerie business for us. Still, I cannot disappoint muh public and I think you Eenglish policemen are too sweet."

At this point Sims joined their group.

Armstrong muttered something. "A damnfool business, if you ask me, sir. What Mr. Strangeways hopes to get out of it, I don't know. Only seems to have half his mind on it, too."

He pointed to where Nigel was talking in a distrait manner with Tiverton.

"Mm," said Griffin, "you'd think he was listening for something–angel voices, perhaps. Still, I'd put a packet on your distinguished coadjutator; he's the dark horse for me. About time we started the race; we're all here. No, we're not. Where the devil is Wrench?"

Nigel came up to them. Armstrong and Griffin got the shock of their lives when they saw his face. Heaven knows, one might have expected a good number of emotions on it, but not what they saw–not, at this point, sheer astonishment. The astonishment gave way to a look almost of consternation. Then a blind as it were was drawn down over it, and he was standing beside them as impassive as ever.

Griffin touched him gently, as one might touch a sleepwalker. "I was just saying to the super., it's about time the race started."

Nigel blinked. "The race? Oh, yes. Yes. We must get on with the race." He seemed to be pulling himself out of a daydream. His face became suddenly stern and formidable. Then he smiled at Armstrong and drawing him away from the others took a medium-sized exercise book out of one of his pockets. "You're looking bored, Armstrong. How about a little light literature? You'll find a full account of the crime–both crimes–in here. It's in shorthand. I hope you don't mind that. But it will be useful should–should anything go wrong with this little tableau vivant of mine. No, don't read it yet. Just curb your indecent curiosity for a moment or two."

He raised his voice and addressed the scattered groups. "Now, gentlemen, the 440 is about to begin. Will you all go to where you stood for the race, and try to imagine that it is actually being run. Try to follow every phase of the race. You've got to *see* the runners—"

"I say, where's Wrench?" said Tiverton.

"Never mind about Wrench. He'll be on the spot in due course. Now, Griffin."

The gamesmaster moved to the starting point, murmuring to himself, "There's a breathless hush in the close tonight." He took out an imaginary list and allotted stations to six imaginary boys. Then he engineered an intensely dramatic pistol-jam failure. By this time the audience was keyed up to a far higher pitch of excitement than that in which they had awaited the original race. Only Armstrong, standing between the group of masters and the school, watching like a cat the door by which Wrench should presently emerge, was outside the sphere of emotional influence.

"On your marks! Get set!" snapped Griffin. The revolver exploded like the crack of doom. "Come on, Anstruther!" shouted Nigel. The white oval on the turf, the drooping flags, the runners falling into line at the first bend–they all came back out of the past, those sunny images holding in a spell the inward eye of the watchers. Even the superintendent, whose ears were stretched as though to hear the feet of Wrench clattering downstairs, glanced involuntarily towards the expanse of turf before him. And then the spell was broken. Somebody was laughing, somewhere behind them; a cool, amused sort of chuckle; a sound that contained at first a hint of bravado, but soon changed to a quietly triumphant key, as though the performer had conquered his stage-fright and knew he was dominating his audience. He was. They whipped round all together. For a second they could see nothing; nothing but the path and the flat stubble of the hayfield. Then all eyes focused on the structure of deck chairs where the haystack had been. A head and shoulders showed above its top. Sims was there, peering benignly at them, chuckling away to himself. He looked like an undersized but confident cleric. He placed his hands on the deck chairs in front of him, as on a pulpit cushion, and gave his congregation the preliminary look-over, half winsome, half compelling, of the popular preacher. Then he began to address them. His tones were level and flowing. An expression of inward joy seemed to illuminate his plain face. One forgot the rabbit teeth and the ridiculous straggling mustache.

"It was quite easy, you see," he said, "every one was so intent on the race. The murderer had only to walk into the haystack, like I did just now, and strangle his victim, and walk back again. There was plenty of time. It was the same at the cricket match. One of the tent-pegs was really a dagger, you know. He just waited for his moment, pulled it out, stabbed once, and put it back again. It only took a couple of seconds. You see, in moments of great excitement, every one's attention is focused on one point and the whole strength of mass-emotion keeps it fixed on that point. Pickpockets work on that principle, of course."

He paused. There was a sigh of sheer amazement, half at his words, half at the strange transfiguration of himself. They almost expected him to raise a glass of water to his lips. Incredulous murmurs began to break out. Sims held up a hand, with an ineffable gesture of authority. In the renewed silence he began to speak again, his voice gathering power and volume.

"You are doubtless eager to know who the murderer was. I will keep you in suspense no longer. To evolve such schemes required brilliance–I think I may even say genius: to carry them out, a nerve and resolution beyond the capacity of most men. But there was someone you had always overlooked; one who appeared insignificant, incapable of brilliance or resolution. You ignored him or despised him, according to your natural bent. That was very silly of you. And he did something none of you could have ever contrived or dared to do. You see, gentlemen, I killed Wemyss and Vale. I hated them and I killed them–right in front of your noses. That is all, I think."

There was a second of blank and ravaged silence. Then Armstrong darted forward. But Sims reached unhurriedly into a pocket, gave them all a last flashing arrogant smile, drew out a revolver and shot himself dead. He had had his triumph.

Chapter XIV

Memoirs and Commentary

"Yes, hate. Just as in the celebrated Cain-Abel case. But the motive was too simple, too primitive for our sophisticated Armstrong. Murder for love; murder for money; murder to cover up a guilty secret; these are common coin for us nowadays. But to go and kill someone just because you hate him, that has become almost unintelligible to us. Which is why poor Sims so very nearly got away with it. He would have, too, if he hadn't tried to get two separate hates off his chest simultaneously."

"Wemyss and Vale? But you can't call that 'simultaneously.' "

"Oh no. I mean Wemyss and Vale on the one hand and you two on the other."

It was after dinner on the day of Hugo Sims' first and last public triumph. Nigel, Hero and Michael were talking in the drawing room. They were feeling exhausted and happy. Nigel had a successful case behind him, and in front of him a large earthenware pot of tea. Hero was sitting on the floor by Michael's chair, with a hand in his and her golden hair shining against his knee; she looked wan still, like Eurydice just emerged from the shades, but the strain was gone; her body and her heart were relaxed. Michael looked down on her with infinite tenderness. It was as though she had come safe through childbirth; then he turned a rather bewildered glance on Nigel.

"Us two?"

"Mm. He bit off a little more than he could chew there." Nigel applied himself to his tea-drinking. Michael stirred restively, and Hero looked up at him—a sleepy look, that seemed to swim up from great depths, half-drowned with love.

"No doubt in your infinite wisdom you will vouchsafe us some explanation. Or is it one of the things we are not meant to understand." Michael spoke in the friendly, challenging, slightly acrid tones he and Nigel had used in their night-long controversies at Oxford. His friend, smiling, replied in the same vein.

"You wish to pose a question? Proceed. You have our ear."

"Dozens. But first, what's all this about Sims hating Hero and me? I know every one treated him like a subnormal child, but we were no worse than the rest, surely?"

"Ah, no, it wasn't that. As a matter of fact, I may have been a bit inaccurate in talking about pure hate. In your case, at any rate, the motive was more complicated. I daresay one would find that Sims was descended from a long line of evangelical missionaries," Nigel added inconsequentially.

Michael stared. "Why, his grandfather was a missionary in China, I know that. But what on earth—?"

"It fits in. Missionaries are and always have been the most intolerant people on the face of the earth. They have to be, I suppose," Nigel broke off and apparently lapsed into reverie.

"You know, if you'd lived in ancient Greece, the Delphic oracle would have had to go out of business. Do cut out the cryptic stuff; we're simply itching to hear all about it. Begin at the beginning, go to the end, and there we may allow you to take a breath."

"The beginning? That would take too long. It began before Sims was born." Nigel fumbled in a pocket and drew out some sheets of paper. "The early Christian fathers sowed a new instinct in the heart of man, and it was watered by their spiritual heirs, the Puritans. Instinct is not the right word, I know, but that fear and hatred of the body is so strong and pervasive, one can scarcely give it any other name. It comes out in all of us at times, often in the most curious forms, and with Sims it was a sleeping volcano. We've found a secret diary he kept during the last two months; the superintendent let me make extracts from it. Extraordinarily interesting for an alienist's casebook." He waved the sheets of paper vaguely in the air.

"When does the lecture finish? I'm going out for a drink."

"Now, now; am I conducting this case or are you? Control yourself, old boy, control yourself," said Nigel coldly.

"You *are* sweet," Hero exclaimed suddenly, full in Nigel's face. He looked startled, then smiled delightfully back at her.

"Oi! Oi! This has got to stop! You can't talk like that to every stray male you meet," protested Michael.

"Stray male to you, sir. That's just what Sims wrote in his diary–'this has got to stop,' I mean. You see, he had seen you and Hero making love to each other; he deliberately followed you and watched you after a bit. It was a kind of self-torture to him, I expect, but he kept whipping up his Puritan blood like that till in the end he believed himself the instrument of God to punish the sinner. That's why he tried to throw the guilt of the murders on you. It's all in this diary of his, but I don't think I'll read out those bits; he's terribly outspoken on the subject, and there's nothing quite so nasty as the Puritan's fascinated horror of sex, when he finds words for it."

"Good Lord! Good Lord! the poor devil," Michael said slowly, with strange compassion in his voice.

"But I don't understand," said Hero, "how could he have spied on us? Surely we would have seen him? And we weren't as blatant as all that."

"He did, anyway. You'll understand in a minute how he was able to. It's a terrifying thought; that mild, insignificant-looking little man going about with a positive hell of disgust in his heart, fanning the flames with the images of his own furious imagination–horrible. But there's no use us being morbid, too. I'll get on with it and read some extracts from the diary."

Nigel began to read:

"*May 9th*. In Batford woods again. Chiff-chaff, willow-warbler, wood-warbler, white throat, several tree-creepers; the bullfinches; the redstarts' nest finished. A lovely day–warblers and woodlarks in full songlike Eden– 'where every prospect pleases and only man is vile'–E. and his whore here again–the serpent of sin in the garden–wanton–filthy—"

"And then there's a good deal of plain speaking and–er–detail, which may be omitted," said Nigel.

"So that's how he found out," whispered Michael slowly, "birdwatching ... his field glasses, of course."

"Yes," replied Nigel, "and that's how *I* found out–or rather, how the possibility first entered my head."

"Meaning—?"

"That conversation you told me about. In Tiverton's room after the first murder. Don't you remember? Sims saw a yellow-bottomed gorse-tit or something, so we had to stop while he stalked it.... And talking of birds, where's Wrench? Stalking the fair Rosa, I expect. And then the scene Sims made about that–people behaving like animals–quite a militant outburst, you told me."

"But he was drunk. He'd just had a few with Gadsby."

"Exactly. *In vino veritas*. Repressions pushed aside, timidity left standing, the real man appeared, and his ruling passion, or one of them."

Hero stirred and looked up at Nigel. "But I still don't follow just how that put you on the right track."

"Well. This is taking things out of their right order. Still, the more I looked at the facts, the more one interpretation seemed to emerge. You see, the whole haystack business smelt of stage-management. It was altogether too much of a coincidence that you two and a corpse should visit a haystack within a couple of hours. Armstrong drew the natural inference, that you were the cause of the corpse being there. I, with a possibly misplaced confidence in Michael's freedom from homicidal tendencies, refused to play. There was only one other explanation, that the corpse was the cause of you being there; in other words, that you had been framed."

"Look on this picture and on this," interrupted Michael.

"That will be all from you. So, to cut it short, I had to find out who had it in for you, and why. It was Sims' great mistake, trying to kill two, or rather three, birds with one stone. It gave me a line. The fact that the scene was laid to compromise *both* of you was where Sims fell down. Too ambitious altogether. It narrowed the issue to someone who knew about your being lovers and objected to it. Judging from the madcap way you were behaving, there was nothing to prevent anyone *knowing*. But there seemed no one, except Hero's husband, who would have any reason for objecting. I mean, for letting his objection carry him to such lengths."

"Quite good for a beginner, isn't he, Hero?" said Michael.

"So Percy Vale was the obvious suspect. Yet I couldn't take that. For two reasons. First, the injured husband killing a boy in order to take revenge on his wife and her lover. Too tortuous. Too melodramatic. It simply isn't done. Second, Vale had plenty of money and an assured position; the revenge motive was not likely to be reinforced by a gain motive. Anyway, he wasn't the right type, not for this type of murder. I could imagine him killing from fear–the cornered rat. But not for gain or out of passion. If he knew about you two, his reaction would be self-pity, followed by spite, cruelty, cat and mouse stuff, refusing to allow divorce proceedings–not murder."

Nigel broke off, looking apologetic. "I say, Hero, I'm terribly sorry. You must think me a cold-blooded automaton, going on like this."

"It's all right," smiled Hero. "I don't at all. It's like–well–talking about a dream, or a previous existence. Go on."

"That left me with X. Someone with a motive for killing Wemyss and an equally strong motive for putting you two away. It had to be that, or a most indigestible coincidence. Moreover, it had to be something more than the ordinary conventional objection to 'immorality'; that would have been satisfied by exposing you to Vale. It had to be the kind of frenzied moral indignation which is rooted so often in sexual perversion or frustration. When I heard about Sims' outburst in Tiverton's room, I knew at once he was a possibility. The more so because of his timid, unassertive exterior. Of course I kept my eyes open for other candidates; Wrench and Tiverton were both in my mind for a little; Wrench especially, he seemed to have the most likely motive for both murders. I admit I was at first as badly beaten as the superintendent by the simplicity of Sims' motive. But the diary comes in useful here."

He began reading again.

"*June 12th*. A queer thing happened today. In form. Wemyss had played a most vicious and unpardonable trick on me. They are all against me—boys, masters, every one. Every one always has been. But he is the worst. And now I know why. Now I know what I have got to do. I thought I was going to faint. As though my head was going to burst. Then it was like some obstacle there being swept away, like a logjam breaking up. Everything became quite clear. It was funny I didn't see it before. The boy has a devil, of course. It contaminates all around him. I know what I have to do. Kill and spare not, saith the Lord. And I am his chosen instrument."

There was a long silence in the room, as though a visitor from a different world had entered. Then Michael spoke, with something like awe in his voice:

"Good God. He was—he must have been a religious maniac, I didn't know they existed—like this, I mean."

"They were common enough not so long ago," said Nigel, "and no one thought of calling them maniacs. Many of the Old Testament prophets, all the inquisitors, were made like that." He turned to the diary. "I'll pass over the next few entries. They are rather appalling reading. You can see his feeling about Wemyss and his feeling about you two converging, till they met and the explosion came. But here's an interesting passage, showing another aspect of his psychological structure."

"*June 16th*. If only they knew what they had in their midst, what I really am! The drunkard Gadsby; the lecher Evans; Tiverton, with his damned patronizing airs—if they only knew! And you, Percival Vale, pedant and cuckold, you'd change your tone pretty quick. But I'll show them. Which of them would dare to contemplate what I am contemplating, or to do what I shall do? And I'll do it before all their eyes. But I must wait for guidance, for the appointed time. I will be patient, I can afford to wait, they will not escape me. I don't mind now that they will never know—not till I'm dead and my Doomsday Book is brought to light. I shall have given life and I shall have taken away. I shall have ruled their lives in secret. That will be my present satisfaction."

Nigel paused. "That explains everything, really. You weren't there when he delivered his own funeral oration; it was on the same lines. You see, even his religious mania was not the fundamental thing. In fact, it was not much more than a rationalization, the way his murderer's state of mind justified itself to him. No; at the bottom of the heap we find that old chestnut, the inferiority complex. Subject for newspaper symposium, 'Can a worm turn? Mr. Nigel Strangeways, the celebrated vermicologist, says "Yes." ' But seriously. Didn't Cleopatra call her asp a worm? Anyway, the serpent is the perfect symbol of inferiority feeling; for ever humbled in the dust, trodden under foot, despised, nursing its venom secretly, deadly when goaded into action."

Hero spoke, rather shakily, "You know, I don't think I can bear any more of that diary. Won't you tell us your part in the business instead?"

"Very well. Sims was my chief suspect. The opinion I began to form of his character and the conclusion I was gradually compelled to adopt as regards the time and method of Wemyss' murder, fitted together. After a bit it became evident, by a process of elimination, that he must have been killed while the 440 was being run. Now it's perfectly true that, at moments of great emotional stress–an exciting race, for instance–every one's attention is likely to be wholly absorbed in the spectacle before their eyes. But no ordinary murderer would take the risk of there being no exceptions to the rule. Ergo, the murderer was extraordinary, mentally deranged. Secondly, apart from the risk, there was the fantastic nature of the setting. There must have been a hundred other ways in which a murderer could get rid of Wemyss and involve you two. But he chose the most public, the most theatrical. It was a clear case of exhibitionism, and the inferiority-ridden person often tends to be exhibitionist in action. Other points in favor–no use for a jury, of course–Sims' asking to be relieved of the stopwatch, and his behavior after the race."

"Good lord," interrupted Michael, "when he came up to me, all worked-up and excited and breathless, it was—"

"Yes. It was not what you supposed. He had popped back into the haystack, strangled the wretched boy, tied a cord round his throat to make certain and returned. Quick action and liable to impart an air of excitement to the agent, but by no means impossible. In fact, not so foolhardy as it sounds. He probably walked backwards, so that he would notice if anyone in the crowd turned round, and he was sheltered from all other sides. If he had seen someone turn round and observe him, he could simply go into the haystack, lug the boy out and ask him what the hell he was doing there. As in the second murder, there was nothing in his actions to rouse suspicion till the very moment of killing."

"Hold up a minute. We haven't mastered the first problem yet, sir. How on earth did he know Hero and I were going to the haystack, and how did he get Wemyss there?"

"That's easy. You must remember he had been trailing you about for some time. He discovered Hero used the loose brick for a pillarbox; he saw her put a note there that night–the night before the sports–took it out and read it. That was his cue. He sent off a Black Spot summons the next morning to Wemyss." Nigel explained the procedure and gave a restrained account of how he had stumbled upon it; the episode of the brazen "nimph" still gave him prickly heat to remember.

"And my silver pencil?"

"The diary doesn't mention it. It was probably just your bad luck, not his stage-property. I asked several of them about it, by the way. Tiverton thought he had seen you using it after the hay battle–his mistake. Sims was noncommittal; I supposed that was his cunning; it would have been a little too obvious if he had sworn to seeing you using it just before the murder. But apparently it was just ignorance. Oh, and I was forgetting. I also announced my discovery of the workings of the Black Spot to several of your fellow-beaks. Sims almost immediately drew the connection between it and the method used to get Wemyss into the haystack. Wrench, who is more intelligent, was definitely slower off the mark. That was one up to Sims; it diverted some of my suspicion temporarily to Wrench. A good double bluff."

Nigel paused, and gazed pathetically into the empty teapot. Hero, affecting not to notice this, said:

"By the way, did you find anything out about that note to James Urquhart."

"Oh yes. That's all in the diary. It was just a second line of defense supposing you two somehow wriggled out of suspicion. Sims had been to dinner with him several times, noticed the disparity between his apparent expenditure and his presumed income, and drew the same inference as Armstrong did. He typed the note on Michael's typewriter, so that suspicion was neatly contrived to fall either on Michael or Urquhart. If Urquhart kept the note, Michael would be in the soup; if he destroyed it, he automatically became a suspect himself; the police would be bound to question whether it had ever existed. Of course, the whole plan had to be thought out at lightning speed. He found Hero's note on the night of the nineteenth, read it immediately after she had put it behind the loose brick, and at once sent off the note to Urquhart, so that it reached him by the morning post. He must have stayed awake into the small hours, working out the other details."

"So you had Sims marked down quite early on?"

"Yes. I hadn't really much doubt. Not after I'd heard of his outbreak about sex, and seen the kind of reading he favored–evangelical divines, hellfire, and so on–to back it up. But I hadn't any proof either, not a stitch of it, to clothe my shameless skeleton of theorizing. In fact, he'd probably be alive now but for his vanity—"

"What on earth—?"

"Don't you see? A repressed character, all shut in on himself, no confidantes. What does a person like that do? Keep a diary, ninety-nine times out of a hundred. Same character commits a brilliant, daring exhibitionist murder; asserts himself at last, but he can't ask anyone to give him credit for it. What does he do again? Puts it down in the diary. The unrecognized genius. At any rate, it will be published after his death. Posterity will recognize him. Oh yes, I'd banked on that diary, but I couldn't think where the devil he kept it. You see, the police searched all the masters' rooms after the first murder, and they don't miss things. Of course, it was the old protective coloring trick again. Had me beat. You remember that story of Poe's–the important letter hidden in the letter-rack, staring every one in the face while they tore carpets up and panelling down—"

"Will you stop this meandering," Michael interrupted. "We don't want an informative talk on American literature. We shall expire if you don't tell us this instant where it was."

"Keep calm! News is coming. It was an ordinary school exercise book–his Black Book. He kept a tally of his impositions in it, too."

"But do you mean to say he carried this keg of dynamite about with him, brought it into class, and into the common room? Why, it's crazy."

"Well, he was crazy. More things than perfect love can cast out all fear. And it was all of a piece with the two murders. Wildly risky, on the face of it; but actually safeguarded from every point, so to speak, except the frontal attack, the red-handed discovery. And of course the fact that it was in shorthand made it pretty safe in your ill-educated community. I got on to it first when I went into his classroom to ask about the pencil. He made an involuntary movement towards his pile of books, as though he wanted to cover one of them up. It gave me an impression of guiltiness. Then I remembered the tiff between Gadsby and Tiverton, about the sacrosanctity of masters' lockers in the common room, and it occurred to me that would be a good place for him to keep the diary. A damned sight too good in fact. I couldn't poke about in them during the day for there always seemed to be someone in the common room, and he had the sense to bring it up to bed with him at night and, anyhow, it was still only a vague notion in the back of my mind. I didn't feel certain I was right about this till just after Vale was killed. Armstrong said they'd just searched the common room; that was a nasty jolt for Sims, he looked sick as death. Every one thought it was reaction from the murder, but it was chiefly reaction to the horrid thought that they might have found his silent friend. He needn't have got so bothered about it, if he'd thought twice, of course. They were looking for a weapon, not a full signed confession."

"How did you get hold of it?" asked Hero.

"That will transpire in due course, ma'am," said Nigel, and went on to the murder of the headmaster and the final discovery of the weapon. "I must confess I ought to have been able to stop that. But I was looking for his next move in the wrong direction. I thought it would be against one of you, if he made it at all. Yet the motive had been right under my nose. I had heard Vale giving him the most devastating ticking-off. Remember thinking to myself, 'I'd crack his head for him if he spoke to me like that.' That's the sort of thing all of us say, but only a Sims puts into practice. Vale had been browbeating and patronizing him for years, but this was the point at which Sims boiled over. He probably was also afraid that Vale might sack him for incompetence. But he might never have gone to the lengths of murdering him, if it hadn't suggested to him a magnificent way of incriminating you. Yes, he really struck the top of his form there," Nigel added enthusiastically.

"So glad you enjoyed it," murmured Michael in society-hostess tones.

"It was more brilliant even than the first murder, and absolutely safe except for the moment of impact. At the crisis of the match he bent down, as if to do up his shoelace, snatched out the tent-peg dagger with his left hand, struck through the back of the deck chair, you get no spurt of blood with a very thin weapon like that, wiped the dagger on the grass, and thrust it back through the loop of the guy-rope. The whole thing would take three seconds. If there had been no really exciting point in the match to distract every one's attention, he simply would not have acted; just substituted a real tent-peg that night and no one any the wiser. As he says in the diary, he could afford to wait. He knew, of course, where Hero and her husband would be sitting. He could rely on Michael being somewhere near. He didn't know, on the other hand, that Hero would faint; that was his greatest triumph of tactics. The original plan was for him in some unobtrusive way to call the attention of the police to the tent-peg, a few hours after the murder. Its proximity to Hero's chair, plus the motive she had for getting rid of her husband, would have clinched the case for the police. When she fainted, he altered this plan in a twinkling, called out 'Fetch some water,' a perfectly innocent remark on the face of it, knowing that knight-errant Evans would hurry off for some, and at once be suspected of carrying the weapon with him. If the police had stopped him, searched him and found no weapon, then Sims could fall back on the first plan. Oh yes, the whole performance was alpha plus. His mania had sharpened his intelligence to a very fine point indeed."

Nigel paused. Hero shivered a little, moved closer to Michael. Even in retrospect these things kept the edge of horror. She looked at Nigel. His dispassionate, scientific admiration for the methods of a killer frightened her. His face seemed inhuman to her at this moment, like a clever machine in repose after a day's work. She shook herself. This was a nice way to feel towards someone who had saved her life and Michael's.

"You haven't answered my question yet," she said.

"What? Oh, the diary? Yes, it was very difficult. I still hadn't a vestige of material proof that Sims was the murderer. And Armstrong was begin-

ning to tug pretty hard at the leash. I couldn't give him any reasons that
would be satisfactory to him for holding Sims. So I asked him to arrest
you, just to keep him quiet, and to keep Sims quiet too, of course. The
diary was an hypothesis; I determined to try and prove it. The trouble
was, Sims might very well have realized that it was a luxury he couldn't
afford now, and burnt it. If he hadn't, he'd be pretty sure to keep strict
guard over it. Anyway, Griffin, young Stevens and I staged a fire-alarm.
That got Sims and every one else out of the common room without arousing suspicion. The diary *was* there, in his locker. Half a minute at it, and
I knew we had won." Nigel's voice changed. "Poor devil. None of us can
have the remotest idea of the agony it is to be despised and rejected of
men; a cancer in the soul. And then madness; the feeling of there being a
curtain, more invisible than gauze, stronger than iron, between oneself
and one's fellow men. To cry out of the abyss, and to know that there will
be no answer, that one is buried alive."

Hero whispered involuntarily. "So you are human, after all."

Nigel started, and looked puzzled, "What on earth—" he said slowly.

"I think I understand," said Michael. Then, with seeming irrelevance,
"Do you always leave your revolver under your pillow? Careless habit.
You should break yourself of it."

"I see there is no getting past you," answered Nigel. "And for goodness' sake don't let this go past you. I should be ruined if Armstrong got
to hear of it. He can't understand how a detective of my calibre should
make such an almighty gaffe as to announce in front of a murderer exactly where he keeps a revolver—"

"What's this?" asked Hero. "Was it your revolver he shot himself with?"

"Yes. I can tell you, Armstrong is pretty sore about that. He'd be a
damn sight sorer if he knew–oh well, I'd better explain. Armstrong imag-
ines that Sims noticed his diary was missing, knew everything was up,
and took advantage of my alleged carelessness with firearms to stage a
grand finale. Actually it wasn't as simple as that. I'm not so tired of life
yet as to leave my revolver about in reach of murderers. And Sims did not
miss his diary till I told him I'd read it; I placed a notebook of the same
pattern in his locker, when I took the diary, and he hadn't had time to
discover the substitution. I had no intention of letting him get away with
suicide then, not till I read the diary; then–well–my views changed. I
knew he would not be hung with that evidence before a judge; he'd be
sent to Broadmoor. And I simply have no use for keeping lunatics alive,
criminal or otherwise. So I had a chat with Sims; told him it was all up,
and where I kept my revolver–*not* under my pillow, I may say–and left
him to it. He–no, I think I will not describe the interview in detail. Anyway, I took everyone off to reconstruct the first crime. That was really for

my own satisfaction. I wanted to prove that he could have moved to the haystack and back during the race without being noticed, and–er–I like a little exhibition now and then. I intended, of course, to play the part of the murderer myself. You can imagine it shook me up all right when I saw, just before we kicked off, that Sims himself had turned up. I'd only left one shot in the revolver. But it looked as if he might propose to fire it into the wrong person. I was just on the point of jumping on him when it occurred to me that what he had come for was not my life but a triumphal exit. It was rather rash of me, I suppose, but I staked on my knowledge of his mental processes, and luckily I was right. We went ahead; Sims reenacted his own part, and had his crowded hour of glorious life, and here we all are."

"Well, you've certainly got a nerve," said Michael.

"I don't know how we begin to thank you," Hero said gently.

"A fresh pot of tea would be quite a good start."

THE END

About the Rue Morgue Press

"Rue Morgue Press is the old-mystery lover's best friend, reprinting high quality books from the 1930s and '40s."
—*Ellery Queen's Mystery Magazine*

Since 1997, the Rue Morgue Press has reprinted scores of traditional mysteries, the kind of books that were the hallmark of the Golden Age of detective fiction. Authors reprinted or to be reprinted by the Rue Morgue include Catherine Aird, Delano Ames, H. C. Bailey, Morris Bishop, Nicholas Blake Dorothy Bowers, Pamela Branch, Joanna Cannan, John Dickson Carr, Glyn Carr, Torrey Chanslor, Clyde B. Clason, Joan Coggin, Manning Coles, Lucy Cores, Frances Crane, Norbert Davis, Elizabeth Dean, Carter Dickson, Michael Gilbert, Constance & Gwenyth Little, Marlys Millhiser, Gladys Mitchell, James Norman, Stuart Palmer, Craig Rice, Kelley Roos, Charlotte Murray Russell, Maureen Sarsfield, Margaret Scherf, Juanita Sheridan and Colin Watson..

To suggest titles or to receive a catalog of Rue Morgue Press books write P.O. Box 4119, Boulder, CO 80306, telephone 800-699-6214, or check out our website, www.ruemorguepress.com, which lists complete descriptions of all of our titles, along with lengthy biographies of our writer